Caramel Hearts

Caramel Hearts

E.R. Murray

ALMA BOOKS

ALMA BOOKS LTD
3 Castle Yard
Richmond
Surrey TW10 6TF
United Kingdom
www.almabooks.com

Caramel Hearts first published by Alma Books Ltd in 2016

© Elizabeth Rose Murray, 2016

Cover image © Jem Butcher

Printed in Great Britain by CPI Group (UK) Ltd, Croydon CR0 4YY

ISBN: 978-1-84688-392-7

FOR MY SISTER
TRACEY

Caramel Hearts

Before We Begin, I'd Like to Share a Memory...

It's a cold, blustery day and sand whips against my face. But I don't mind. Whitby is almost two hours away from home, and on its beach I'm as free as the howling winds.

I reach into the scrunched newspaper in Mam's hand and take another steaming-hot chip loaded with salt and vinegar. Popping the chip into my mouth, I wait until Mam's distracted, then turn to my sister Hatty and open my jaw wide, showing the contents.

"Yuck! You're disgusting!" cries Hatty, copying in return.

We giggle, one eye on Mam, but she's completely unaware. Her eyes are closed, her lashes fluttering contentedly as she faces the North Sea, as though remembering something special. I take Hatty's hand.

"I told you, Liv," whispers Hatty. "She's getting better."

I turn a wobbly cartwheel, and my hair leaves snake trails in the sand.

"Yay!" cries Hatty.

Mam joins in the celebrations. We must have disturbed her. We check she's not cross and touch our left ears – our signal that it's all clear.

"Olivia Bloom, youngest of the Bloom sisters, takes gold!" says Mam in a commentator's voice.

Not to be outdone, Hatty kicks up her right leg and spins her body in a perfect arc.

"Harriet Bloom performs a stellar round also! It's joint gold for the Bloom sisters!"

Mam lifts her arms high into the air and nearly upturns the chips. We scramble through the deep, powdery sand to rescue our lunch. Mam's quick: she turns tail and runs towards the cave. We follow in hot pursuit, laughing and shrieking, but by the time we reach the cave, Mam's mood has changed. She stares blankly at us as we catch up, panting. The air is flat and damp. The wild, free winds are left outside.

"Mam, do you want to rest for a while?" offers Hatty.

"I want Max," says Mam, bursting into tears.

We sit next to her, close enough for her to know we're there but not close enough to touch. And we wait. To pass the time, I gather Hatty's treacle-coloured locks and plait them into seahorse tails. I think, *Please don't let Mam get angry.*

Mam stops crying and turns her soggy face towards us. Her fringe sticks to her forehead in swirls.

"If your dad was here, I wouldn't get these moods."

I stop plaiting, draw my knees up and rest my chin on them.

"If you hadn't driven him away, Liv, everything would be fine."

"Sorry, Mam," I say.

They split up when I was two. That's six years ago.

"If only you'd been a better baby. If only you hadn't scribbled on the walls. Thrown your food bowls."

I squash my chin onto my knees as hard as I can, trying to make a bruise. A bruise helps to take your mind off things. When you poke it, all you think about is the pain, and you forget the bad stuff you've done – like driving your dad away.

"Hatty never threw her food bowls. Max didn't leave when there was just me and Hatty."

"I did other naughty stuff though, Mam," says Hatty in a shaky voice.

It's as though Mam hasn't heard her at all.

"You always were a naughty child, Liv. He couldn't cope with it. He had to leave."

"Sorry, Mam."

I feel the soft touch of Harriet's fingers searching out my own, followed by a warm, gentle squeeze. I know it's meant to mean "don't listen", but I can't help it.

"You'll always be that way, I guess. You've got my blood, Liv, that's the problem. Bad blood."

She shuffles closer to me, so I turn my eyes to Hatty and wait for the signal. Mam hugs into my back, whispering, "Sorry, love, don't mind me. Don't pay any attention," and eventually Hatty touches her ear. When Mam pulls away, she's all smiley again.

"Who's for more chips?" she says and, squealing, we all run back into the daylight.

Chapter One

Delicately, as though Handling a Bird's Egg

I drop the crumpled postcard from Whitby back into Mam's knicker drawer and quickly cover it up: staring at a six-year-old memory won't bring those times back, even if my mouth waters at the thought of those salty, tangy chips. The sleeves of my dressing gown catch on the drawer handle as I carry on rummaging, uncertain what I'm looking for but determined to find it anyway. Ever since Mam went into Ashgrove House Recovery Centre for Women, I've been searching for something that reminds me of her before the drink took over. But a postcard of the Whitby whalebones doesn't quite cut it.

The floorboard creaks underfoot, and although I'm hidden in shadow, my heart still pounds. If Hatty finds me going through Mam's things, she'll lose her head – and it wouldn't be fair to wake her when she's trying to catch up on her assignments. My sister's almost twenty-one and should be completing her studies at Edinburgh University, but instead she's looking after me while Mam recovers – if you can call it that. Mam's track record isn't great, and although Hatty swears she'll dry out this time, I can't help being a little sceptical. This is Mam, not *EastEnders*.

I hold my breath for what feels like eternity, straining my ears for any sign of movement. Certain it's all clear, I rifle through the last few drawers and check under the bed. Reaching out, my hand touches something cool. It's only an empty whiskey bottle.

"Should have known," I whisper, before returning it.

Disappointed, I lie down on Mam's bed, face towards the ceiling. My hair spills across Mam's pillows as I close my eyes and try to make myself tired, but thoughts race through my brain at lightning speed and there's no way I can sleep. I try the relaxation method my counsellor showed me – slow breaths, counting to three as you inhale and three as you exhale – but it doesn't work. Flipping onto my stomach, I cuddle the pillows instead. My fingers bash against something hidden in the pillowcase; this time, it's not made of glass.

I tease out the object delicately, as though handling a bird's egg, and light the reserve torch Mam keeps in her bedside cabinet for when we can't afford the 'leccy bill. The dim yellow beam reveals a chunky book. Its wrinkled cover is made of rough cream card, decorated with dried leaves and real pink rose petals. As I lift the book closer, I spot a neat, handwritten title: *Recipes to Make Happiness Bloom*.

It's Mam's handwriting.

Flipping open the cover, I realize I'm holding my breath: it's not like I'm reading her diary, it's just a book of recipes, but my hands are unsteady as I peek inside. On the front page, there's a recipe for "Lovers' Lemon and Choc-Chip Shortbread" in the same careful hand. She's decorated it with loads of cute drawings of ingredients and a nicely shaded sketch of the finished product. I'd almost forgotten that she could draw. She used to make colouring pictures for us when we were kids – they were always much more pretty and intricate than the ones you got in books – but that feels like a lifetime ago.

"Why would Mam write a cookbook?" I whisper to myself. "She only ever goes to the kitchen to pour another drink or microwave some beans."

I fling the book aside; I'd been hoping for something better. But then I feel mean for thinking such negative thoughts about Mam. At least she's trying. Snatching the book back up, I flick through the pages to give it a second chance. This time, I notice the inscription on the inside cover.

To the love of my life, Abigail "Happiness" Bloom. May we have many adventures together. Yours always, Max. Christmas 2000.

I lift the cookbook higher to inspect it more closely. Max is my dad's name – now we're getting somewhere. When Mam's around, she's the only one that's allowed to mention Dad. Like she's the only one that feels his absence.

Tracing the words with my fingertips – the words my dad wrote – my stomach feels like it's full of eels. Hugging the cookbook to my chest as I drift off to sleep, I swear I can smell baking shortbread, cold sea air and a man's cologne seeping from its pages.

Lovers' Lemon and Choc-Chip Shortbread

Guaranteed to set anyone's taste buds tingling and their dreams soaring, this is the perfect antidote to grey clouds and cold winds...

INGREDIENTS

115 g/4 oz plain flour, plus some extra dabs for dusting
125 g/4½ oz yummy butter
60 g/2 oz caster sugar
1 tsp aromatic cinnamon
Pinch of salt (unless the butter is salted)
Zest of 1 lemon
Big handful of chocolate chips (the more the better!)
Dainty splash of icing sugar

HOW TO MAKE THE MAGIC HAPPEN

1. Preheat the oven to 220 °C/425 °F/Gas mark 7.
2. Use a wooden spoon to cream the butter and sugar together. Then add the flour, cinnamon and salt, a little at a time, and combine together in a bowl, using your fingertips. Keep going until the mixture looks like breadcrumbs – breathe in those delicious smells!
3. Add the lemon zest and chocolate chips, stirring well to combine the ingredients. When doughy, collect the shortbread mixture and plop it on a lightly floured surface, then knead for 2–3 minutes.

4. Roll that pastry! Make it about 1½ cm/¾ in. thick, depending on how you like it (it won't rise much when cooking). Use a heart-shaped biscuit cutter to get as many biscuits as you can out of the dough. Pop them on a baking tray and bake in the oven for 8–10 minutes, or until golden-brown, like summer hayfields.

5. Cool on a wire rack, dust with icing sugar – and whatever you do, don't forget to *seal with a kiss*.

Chapter Two

That's OK – Sisters Together?

Waking to the sound of the shower running and the boiler creaking, it takes me a moment to realize where I am. I sneak out of Mam's room and across to my own, *Recipes to Make Happiness Bloom* tucked inside my dressing gown. I hadn't meant to sleep in Mam's bed all night – or at all, if I'm honest – but I'm grateful for the decent kip. For once, my brain feels alert and my eyes don't sting.

Before I do anything else – drink a glass of water or brush my teeth, even – I cover the recipe book in polka-dot paper like my schoolbooks, as a disguise. Then I plump the pillows on my bed and open the book to see what gems are hidden inside. There might even be more messages from my dad. Scouring the lists of ingredients, my taste buds tingle. There's nothing boring in there, like salads or shepherd's pie – just sweets and puddings. Mam always had a sweet tooth. Each cake, biscuit and dessert sounds tastier than the last, and the instructions are almost poetic – telling stories that make the recipes come to life. Stories from a time when my mam and dad didn't hate each other. Just by reading, I can imagine how delish everything will taste. I wonder what it would be like to try and bake some cakes; imagine the smells wafting from the kitchen and filling the house, hiding the smell of damp.

At school, our English teacher, Miss Clyde, says that smells bring back memories more acutely than any other of our senses. She always makes us add aromas into our creative writing to help our readers feel what's going on. I close my eyes and think about the smells I love: hot chips, acrylic paint, new books and cinnamon bubblegum. Then I think about Mam – violet perfume, face cream that smells like freshly cut grass, plummy red wine, whiskey stale and sour on her breath – and I decide not to go down that route. When I try and think about Dad, it's just a void, so I return to my recipes.

After a while, my stomach starts rumbling and I realize it's almost noon. I hide the recipe book under my pillow and race downstairs for food. The cereal boxes are empty so there's only toast to eat. I conjure up images of croissants and *pain au chocolat* – like they eat in France. Imagine living in a country where you can eat cake for breakfast!

As the slices of bread warm between the hot filaments of the toaster, my mind races. I fantasize about serving the treats up to Hatty on elaborate silver trays, and making boxes of them for summery picnics. It'd be a "thank you" for all she's done. Just like a scene from one of those period dramas that Mam likes to watch, snuggled under a blanket on the sofa with a bottle of wine. I'm not a huge fan myself, but I do like sharing the blanket and seeing Mam's eyes light up when the handsome hero comes back for his girl.

As soon as my toast is ready, I slather on butter and run up the stairs two at a time, trying to figure out how to make this fantasy a reality. There must be a bit of spare cash to get some ingredients – and it would feed us, so it'd be an investment. I decide to ask Hatty for help, so I can cook Mam's recipes in the order they appear in the book – it's the closest I've felt to Mam in ages. Something tugs at my memory – a vague reminder of how she was before the drink took over. "Lovers' Lemon and Choc-Chip Shortbread" is first, and you never know – if I make some for Mam, it might trigger something in her alcohol-riddled brain and help her recover. So long as I keep quiet about the fact I was in her room and going through her things. I'd better not mention it to my sister either, if I want her help.

* * *

"What are you doing?" asks Hatty, as she catches me rifling through the backs of the cupboards that evening.

Amazingly, I've gathered most of the ingredients I need, except for icing sugar and a lemon. The stuff's mostly out of date, but seeing as I've never even held a wooden spoon, I'm not going to fret about details like that just yet.

"Do you like shortbread?" I ask.

"Yeah, why – have you found some?"

Her voice is so excitable, I can't help grinning.

"Nope," I say, and Hatty's shoulders deflate. "But I was thinking of making some."

"Make? Like, from scratch?"

"Yeah, from scratch."

Hatty's eyebrows lift high on her head.

"You know how?"

"I've got a recipe. How hard can it be?"

Hatty laughs as she puts some fish fingers under the grill.

"So long as you don't go nuts and make a mountain of the stuff," she says. "I'm watching my weight, remember."

Like I could forget. She's been watching her weight for ever. Always fussing over calories and fat content – but then she just eats it anyway, cos we can only afford cheap food and neither of us can cook anything except bolognaise. And even then we use a jar. I don't know what she's worried about anyway – she's a size 12, and I think it suits her, but she's obsessed with getting skinnier. Believes everything in life will get magically better if her waist shrinks a few inches.

"I don't have to make any…" I say, shrugging.

She turns the fish fingers.

"I didn't say that, did I? It'd be a shame not to try…"

We both chuckle, then stand and watch in silence as the breadcrumbs sizzle and brown under the grill. Hatty piles half of the cooked fish fingers on some bread, squirts wiggles of ketchup along each one, exactly how I like it, then tops it with more bread and cuts it into triangles. She hands it across to me, before making one for herself, ketchup-free and sliced into rectangles.

"If you're serious about these biscuits, let me know if I can help," she says, taking a bite.

"How about a lemon and some icing sugar?"

She rifles in her jeans pocket and hands over £1. I'm amazed how easy this is – it must be fate.

"If they have it cheap in Asda, it's a yes. And if I get this job tomorrow…"

"I'm sure you will, Hatty," I say, pocketing the money. "Then I'll make you all the shortbread you can eat."

"A moment on the lips," says Hatty, tapping her hips and I shake my head, laughing, as she disappears back upstairs to her books.

* * *

It's late by the time I get round to gathering my school stuff together; it took me ages to get the icing sugar and lemon at Asda because the baking section was so intriguing. I had no idea that there were so many fancy tools required – silicone cookie cutters, rolling pins you can fill with water, decorative cake cases in all shapes and sizes and special sugar thermometers. When I got home, I read the shortbread recipe over and over to make sure nothing could go wrong. And then I remembered about my Maths homework. Only when that was finished did I think to check whether my uniform needed ironing.

Peeking upstairs, I'm relieved to see the light is still shining under Hatty's door. One of the coolest things about Mam not being here is that I've got total freedom when it comes to staying up late. We had this big chat when Hatty first came home about how she's not trying to replace Mam: she's still my big sister and we're in this together, so we have to work as a team. No "Mam rules", so long as I pull my weight and act responsibly.

"Hatty, have you done my school uniform?" I call up the stairs. "I can't find it."

A short silence follows – then I hear a book slam and Hatty's feet pad across her bedroom floor. It's the only room without carpet. Mam's been promising it for years, but when Hatty went to uni, other things took priority. Drink included.

"I'm sorry, Liv," Hatty says, biting her bottom lip. "I completely forgot. I'm so behind in my assignment... it must still be in the wash basket."

On my bedroom floor, more like, I think, but I decide it's best not to mention that fact.

"But what will I wear tomorrow?"

Sighing, Hatty starts down the stairs, a pen tucked behind her ear. She looks knackered – I hope she'll use plenty of slap for her interview.

"Even if I put a wash on now, it won't be dry in time. You should have reminded me on Friday."

"I did. You said to leave it with you."

"I did? You should have reminded me again this morning. Or better still, done it yourself. I can't remember everything."

"Can you give me a note so I can wear something else?"

I see the worries flying through her brain as she mulls my request over. Hatty's scared of the slightest thing going wrong, in case it upsets the Social Services and she's declared an unfit guardian.

"Don't worry about it," I say. "I'll just clean the tide-marks off the shirt collar and hope it dries. No biggie."

Hatty frowns. "That's disgusting."

"It's only one day. I'll stick the wash on after school tomorrow – sisters together, right?"

"Right. Sisters together." Harriet checks her watch, and her tired smile melts away. "It's almost midnight. Hadn't you better think about getting some sleep?"

"Sure," I say. "I'll just wash my shirt first."

Nodding, Hatty climbs back up the stairs. "Goodnight, lil sis."

"Goodnight."

It's almost one o'clock in the morning by the time I finish scrubbing the shirt collar clean – and I can't resist a final peek at the recipe book. I fall asleep in seconds. I get the best night's sleep I've had in months. No nightmares or twisting in the covers. Instead, I dream of buttery smells and warm, sunny kitchens.

Chapter Three

It's Not Fair to Stress Her Out

I wake up with biscuits on the brain, only to find my shirt collar isn't dry. I give the shirt a good sniff and it reeks. I spray it with deodorant and hope for the best, but the results aren't quite what I was expecting. I knock on Hatty's door, hoping she's awake. The door creaks open, and Hatty peeks out.

"Morning," she says, yawning.

Behind her, I can see a pile of books sprawled across her bed, her laptop open and glowing.

"Did you sleep at all?" I ask. "You've got that interview—"

"Did you come to give me a lecture, or do you want something?" she asks.

"Smell this." I hold out my shirt. Hatty gives it a sniff and pulls a face. "I can't wear this. Will you write me a note?"

"I don't want the school thinking we can't cope, Liv."

"I'll get picked on if someone gets a whiff of this. And I'll get grief all day off the teachers if I wear something else without a note. Please?"

"OK. But just this once." Hatty scribbles on a piece of paper and hands it over. "So, you'll wash your own uniform from now on?"

"OK," I say, not really meaning it. "Though I'm pretty sure that's a form of child abuse."

I turn and head away before she can say anything.

"That's not funny, Liv," she calls after me.

I don't have many clothes that would be considered suitable for school, so I decide to go in with a bang. Picking out my favourite green and white striped tights, black dress and fake Dr Martens, I shove my burgundy school jumper over the top and check in the mirror. *The teachers will pee their pants when they see this, but they won't be able to do anything with a note!* I chuckle to myself, fix up my eyes with some eyeliner and mascara, and plait the front left side of my hair. Feeling rather pleased with myself, I tiptoe past Hatty's room, then quickly make toast, stuffing it down my throat as I head up the street. I haven't gone far when one of the most popular lads from my class, Chris Murchison, passes by and gawks.

"Are you going to school in fancy dress?" he says, laughing.

"Whatever," I say.

What's he even doing over here? Chris is from the posh part near school, but it looks as though he's just come from Egerton Mount – the dodgiest of the Egerton estates. Known for theft and drugs, it's the kind of place the bus won't pass through in case it loses its wheels halfway. Neighbouring Egerton Hill – where I live – is rough enough, but some people have jobs and there's a Neighbourhood Watch scheme, so there's a bit less crime, and people try not to chuck their litter into your front garden. Egerton Park, where school is based, is snobbier; it sits facing our estates like a referee separating two boxers. People say places like the Mount and the Hill give the North-East of England a bad name. They're no oil painting, but they're not that bad.

"I wouldn't be seen dead in that outfit. Are you some kind of goth?"

I ignore him so he can see I couldn't care less what he thinks.

But maybe he's right. Maybe it wasn't such a good idea to wear this outfit after all. I slow down, let Chris get well ahead, and then I turn back. Dawdling, I try to think up a good explanation to give Hatty – a reason why I thought these clothes would be suitable attire. And why I changed my mind. But my brain keeps wandering back to the recipe book and the shortbread, so when I reach home, I've nothing to say for myself and I daren't go in. Even if I get changed really fast, I'll be late for school, so I'll need another note. Hatty won't be best pleased, and it's not fair to stress her out when she's got her assignments and an interview.

Thankfully, a better idea comes to mind. I send a text to my best friend, Sarah, so she won't be waiting for me to walk to school.

NOT COMING IN TODAY. I'VE GOT THE LURGY. L X

The reply comes back immediately.

OK. GET BETTER SOON. S X

I know nicking off school isn't the smartest move, but it's not like I planned it. Those biscuits are dying to be baked, and with Hatty at her job interview in the supermarket in town this afternoon, it's the ideal time to get started. It would be a nice surprise for Hatty after a stressful day – I'll pretend I made them at school.

I walk around the estate for a couple of hours, then hide near the garages at the end of our road when Hatty is due to leave for the bus. As soon as I see her pass, I give it a few minutes and then I head home and watch some TV before rolling up my sleeves. I'll still be done and out of here before she gets back, and the risk of getting caught is pretty much zero.

Chapter Four

Like Magic, It Begins to Mould Together

I set the recipe book in place, open the oven door, and a rancid smell of stale fat rushes out. When was the last time Hatty cleaned this thing? A thick, tar-like substance has frozen mid-drip on the shelf's slats. It's disgusting, but as Mam says, "beggars can't be choosers", so I light the gas anyway, and get to work. Without any weighing scales, I guess the measures, using the overall quantities on the packet as a guide. I place the butter and sugar in a bowl and, without a wooden spoon to hand, try a fork for whisking instead.

It's a disaster.

The fork handle gets covered in butter and loose sugar granules spray out of the bowl like water from a sprinkler. A metal spoon isn't any better. The thought of sticking my hands into the butter is gross, but time is ticking, and if I want it to work, I have to chance skipping to the next step. I'm surprised to find the cool stickiness is actually quite nice as I mix the ingredients together. But it's hard work. The recipe book doesn't mention anything about that. My shoulder goes dead after a few minutes and the sugar grazes my skin like sand. The butter's so hard I think my arm might snap with the effort, but soon everything begins to warm and soften, dissolving the sugar in a buttery embrace. When everything is mixed, I can't resist sucking on a finger. It already tastes amazing.

Mouth watering, I carry on. The recipe says to add a bit of flour at a time, but to speed things up, I dump it all into the bowl. White powdery clouds billow out, catching in my throat and making me choke.

"Dammit!"

Using all my strength, I work the ingredients between my fingers. Like magic, it begins to mould together – not like any breadcrumbs I've ever seen, but it'll have to do. I check my flour-stained phone for the time. Hatty should be back in about an hour, leaving just enough time to bake, clean up and get out of here undetected.

As I add the lemon zest and chocolate chips, my nostrils suck in the smells and my stomach rumbles loudly in complaint. I had to skip lunch, so I can't wait to get stuck in. All morning I've been imagining the warm shortbread crumbling in my mouth and melting away. It even took my mind off my next counselling session with Rachel for a while. Sometimes talking about stuff helps, but it's like Rachel wants to know everything that's in my head. She's just trying to help, but it's freaky. She even started talking to me about sex and periods the other week – like they've got anything to do with Mam! And she's a year too late for the periods. I guess I don't mind. It's not like anyone else is going to talk about these things – Hatty gets too embarrassed – but still!

I realize I've been daydreaming and the dough has turned lumpy. I turn the mixture out onto the kitchen surface and start to knead, hoping this will help. Every time I lift my hand, the dough sticks and, no matter what I try, I can't make it stop. Taking a deep breath and checking the recipe, I realize I haven't floured the surface. Annoyed at myself for missing such a basic detail, I grab a fistful of flour and wiggle my fingers so it falls like snow. The dough works better this time, and I relax into the kneading, enjoying the rhythmic strokes – until I realize I'm missing a rolling pin. When did I get so crap at following instructions?

I grab the first heavy item I can find – a supersize tin of beans – and lay it flat on the dough. I try to roll. But once again, the mixture sticks. It lifts with the tin, breaking into gloopy blobs and slopping back down onto the surface. Sweating and cross, I squash the dough together as best I can and pound it into shape with my fists. The citrusy, chocolatey aroma makes my mouth water. I pull a bit of the dough off and let it melt slowly on my tongue. The velveteen mixture's dead tasty. These are going to be divine! Hurriedly, I check the recipe one last time: "*Use a heart-shaped biscuit cutter to get as many biscuits as you can out of the dough.*"

That's a laugh – and I can't even imagine Mam writing it. There's nothing heart-shaped or patterned anywhere. "False hearts and broken promises are the reason I drink," Mam always says. When she's not blaming me. But the recipe is proof that she must have believed in love once upon a time, and I can't help wondering why she changed her mind. She says it's Dad's fault, of course – we all know nothing is ever down to her – but she's never actually explained why they split up. You get the feeling she's hiding something.

After fashioning my own heart shapes with a dinner knife, I place them carefully on the baking tray. I reread the bit about the icing sugar – "*seal with a kiss*" – and a boy's face from school unexpectedly pops into my head: Jack Whitman. Even though I'm alone, my face burns. Pushing him out of my mind, I splash sugar on the biscuits and pop them into the smoking oven. Ignoring the acrid burning smell, I set about cleaning up.

The tidying takes longer than expected. Flour dusts the floor, the worktops and my hair. Wherever I turn, there's another doughy handprint or footprint. I've trampled it everywhere and, to make matters worse, the dough isn't easy to wash away. Like the clay we use in Art class, it clogs the sink.

"Hatty's going to kill me…"

I check the time. My sister's probably due back any minute. And I'm meant to be at school. A loud whoosh catches my attention and I turn to see flames lapping out of the oven.

"Holy crap!"

I bust the oven door open. Angry blue and yellow tongues flick out. The fat on the shelf has caught fire. I'm definitely dead meat now. I cross my fingers and hope that Hatty will be too busy celebrating her new job to get angry with me. Grabbing a bunched-up tea towel – I've discovered we don't own an oven glove – I try to snatch the baking tray out of the fire but the heat is too strong. The flames lap higher, blackening the ceiling. Smoke fills the kitchen, spilling into the passageway.

"Liv, is that you?" I hear Hatty call out. I hadn't even heard the front door slam. "Liv? What are you doing home? Pauline next-door called me – said she'd heard noises… What the—?"

Hatty runs full speed into the kitchen and flings her bag across the floor.

"Quick, get me a damp tea towel!"

I do as I'm told. Within seconds, Harriet has everything under control – shortbread and tray dumped into the sink, oven shelf quickly following.

"What are you playing at? You know that if we don't keep things under control, they'll take you away. Is that what you want?"

"Of course not."

"Well you've a funny way of showing it. I thought you were going to act responsibly?"

"I am! I was just—"

"Nicking off school and setting the place on fire?"

My heart sinks. I only wanted to make Harriet smile.

"If Mam hears about this," continues Hatty. "It'll set her right back."

"And it'll be all my fault. You sound just like her." It's too late to stay out of trouble and I can't seem to stop my mouth. "Maybe I'd be better off if the Social Services did take me away?"

"Sometimes I wonder why the hell I bother!" snaps Harriet.

I roll my eyes. "Go back to your precious uni. I don't need you to look after me."

Harriet grabs me by the shoulders and shakes me harder than I expect, her face puckering with anger.

"Don't be such an ungrateful bitch!" she spits.

My ears and teeth rattle, but I don't bother to fight back. Instead, I focus on the points of her fingers digging into my flesh, my eyes resting on the sink where my ruined shortbread lies black and smouldering. My stomach growls as I watch the red cinders of my shortbread die out, one by one. Why can't Harriet see I'm trying to do something nice?

Wriggling free, I snatch up the recipe book and stomp up to my room.

"I'm a bitch? Then what are you?" I shout down the stairs before slamming the door.

It's our first fight since Mam went away and the lovely lemony flavour turns sour in my mouth. I ball my fists and punch into my mattress. Only when my knuckles start getting sore do I feel a bit better.

"It's all your stupid fault," I say, flinging the cookbook across the room. "It was a ridiculous idea."

The book slams against the wall and lands on the floor, open on the inscription page. I can see my dad's words from here, full of love and tenderness.

"Why did you have to leave?" I say, my voice cracking.

Pushing my face into my pillow, I let the tears fall, resolving to never set foot in the kitchen again.

Chapter Five

The Three Amigos

It's almost 8.15 a.m. when Hatty shakes me awake, a freshly laundered and ironed uniform in her hands. She drops the uniform on my bed as I clamber out, but there's no sign of any note to explain my absence. I'm expecting fireworks and lectures, but it doesn't happen. Instead, her voice is cool and clipped.

"You know you can't keep nicking off school, right?" says Harriet, her best frown in place.

"Right," I agree, my head hung low.

"I know you were trying to do something nice, and it's good you've got an interest, but…"

"But?"

My voice is more defiant than I mean it to be, but there's bound to be something bad coming. Like getting grounded or being walked to school to make sure I get there. For the rest of my life.

"We have to keep our noses clean if we're to keep things as they are."

"You don't even want to be here!"

It's hard to keep my voice from wobbling. My head feels heavy, my heart heavier still, and my hands shake as I turn my back to my sister and start getting dressed. My shirt smells of wild flowers, and I breathe it in.

"I'm sorry for what I said, but I was worried – what if the place burned down? With you trapped inside?" She reaches out and touches my shoulder. "Where would I be without my lil sis?"

I pull away, but only because she's making me feel bad. I'm the one that messed up, and she's apologizing!

"I'm sorry too," I say, the words sticky in my mouth. My shoulders feel lighter as the words come out. "But it was an accident."

"I know that. But that doesn't excuse—" She pauses, gathering herself. "You've got to start pulling your weight, Liv. Taking control of your own life a bit more. I can't always be here to pick up after you and wash your clothes. You're old enough to do it yourself."

"Fine," I say. "Why didn't you just say?"

"I did," she replies. "And I'm sick of repeating myself. Just do it, please."

As Hatty leaves, I spot the recipe book discarded on the floor, still open, and I blurt out, "What about the baking?"

Suddenly, giving up doesn't seem like an option. Why should I? The recipes are the only thing I've looked forward to in ages. And if I'm going to be treated like a slave, I might as well do something I enjoy.

"What about it?" asks Hatty, pausing on the landing.

"Will you still help me out?"

Her eyes go wide and her eyebrows lift so high, they look like they're trying to escape her forehead.

"You're kidding, right?"

"No. You said—"

"That was before you abused my good nature, played truant and almost burnt the place down."

"So you're stopping me from doing the one thing I'm interested in? You're always telling me to have more hobbies."

Harriet puts her hands on her hips.

"I'm not stopping you, Liv. You want to bake, you bake. But you have to learn some sense of responsibility for your actions. So, you get the money for the stuff, and you can bake as much as you please. But not in school time, and not without me around. OK?"

"How am I meant to get money, if not from you?"

"Get a part time job. I used to babysit when I was your age."

"If only I was as perfect as you!" I say, and close the door in her face.

* * *

When I get to the traffic lights, my best friend Sarah is already waiting. Sarah's face is flushed pink, and the dark shadows under her grey eyes show she's had a restless night's sleep. Her long, usually straight blonde hair sticks out like twigs. I know if I tell her she'll get embarrassed and she'll bite my head off. So I keep quiet, hoping she'll notice it in the reflection of a car window instead.

"Are you feeling better?" she asks.

"Yeah. Sorry I'm late. I slept in." I check my hair in the reflection of a car window. "Are you OK?"

"I-I'm fine." Worry always brings out Sarah's stutter. Embarrassing situations and excitement too. I feel dead sorry for her, cos she can't ever hide what she's feeling. Sarah pauses, takes a deep breath and continues slowly.

"M-Mam had a turn last night, but she's OK now. It's just... you know?"

I nod. I know all right. We've been friends since primary school.

"NFDN," I say. No Further Discussion Needed. "Do you have running practice during lunch?"

We always get our plan straight as we walk to school – especially when our timetables don't match. For the last year, Sarah's been having problems with one of our old friends, Madeline Delaney (who we've secretly started calling Mad Dog). Maddy's from Egerton Mount, and her dad's doing time for aggravated armed robbery. She's tougher than steel, but we were best friends once. Mam used to call us The Three Amigos in primary school – we were inseparable. But she outgrew us. Myself and Sarah were still into dolls and making dances to our favourite songs when Maddy started kissing boys and having a cheeky fumble. Mam said it wasn't her fault that she had to grow up fast. Now she's mixed up with a bad crowd, so we only hang out now and again – when she'll let me. Not with Sarah though. Never Sarah.

"Yeah, I'm running. Meet me at the hall at 12.15 p.m.? We can go on first dinners."

It's a mutually beneficial scam we've been pulling for months: the dinner ladies think I'm running too, so they let me in for the early sitting with Sarah. That way, Sarah has the backup she needs and I get fresher food.

"Deal!" I say.

We turn in the direction of school, taking the long way round across the open fields. Known locally as "the Rec", most people avoid it because a cold wind always blows across its exposed grounds. As the wind blows, the scent of floral washing powder fills my nostrils.

"Chris Murchison said he'd seen you yesterday, dressed as a clown."

I feel my face redden. "He's an idiot," I say.

"Yeah, but cute," says Sarah, a dreamy look on her face.

Rolling my eyes is the only reaction I can muster.

"Aw, c'mon, Liv – admit it. You must fancy him a little bit. Otherwise you're not right in the head."

"Guess I'm not right in the head, then. Seriously – why would I fancy someone everyone else likes?"

"Those big eyes, his posh accent, and he's dead funny – Chris is the hottest guy I've ever seen."

"He's an airhead. I'd have thought you'd know better."

"Well I'd have thought you'd know better than going after the same guy Maddy Delaney fancies."

Stopping in my tracks, I put my hand to my chest like I've been shot in the heart.

"Why would you say such a thing?"

"Are you still denying you fancy Jack Whitman? I've seen the way you gawk at him."

"Yeah, right."

"You go weak at the knees every time you see him."

"I do not! What would be the point? Maddy's much more popular. I've never even been kissed and she goes all the way."

"So you have been considering the idea…" coaxes Sarah.

"All right," I say, waiting until Sarah goes quiet. "I guess he's OK."

"I knew it!"

"But you keep your mouth shut! If Maddy finds out, she'll kill me, then you, then him."

"I'd be first on the list," says Sarah, glumly. "Come on, we'd better get a move on."

Hunkering down into our summer jackets, we speed up. It's nearly the end of May but the wind is harsh. Mam always says the landscape matches the lives of the people here: wild and brutal. But I think it's all right. At least it's consistent, and when your cheeks sting and your eyes water, you feel alive.

* * *

"Sorry about yesterday, miss – I was sick," I say to my form teacher, Mrs Pearl, as I breeze my way past her.

I'm chatting happily with Sarah when a shadow looms over me. It's Mrs Pearl.

"Liv, can I have a word?"

"Yes, miss."

"Outside the class," she says, motioning to the door.

Someone in the class whistles, like I'm really in for it. Sarah gives me a quizzical look and I give her a sly shrug of the shoulders. I wait outside the door, fiddling with my tie, while Mrs Pearl gives the class some instructions. When she joins me, her face is full of concern.

"Would you like to tell me what's going on?" she says.

"I— Erm— About what?"

"Your sister called and said she caught you playing truant yesterday. Is this true?"

I flip my tie over my hand as I stare at her dumbly. Betrayed by my own sister.

"What's going on, Liv?" asks Mrs Pearl, even though it's none of her business. "Should I be concerned?"

I shake my head. Why did Hatty do such a stupid thing? Why can't she colour outside of the lines sometimes?

"It won't happen again, miss," I say.

I just hope Hatty hasn't mentioned the fire. Mrs Pearl would freak and she'd be bound to tell someone. It'll all get out of hand – and we all know where that will lead. Back in care.

"Do you want to talk?"

I shake my head. I'm sick of talking. Hatty, my counsellor Rachel... where does it ever get us?

"Well, I'd like you to see the head teacher," says Mrs Pearl.

"But there's no need!"

"At school, we have a duty to look after you, Liv. I understand you're going through a difficult time, but if you won't talk to me... I'll make an appointment for you to see Mr Morrelly at twelve o'clock sharp."

Before I can return to class, the bell rings for first lesson. My form class nudge their way past me – some glancing, some staring, all trying to figure out what's going on. I spin on my heels and head down the corridor towards Science, pretending I can't hear Sarah when she calls my name.

Chapter Six

My Cool Stakes Will Fly through the Roof

When I knock on Mr Morrelly's office door at 12.03 p.m., I feel like I'm about to be sent down for a crime I didn't commit. Hatty owes me big time.

"Come in," calls a deep, thundering voice.

Mr Morrelly – Old Mozzer to us – is a giant. He's well over six foot. It must be difficult to find clothing that fits because all his suits have weird collars and look like they're from the seventies. He has massive, thick glasses and his hair sits in clumps on his head like a heron. Despite being head teacher, he's all right. As all right as a head teacher can be. But he has this annoying habit of pacing when he's cross. It's a dead giveaway. I take a deep breath and push open the door. Thankfully, he's seated with his hands clasped on his desk. I let out my breath and stand in the middle of the room, swapping from foot to foot.

With his back to the window and his face in shadow, Mr Morrelly looks even bigger than normal, and when he gestures for me to sit down, his hand looks massive, reminding me of the BFG. I have to fight to keep a smile off my face.

"Olivia," he says, in that way which makes it sound like I should be able to read his mind and tell him instantly whatever it is that he wants to know.

"Yes, sir?"

"Home. How are things?"

"Fine, sir."

"And Harriet?"

"Fine, sir."

"Mrs Pearl – she says there have been some... issues. Anything you'd like to discuss?"

"No, sir."

He stares at me for a while and I feel his eyes bore into me. I imagine them coming out on mechanical stalks and tunnelling their way up my nostrils, right into my brain, so he can see the blind panic racing through it. I fight to stay calm but I feel my armpits heating up and turning sticky.

"Very well. But your grades could do with a bit of improvement – and playing truant won't help. I have my eye on you." I squirm in my seat as he peers over his thick rims. Then his tone relaxes. "Your well-being is our first priority – so if you ever feel the need to come and talk, to let off some steam, you know where I am."

"Yes, sir. Thank you, sir. Is that all, sir?"

He pauses for a bit too long, and as a throbbing feeling attacks my temples, I imagine his mechanical eye-stalks retracting and taking a wrong turn, bumping into my brain.

I'm so busy daydreaming, I don't hear his dismissal.

"I said yes, Olivia, that is all," he repeats, a mild frown on his face as I turn and scurry away.

* * *

My throat goes dry as I leave the office behind – so much for keeping our noses clean. Hatty's stupid phone call has got me walking around with bells and whistles on. I blow air upwards, across my face, hoping my skin hasn't turned blotchy like it usually does when I stress out.

That's the trouble with being a redhead – you have the delicate skin to go with it. As I turn into the busy corridor, head bowed, I bump straight into someone – Chris bloody Murchison – and then rebound into his mate.

"Sorry!" I say.

It's only Jack Whitman. There's no hiding the colour in my cheeks now.

"It's OK. I like being a human domino."

I laugh way too loudly, and immediately wish I could stuff the sound back in my gob. I can't believe Jack is talking to me. Neither can Chris – he tries pulling Jack away, but Jack signals for him to go ahead.

"You just been to see Old Mozzer?" he asks, pointing towards the head teacher's office.

I nod. I can imagine the stupid look on my face. I'm just pleased Sarah isn't here. Sarah! I check my watch – I'm already ten minutes late. If I don't hurry up, I'll miss her.

"What did you do?" continues Jack.

"I'm innocent. I was just unfortunate enough to be born into a family of morons," I say, hoping it sounds witty, if a little mean.

Jack laughs. "That sounds serious. But honestly... Seems you've been getting it in the neck quite a bit recently."

And here's me thinking Jack doesn't even know I exist.

"It's too embarrassing to even bother explaining," I reply.

If I started walking towards the lunch hall, I should still be able to catch Sarah. But my legs are glued to the spot.

"I could find a way to get it out of you."

Before I realize what's happening, Jack reaches out and grabs me by the wrist. He tickles me under my armpit – of all places – with a big, soppy grin on his face. I can't help screeching – but when the other kids turn to look, I don't care. They'll see I'm with Jack and my cool stakes will fly through the roof.

Or at least they'll move away from zero.

"OK, OK! Mercy!" I cry.

"Tell, or I keep going for ever."

I'm still giggling when Maddy pushes her way towards us – she must have finished her dinner already. She's not particularly pretty, but she has perfect boobs and deep blue eyes, and is always dead trendy. She always wears the latest fashions because her mam's best friends with the shoplifters. She even manages to make the school uniform look cool. Maddy's eyes flick from my face to Jack's questioningly, and my heart pumps in my chest. I can hear the blood in my ears.

"What's going on here, guys?" asks Maddy – all sweetness, but I can tell by the way her lips tighten in the corners that she's livid.

Whenever she pulls that face, I think about the time the three of us – me, Maddy and Sarah – were playing in the sandpit and her dad came early to take her home from school. Maddy refused to go and, when the teachers weren't looking, he slapped her right across the face. She didn't cry. Didn't even make a noise, despite the raw, red handprint. Just pressed her lips together and followed him out of the room.

"I'm holding Liv captive until she tells me what I want to know."

Maddy raises an eyebrow.

"Why don't you put the boy out of his misery?" she asks, but the tone is more of an order than a question.

Jack doesn't seem to notice. Mam always says men don't pick up on subtleties.

"I got caught nicking off school yesterday," I say quickly.

Jack lets go and feigns complete horror.

"My word, Liv. I'm shocked. That's like so—"

"Lame," says Maddy.

"It is a bit," Jack chuckles, and turns to go, so I blurt out the first thing I can think of.

"What they don't know is that I set the house on fire."

A slight exaggeration, and hardly something I should share, but it makes Jack stop in his tracks. And Maddy too.

"And Old Mozzer knows that?" asks Jack, his eyes widening.

"Not exactly."

"Didn't you know her mam's an alky?" asks Maddy innocently.

Her words cut right through me. Why would she say such a thing? I'd never bad-mouth her family like that, even though they're way worse than mine. I know we're no longer close, but still! I daren't look Jack in the eye. That's the last I'll ever be talking to him then.

"My dad was too," says Jack. "But he's off it now. So I know how it feels."

The way her face crumples, you'd think someone had hit Maddy head-on with a shovel.

"You never told me that," she says, linking his arm and pulling him away without a backward glance.

I can feel the sense of victory fizzing off her – even though Maddy always makes sure she wins, she never tires of it.

Giving them a few minutes' head start, I go in search of Sarah – but I'm too late. I just hope she managed to keep out of Maddy's way.

* * *

Sarah isn't in our usual meeting spot at home-time, but I can see her blonde ponytail bobbing its way across the Rec, so I race to catch up with her.

"Hey, am I late?" I ask, knowing full well that I'm not.

Sarah keeps walking at top speed, her head down. I grab her by her jacket sleeve.

"Hey, what's going on?"

When she looks up, there are tears streaking her cheeks.

"Sarah, what's wrong?" I say. "What happened?"

"Your g-good friend, M-Mad Dog, that's what," she says. "I couldn't wait for you, Liv. She said if she saw me after school, she'd kill me."

"I know she has a pretty nasty mouth on her, but she wouldn't hit you. Her friends, maybe, but not—"

"Oh really?" snaps Sarah, yanking up her coat sleeve.

There's a nasty purple bruise on her forearm.

"She did that? Are you sure?"

"No, Liv, I'm making it up. Of course I'm sure! She followed me out of the dinner hall, got me in the toilets. Said my s-stammer was so disgusting, it was stopping her from being able to eat."

"Was she on her own?"

"Yes. So you can't blame her friends this time."

Maddy's gang of friends can make your life hell if they choose to, and they love that fact that Sarah's stammer gets worse when they mention it. I always see Maddy hanging back, but Sarah's been saying for months that she's even worse than the rest – I thought she was just jealous because Maddy wants to hang out with me now and again. I really wasn't expecting this.

"Do you want me to have a word?"

Sarah looks at me like I have two heads.

"Are you crazy? It'll only make things worse. Why do you hang out with her, anyway, when she's such a cow?"

It's not an easy question to answer. "She's never done anything to me," I say.

Sarah doesn't speak to me the rest of the way home. Even when we part, she ignores my goodbye.

Gooey Chewy Flapjacks

When the clouds are grey and it's raining in your heart, the only thing that can make the skies blue again is a good dose of sweet, chewy flapjack. Golden, sweet and definitely moreish – they'll bring out the rainbows in your soul.

INGREDIENTS

200 g/7 oz unsalted butter
200 g/7 oz demerara sugar – the good stuff
200 g/7 oz runny honey (otherwise known as liquid gold)
400 g/14 oz porridge oats
70 g/2 ½ oz mix of rainbow-coloured treats (remember the old saying – "Richard of York Gave Battle in Vain" – that'll help you remember your rainbow colours!) Try using dried cranberries (red), sultanas/toasted desiccated coconut (yellow) pumpkin seeds (green), sour cherries (that's artistic licence for blue), prunes (indigo) and sugared violet petals.

HOW TO MAKE THE MAGIC HAPPEN

1. Preheat the oven to 180 °C/350 °F/Gas mark 4.
2. Grease a 20 cm x 30 cm (8 in. x 12 in.) cake tin. Heat the butter, sugar and honey in a saucepan, stirring occasionally. Make a wish as you stir – it'll help make the clouds go away.

3. When the butter has melted and the sugar dissolved, add the oats and all the healthy, tasty goodness and mix well. After all, you are what you eat – and you need rainbow colours to make rainbows appear.

4. Transfer the oat mixture to the cake tin and spread to about 2 cm (¾ in.) thick. Smooth the surface with the back of a spoon (and don't freak out when you see your face reflected upside down – you should know by now, this is a crazy world, my friend). Bake for 15–20 minutes, until lightly golden around the edges, but still slightly soft in the middle.

5. Let the flapjacks cool in the tin, then turn out and cut into squares. Take a bite and watch the rainbows explode, right side up.

Chapter Seven

Don't Air Your Dirty Linen in Public

When I get home, I head straight for my bedroom. After she's taken back her promise to help me with my baking, and put me under the spotlight with her stupid phone call, I'm in no mood to talk to my sister.

"Liv, is that you?" shouts Harriet from the kitchen.

"Who else?" I slam my door shut and blast Johnny Cash at high volume, then sit on the floor with my back against the door. When Mam left for Ashgrove House the first time, I took her ancient record player and vinyl collection. That's when I discovered Johnny Cash. Hatty says I'm like an old lady, says the music is too dark and depressing, but I think the melancholic guitar riffs are lovely. It's like the music understands how I feel. So now, whenever Mam goes to Ashgrove House, I commandeer the record player.

The door jerks, banging against my back.

"Liv!"

"What?"

"I need you in the kitchen." The door nudges again but I stay put. "What are you doing in there?"

"I'm getting changed! I'll be down when I'm dressed."

I don't move until I hear her stomp down the stairs. In the kitchen, I find Harriet leaning against the counter, glowering at a couple of bags of groceries.

"What's for tea?" I ask, peering into the bags.

Harriet slams a cupboard shut. Like a loser, I jump.

"What's wrong with you now, Hatty?"

"What makes you think something's wrong?"

"What have I done?"

"Nothing! That's the point! You come in, stomp up the stairs without even saying hello."

"So?"

"So? I had a life in Edinburgh. I should be with my mates or working on assignments. Not playing Mam to a spoilt brat who can't even say hello!"

"All this is because I didn't say hello?" I roll my eyes, knowing how much it winds her up. "I'm sorry. Hell-o-o. There, better?"

"There's no need to be sarcastic. As usual, you're missing the point."

"So enlighten me," I say.

She looks like she wants to shake me but thinks better of it.

"Would it hurt you to help a bit round here? You're fourteen – old enough to stand on your own two feet. When I was your age, I was looking after you. You're too lazy to unpack a few bags of shopping!"

"So that's what this is about. Unpacking shopping. Why didn't you just ask?"

"I shouldn't have to. And it's not just that. It's uniforms, and nicking off school and trying to burn the place down."

"I thought we were done talking about that this morning," I say.

Hatty slumps down on a kitchen chair and rubs the bridge of her nose between thumb and forefinger. I should leave her alone. She looks wrecked. Her hair is straggly and her skin sallow. And she's put on a few pounds. I try to keep my mouth shut as I unpack the food. Bread, beans, cornflakes, cheese, butter, milk, pasta: the essentials to keep us going, but nothing exciting. And all Asda's own brand.

"No treats, I see."

"No, Liv, no treats. We only have your child allowance and my student loan – which is running out fast. If I'd got that job, then we'd have been just about OK."

I stop, suddenly realizing what the real issue is.

"You didn't get it? I thought you said the interview went well."

"It did, but they reckon I'm over-qualified. Called me today, advising me to continue with my studies. Chance would be a fine thing!"

Guilt plucks at my stomach.

"You'll go back to uni, Hatty, and you'll forget all about this place. You'll finish your degree."

"I used to think so."

As soon as the shopping is away, I put the kettle on to boil and make some sandwiches for tea. Spooning coffee into Harriet's favourite "*carpe diem*" mug, an empty feeling wells in my stomach. As I hand Harriet her drink, the emptiness turns into anger. None of this is fair on either of us. Why should we suffer because of Mam? I decide to try and cheer Harriet up by asking about her favourite topic: uni.

"Have you heard from your uni friends lately?"

"No."

"Will you tell me about that time the lad came streaking through the uni bar with his pants on his head? That was dead funny."

"Another time, Liv. I'm not in the mood."

I butter four slices of bread and grate a thin layer of cheddar on top of each. I prefer the cheese in slices but it doesn't last as long.

"So you haven't heard from anyone?"

"No. I'm trying not to call too often."

"Why?"

"I don't want them to get sick of me or think I'm a pest."

"Why would they think you're a pest?"

"They're all so together: nice families and stuff. I don't want to be bothering them with my freaky family."

"Thanks!" I say, only slightly hurt. "But that sounds dumb to me."

Harriet shakes her head and sighs.

"You'll understand when you're older."

She trusts me one minute, then acts like I'm a kid the next. Frowning, I put the tops on the sandwiches and cut them down the centre. Triangles for me, rectangles for my sister.

"If I was you and I'd had bad news, I'd call my friends. Who else can you count on?"

Harriet's face twists into a smile.

"You know what? You're right. I'll call Robin. She's always happy to listen to a good rant."

I follow Harriet into the passageway and lean against the wall, munching one of my sandwiches. As soon as Robin answers the call, Harriet signals for me to skedaddle. I do, but I can't resist listening in from the landing as I read through the flapjack recipe, trying to figure out where to get the stuff from. There's quite a bit needed, and some of it sounds expensive. As I read, I listen in to Hatty's conversation. I have to shove my hand over my mouth every time she says something using Edinburgh slang. But then her words take an unexpected turn.

"Yeah, I'm OK. Tired. And missing Edinburgh. You'll never guess what Liv did this time."

There is a pause. I listen closely, my giggles falling away as I grip the banister.

"Ah no, this is a good one," Harriet chuckles into the phone. "Even I can hardly believe it. She only went and set the house on fire."

There is a long pause this time.

"It wasn't on purpose. It was a cooking accident. Which is weird, seeing as no one in my family cooks."

Shame and anger battle it out in my gut. How dare Hatty discuss me like this? If Mam taught us anything, it's that you don't air your dirty linen in public.

"She was making shortbread and it caught fire. The oven's filthy and the ceiling's all black. I swear she's a right handful."

My anger sizzles and bubbles, threatening to erupt. I should stop eavesdropping, but I can't tear myself away.

"Oh, Robin, not this again! I told you before, I know you're concerned about me, but I can't put her in a foster home. I'm her big sister. I have to look after her."

My jaw drops and it feels like a ton of something cold and horrible has just landed on my head. Whoever this Robin is, she wants Harriet to dump me in care!

Memories of when we were both in foster care for a few months come flooding back. I was just five and the people looking after me were really nice. They took me to the park and on woodland walks, made me jam sandwiches for tea and let me wear my favourite dresses – even though

Mam said they were only for best – but I couldn't stop crying the whole time. All I could think about was Hatty. Her absence was like a big monster trying to swallow me whole. I can't even remember what the nice couple looked like – all I can remember is the emptiness. Robin will never persuade her.

"I know she's making life difficult, but uni has to wait. I can't give up on her. Not yet. She has no one else."

Hurt swells inside my heart, and I swallow hard. Creeping quietly into my room, I whack Johnny Cash up to full volume and throw myself on the bed, face to the ceiling and jaw clenched – not *yet?*

Chapter Eight

A Regular Little Goody-Two-Shoes

It's late when I sneak out of the house to clear my head. The night air feels crisp and fresh, despite the orange tinge to the clouds hovering above the chemical works. I suck in slow, deep breaths and the tension behind my eyes lessens. I sit quietly on the step until I get too cold and I'm forced to walk to warm up.

Heading for the local shops in the next estate – they should be quiet at this time and if there are any gangs hanging around, I can always turn back – my mind is buzzing with questions. How can I get some ingredients now Hatty's not going to help me? Why did I have to be so stupid and nick off school? Is Hatty really thinking of leaving?

The shops are quiet, and the shutters on the chippie are down. I peer into the small corner store, my hand sheltering the reflection from the street light above my head as I squint – trying to find the baking section so I can see how much money I'll need to get the oats, honey, sugar and rainbow treats.

"Fancy seeing you here."

I vaguely recognize the voice coming from the next shop doorway, and yet I jump.

"You frightened the life out of me—"

As I turn, my stomach somersaults. "Maddy, hi… sorry, I didn't mean to—"

"You're all right. You're not interrupting nothing. I'm just having a quick drink. Sit down – I could use some company. Want some?"

Maddy jiggles a small bottle of something emerald-green in my direction. I shake my head.

"Regular little goody-two-shoes aren't you?" Delighted with herself, she slaps her knee and laughs, loud and fake. "Oh yeah, I forgot your mam's an alky."

Sure, I think. *That's why you broke your neck to tell Jack earlier.* But she seems a bit out of it, so I keep quiet.

"Sit down then," she says.

I wish I'd stayed at home – or at least gone to the shops earlier. Unable to think up a plausible excuse to leave, I do as Maddy asks and join her on the step, tucking back into the shadows.

"Want a ciggie?"

She offers a blue and white packet. Again, I shake my head.

"I'm gonna get offended if you keep refusing me," says Maddy, blowing a cascade of smoke rings, thinking she's cool.

I try to read her expression. When she bursts out laughing, I feel my shoulders relax. A bit, but not completely.

"I'm only having you on. Don't look so serious! What are you doing here anyway?"

"An argument with Hatty. You?"

"Now, you should never ask someone their personal business. Didn't your mam ever teach you manners?"

"Sorry, I—"

She laughs in my face. "I'm pulling your leg! Jeez, you've no sense of humour these days, Liv."

Deciding it's safer to look at the ground, I pick at the rubber around the sole of my khaki Converse. The only decent item of clothing I own.

"Sure you don't want some of this? It's got a good kick."

The green liquor sloshes around the bottle as Maddy swallows a glug.

"No thanks."

"It won't kill you. Scared you'll end up like your mam?"

I know if she offers again, I'm going to have to accept. I'm already pushing it.

"Go on – one or the other. I'm not joking this time." There's a hard edge to her voice. "It's no fun smoking and drinking on your own."

It's my get-out-of-jail-free card. I take the cigarette and hold it to my lips. I've done this before and know how to look like I'm smoking without actually taking it back. I take a light drag, let the metallic taste fill my mouth, hold it for a few seconds then expel the smoke into the cold night air.

"You didn't take it back. Look, like me."

Trust her to notice. My heart's thumping as Maddy snatches the cigarette and sucks hard on its tip, relishing the taste. She hands it back to me triumphantly.

"Your turn. Properly."

This time, the smoke scorches my throat and fills my lungs. The roof of my mouth burns like when you're too hungry to wait for your pizza and you bite into the hot, melted cheese. Only it's a hundred times worse. I start choking, making embarrassing retching noises. Mad Dog snatches the cigarette away.

"That's disgusting. You've soaked the end. Slobbered all over it."

But she continues smoking it anyway. The way she sucks and blows on the ciggie makes me feel sick. After a while, she finally ditches it. The red embers glow as the butt arcs through the air, landing a few feet away. I watch the red glow fade and disappear, wishing I could do the same.

"So, what's this argument about?" asks Maddy.

I don't know what to say. I don't mind hanging out with her now and again, but Sarah's the only one I share my intimate secrets with.

"Nothing, really. Just getting some space, you know?"

"I've never seen you here this late before. It must be serious…"

I shrug, making a mental note to stay well away in future.

"Fine. Don't tell me then."

I take a deep breath. I've got to say something. People are volatile when they're half-cut and I can't risk upsetting Maddy.

"Did you see Sarah this lunch time?" I ask.

Of all the things I could say, why did I choose this? Now is not a good time. Maddy puckers her lips and stares into the distance. It's a while until she replies.

"Yeah. I saw her."

"Only—"

"What, Liv? What's she been saying about me now?"

"Nothing," I say, quickly retracting any plans to mention the bruise.

"Yeah, well I heard otherwise. She was overheard calling me a nickname – Mad Dog, that's it, isn't it?"

Trembling, I shrug.

"So I had to have a word with her."

"Just a word?"

"I said so, didn't I?" But the way Maddy's lips press together as she glares at me, I know she's lying. "While we're talking about having words… what was that crap you were telling Jack earlier? About setting the house on fire."

I'm glad she's dropped the other subject, but I know we're on dodgy territory with Jack, so I try to dismiss the conversation quickly.

"Oh that? I was baking and set the place on fire, that's all."

"You set the place on fire? Brilliant!"

"Just the oven. By accident."

"Shall we set this place alight? Burn it up?" She holds her lighter flame close to the shop door. The paint scorches and starts to blister. When I see smoke, I knock the lighter away.

"Don't!" I say.

Maddy laughs and puts the lighter back in her pocket. "Will you make something for me?"

"I dunno if Hatty will let me bake again," I say.

Maddy raises an eyebrow.

"I bet you would if Sarah asked you."

My legs tingle and turn weak. I wiggle my toes inside my shoes to make them feel a part of me again.

"It's not that. It's just convincing Hatty…"

"Must be nice to only have baking to worry about. I'd happily swap places."

She knows damn well Mam's in recovery and I've a lot more to think about than just baking. I open my mouth to say something, but decide better of it. Despite Maddy's bravado, there's a hint of sadness on her face as she stares off into space.

I think back to the times we'd be playing and her brother would come running up to warn her their dad was on his way home so she'd better get there quick. Sometimes she'd invite us to play with her in her garden, and although her mam was nice enough, there was no way we were going near her psycho dad. She always looked so hurt as she hurried off, looking back now and again to where me and Sarah played. I always pretended not to notice.

"You should tell your sister to get lost," says Maddy after a spell. "That's what I used to tell my brother, before, you know..."

Her voice trails off and I wrack my brains, trying to figure out whether it's her brother's birthday or the anniversary of his death. He was killed in an accident in our first year of secondary school, heading home from rugby try-outs. A motorbike lost control and ran into him. That's when Maddy's mam had a nervous breakdown. She's the same age as my mam but looks ancient, and she's always off her face on pills these days. When she's not, she's scared of her own shadow.

"But what I want to know is..." continues Maddy, stabbing my chest with her finger. I don't let her see that it hurts. "Are you going to stick up for yourself or what?"

"I do. But it doesn't work. She's in charge. And it's not like I can bake without ingredients."

Mad Dog snorts, slaps her leg and shakes her head.

"So, does Sarah help you bake?" she asks, lighting another ciggie.

I turn my head from the smoke.

"Nah. I've only tried it once. On my own."

"You make it sound like shagging or sniffing glue."

I can't help laughing. She's right.

"Here, you and Sarah, you're not lezzers are ya?"

Wishing I could tell Mad Dog where to go – like, who cares about that stuff anyway – I shake my head.

"No. Just mates."

"I've got loads of mates, me," says Maddy. "Can't stand hanging out with just one person. It gets on my tits."

"I couldn't get sick of Sarah."

"Even though sh-she's a l-loser?"

I feel like a rodent cornered by a hyena, but for some reason I can't stop my mouth.

"What have you got against Sarah these days, anyway? You'd still like her if you gave her a chance."

Snorting, Mad Dog raises her hand up to my face, fingers splayed.

"No way! I only have cool friends. Now shove off. No offence, but you're starting to get on my tits too."

I don't need telling twice. I jump to my feet.

"It was nice chatting with you—"

"Wish I could say the same," says Maddy.

"Right," I say, quickly turning the corner.

As soon as I'm out of earshot, I leg it all the way home. Tucked safely up in bed, the conversation with Mad Dog plays over and over in my head. I reread the next few recipes and I wrestle my brain for options, but can't find any. Then it comes to me: Mrs Snelling, the school's head cook. She's dead nice and would probably be delighted to know a student was interested in cooking. I decide to tackle her the next day.

Chapter Nine

Some of Us Would Like to Eat Today

As soon as I see Sarah twitching in the dinner queue, I know Mad Dog's nearby. Checking behind me, I spot Maddy on her own, two people down in the line. I smile at Maddy, but she ignores me, and her eyes lock onto Sarah's profile. Taking a step back, I nudge Sarah into my own space in the queue.

"Here, you're in a hurry. Go first."

Sarah's features relax a little and she smiles appreciatively, but I daren't look in Maddy's direction. She'll see it as me taking Sarah's side again. As we move along the counter selecting our food – burger, chips and beans for me; beef, roast potatoes and carrots for Sarah – I feel my heart beat faster and my palms grow sticky. The counter where the head cook serves is getting close. Mrs Snelling – a short, fat, ginger-haired woman who always laughs too loudly – is my only hope if I'm ever going to continue baking. There's a lot at stake here. I have to handle it right.

When we reach the dessert counter, I act like I can't decide – even though I always choose sticky toffee pudding. Sarah's not convinced.

"It's this morning's double Science," I say. "It's got my head in a muddle. Grab us some seats and I'll be right over."

Sarah sneaks a glance in Maddy's direction. She's busy chatting with the dinner lady so Sarah scuttles off. Meanwhile, I flash Mrs Snelling the biggest smile imaginable.

"How are you today, Mrs Snelling?"

Mrs Snelling guffaws and throws up her hands.

"Well, I never been asked that before – not in here anyways." She turns to the lady in charge of vegetables. "Have you ever heard the likes?" She laughs like a madwoman and slaps a hand on the counter. "I'm very well, thank you. How are you today, missy?"

I can feel the other kids watching.

"Liv... my name's Liv. I'm good too – except..." I leave the sentence hanging, like I've got something really important but difficult to say.

"Except what, dear?"

Mrs Snelling's round, ruddy face is full of concern. It's all going to plan – except for the other kids staring.

"I've a Home Economics project and I'm short on ingredients."

Mrs Snelling leans back and sets off laughing again. A hush travels along the dinner queue like a Mexican wave. I spot Jack towards the end of the line, fiddling with his cutlery. He flashes me a big smile, and then mimes flicking open a lighter, followed by an explosion. Maddy sees him and giggles, but shoots me an angry look.

"A few more people your age could do with taking an interest in cooking," says Mrs Snelling, and even though I want to shut her up so I can hurry on, I can't. I need her help. Mortified, I listen. "People say it's lack of education and high unemployment what causes problems, but..." She throws a judgmental glance along the queue that I hope Jack won't see. "The real issue is that people are losing basic skills. They're not being shown at home, so they don't take any interest."

Trying to keep smiling, I nod. I'm attracting too much attention. Down the line, they're getting fidgety and several kids step back to see what's causing the delay. Fights start breaking out about who belongs where in the queue.

"What's the hold-up, Liv?" shouts Mad Dog. "Some of us would like to eat today, y'know."

I keep my eyes averted. I don't want to seem like I'm offering a challenge.

"What ingredients are you missing, dear?" asked Mrs Snelling.

"I'll have to check the recipe – there're just a few things," I lie.

My face is hot with blushes. Thankfully, Mrs Snelling holds up a podgy hand, ripe with oven burns. I make a mental note to use oven gloves.

"Well, I'd never leave a fellow chef in the lurch! Come back when you're ready – about half three's usually a good time, before I head home – and we'll see what we can do. And here – have an extra-big portion of sticky toffee pudding to keep you going in the meantime."

"Thanks," I say, preparing to leg it.

"Can I have an extra-big portion too?" asks Maddy.

"Friend of yours?" asks Mrs Snelling. I feel Maddy's eyes burning into me, and nod. "Then of course you can, dear," says the cook, laughing once more.

I take the opportunity to make my escape. As I flop into the plastic chair opposite Sarah, I see her cheeks colour slightly.

"I see you and Maddy are best friends again," she says as greeting.

"I bumped into her last night," I say, realizing Sarah is wearing her jumper, even though it's a warm day. "How's your arm?"

"Fine. Forget it."

"I tried to have a word with her... She denied it of course."

"You did what? She'll kill me."

"Don't worry. I was subtle. But I knew you were telling the truth this time, not her."

A strange look crosses Sarah's face. She puts down her fork.

"Wait – you thought I was lying?" she asks, like the idea had never occurred to her.

"Not lying exactly but... exaggerating maybe?"

"That's nice, Liv. Real nice. Speaking of lies... What's all this about doing Home Economics?"

"Supersonic ears!"

I tuck into my burger, using it as an excuse not to talk. Although Sarah's my best friend, she doesn't have to know *everything* – especially when it's something I can't even explain to myself.

"Fine. But when you get that look on your face, you usually end up in trouble."

Waving my burger in the air dismissively, I stuff my mouth with chips. There's no way this plan can go wrong. It's just a few cakes and biscuits. A way to remember Mam and get back into Hatty's good books. What harm can it do?

Chapter Ten

Shame Hangs Over Me Like a Cloud

On Friday at three o'clock, I hand over the list of ingredients to Mrs Snelling, having spent ages copying them from the recipe book. The kitchen machinery hums as she reads the list slowly, nodding as she goes. I cross and uncross my legs on the high stool, my back as straight as I can muster under the embarrassing circumstances. Mrs Snelling gets so far down the list, then stops and frowns.

"There's quite a bit here – don't you have any of it?" she asks.

Mortified, I shake my head.

"Well, I have most of it," she says. "But sugared violet petals? We don't have any of those here. Too expensive."

"Don't worry about them – I'll do without," I say.

"Improvisation. The sign of a great cook."

As she winks, I give her a big grin, thinking what a dead nice mam she must be. Her kids are lucky.

Mrs Snelling disappears off into a huge cupboard in the back, and I spin on my chair, taking in the kitchen's shiny surfaces and industrial appliances. It would be impossible to set this place on fire! When Mrs Snelling returns, she has a small carrier bag of ingredients for me, which she hands over with a smile. I stuff it inside my rucksack, and get ready to leave.

"I'm glad I could help," she says. "But have you thought about how you'll get stuff in future?"

I had been hoping to ask her, but I guess that's not an option.

"Mam will be able to help me next time. Things were a bit tight this week," I lie.

Out of nowhere, anger bubbles up inside me and I clench my fists and jaw to hide it. I'm angry at Mam, at Hatty; I'm furious with my dad, who wouldn't even recognize me in the street. I shouldn't have to be begging for oats and honey. We're not living in the dark ages. A pitying look creeps over Mrs Snelling's face, and the room suddenly feels too noisy and too hot. Thank goodness it's the weekend, so I don't have to face her tomorrow. I jump to my feet and edge my way to the door as Mrs Snelling starts chatting about edible flowers and how they shouldn't be so pricey. I wait as long as I can, but not until she's finished, before calling out "Thanks for these," and rushing off.

* * *

I don't return to class – there's no point with just a few minutes to go till the bell rings. Instead, I go outside and gulp the fresh air, resting against the wall so the cold bricks penetrate my clothes and cool my skin. I should be delighted – I've got what I wanted – but a sense of shame hangs over me. I close my eyes, let the gentle sunlight warm my eyelids for a moment. The bell screams out and footsteps pass by as other pupils start streaming out of the building, chattering excitedly about their weekend. I try to concentrate on my breathing, let their voices merge and wash over me. I'm dreading the weekend. We have to go see Mam on Sunday.

The chatter passes me by and I'm just starting to relax, with spots of green appearing behind my eyelids, when a voice rings out – too loud and too close.

"What on earth are you doing? You get weirder every day, Liv."

It's Maddy. I open my eyes and leap away from the wall. She's with her cronies. Emma, a tall thin girl with cat-like green eyes and a frizzy black Afro; Zadie, an African girl who was picked on for years in our primary school but is now almost six feet tall, the perfect height for exacting revenge on the world; and Lorna, one of the school's top athletes, who is built like a shot putter but blessed with gorgeous brown curls. They're all there, watching.

"You wanna hang out with us?" asks Maddy.

I should go meet Sarah and walk home. Getting mixed up with this crowd is never a good idea. But it's ages since Maddy asked me to hang out with a group, so I can't help being tempted.

"Where are you going?"

"To the cemmy. Getting some cider. It'll be a laugh."

"I don't know…" I say.

Then Jack and Chris turn up.

"You hanging out?" asks Jack.

"Nah. She's being boring," says Zadie.

I swallow, and look out towards our usual meeting spot to see if Sarah's waiting. Of course she's there. I see her leaning on the fence, checking her watch. A few more minutes and she'll leave. Maddy follows my gaze, and a small smile plays on her lips as she hooks her arm into mine.

"You leave Liv alone," she says, and Zadie's face drops. "We've been friends since primary school."

She starts walking us away from Sarah, towards the direction of the cemetery, and I cross my fingers, hoping Sarah won't notice. It can't harm hanging out with Maddy; if I get back in with her, maybe I can convince her and her friends to leave Sarah alone.

I check behind me and see Sarah fidgeting. She checks her watch one last time and is just about to give up on me when Maddy calls out, "Have a nice weekend, Sarah."

Spinning on her heels, Sarah's eyes meet mine and my heart sinks into my stomach. I try to give her a smile but she's already turned her back and is heading towards home, her head held high but her steps slow and measured.

"Can't we ask Sarah too?" I say.

"No way! That stutter m-makes me s-s-sick," says Maddy, and everyone laughs. Even me, though I don't know why.

* * *

I can't text Sarah or Hatty because my battery is dead. I should probably go home, but when Jack offers me some cider, I take it. I know I shouldn't, but it's not like I have any better plans. Every time Jack looks over from the group of lads he's sitting with – Chris, and some guy called Macca who hasn't even acknowledged me – I take another slug.

It turns out Maddy and the girls aren't as bad as Sarah makes out; they're actually quite nice when you spend time with them. They do their best to include me at first, but after a while, they fall into their usual conversations and in-jokes; when Maddy, Zadie and Emma start talking about some new perfume I'll never be able to afford, I leave them to it and find myself a quiet spot, equidistant from the lads and the lasses. The last thing I expect is for Jack to notice and follow me.

"So, what's your mam like?" asks Jack.

He's a little bit wasted by now, and his voice slurs.

"Dunno," I say.

He laughs, globs of spit escaping his mouth. It doesn't even make me feel sick. It could be the cider, or it could be the fact that he's gorgeous and I've got him all to myself.

"I used to sound like you. Don't be embarrassed – my dad was a raging alky. Used to beat up my mam and stuff. It was a nightmare."

He shakes his head. The cider has made me brave – I wouldn't dare sit and chat with him like this usually – and I wonder if this is the feeling Mam looks for when she drinks.

"I used to dread him coming home," continues Jack. "Now, I wish he would."

"Your dad's not around?"

"No. Remember when I was getting into trouble all the time and being a complete idiot?" I nod. That's when he started hanging around with Maddy. That's when he suddenly got taller and his voice got deeper, and I really noticed him. "Mum booted him out. He kicked the booze, but there are some things you can't make up for."

"I had no idea. Sorry…"

I feel like reaching out, stroking Jack's hand or face, but of course I don't. This isn't some romcom, this is real life. He'd probably push me away, disgusted.

"It's OK. Mum didn't deserve the beatings, and I couldn't do anything to help her at the time, so it's only right I should support her now. Your dad's not around either, right?"

"Right," I say, spotting Maddy on her way over, and hoping that'll end the conversation.

"You might not talk much, but you're a dead good listener, Liv. Thanks," says Jack.

His words hang in the air. I shrug and take another swig, accidentally inhaling it so I start choking on the cider just as Maddy arrives.

"What are we talking about?" asks Maddy, narrowing her eyes at me.

She sits next to Jack, making sure her leg touches against his. He doesn't move away.

"Absentee fathers and pissheads," says Jack, and falls about with laughter.

Maddy looks at him for a second, then starts falling about with laughter too. I have no choice but to join in.

"We can all relate to that," says Maddy, and she takes Jack's drink from him and has a big gulp, staring at me as she does so. "I thought we might be talking about how come Liv's suddenly drinking. Wouldn't take a drop off me the other night."

I feel my insides tremble and my stomach lurches. The cemetery turns wobbly, like the gravestones are ready to topple. I take a deep breath, but that just makes me feel even more sick.

Jack laughs. "I guess I'm better company."

I try to protest, but before I know what's happening, the cider is rushing back up my throat and out of my mouth. Projectile vomit spurts towards Jack and Maddy pulls him out of the way, into her arms, just in time.

"Urgh! Disgusting! Everyone, Liv's chucking up."

I heave and heave, the stream of acidic liquid seemingly never-ending, and I make these embarrassing retching noises that sound like a goat being strangled. Zadie, Emma, Chris and some other lad that's joined us; they all come to watch. Chris pats my back.

"Get it out, lass," he says, making me throw up once more, much to everyone's amusement.

When I stop retching, everyone claps and cheers, then they return to their own drinking. I try to get to my feet, but it's like my legs are disconnected from the rest of me. Thankfully, Maddy leans in and hooks my arm.

"I saw Jack first, so he's out of bounds. NFDN, remember?" she hisses in my ear, then adds loudly to the group, "Jack, darling, get the other side."

Jack does as Maddy asks, and the two of them walk me around the cemetery several times until I'm feeling better. Emma brings me some water, and then we do one last lap of the leafy grounds. I could easily walk without help by now, but Maddy seems intent on making a good impression by playing mother hen. Something tells me it's not for my benefit.

The sky is getting dark and it's time to leave. Hatty will be worried if I'm much later, especially seeing as I didn't send her a text. But how do you leave when there's a big gang of you and you've a lonely night ahead? Lorna is getting off with Macca, and I fidget awkwardly, trying not to watch, waiting for a break in the conversation of the others. As soon as there's a breather, I jump in.

"Right, I'm off," I say, hoping Jack will come too.

"Bye," says Maddy, her voice cold and unfriendly.

The other girls pick up on it straight away.

"Yeah, see ya," they say in unison.

As I start walking away, Jack shouts after me.

"Want me to walk you home?"

"No, I'll be fine," I say.

"You sure?"

"She'll be fine," says Maddy.

As I make my way home, the road sways and I realize I'm not as sober as I thought. It may be wobbly, but the ground feels like air. I just spent my evening talking to Jack Whitman! When I get in, there's a crack of light showing under the living room door.

"I'm home," I shout, and go straight up the stairs.

That's the last I remember. Next thing I know, it's morning, and I'm sweating in bed, fully dressed, with only my shoes missing.

Chapter Eleven

Richard of York Gave Battle in Vain

I stay in bed to avoid Hatty for as long as I can, in case she could tell I came home drunk. My head feels thick and sludgy, and my limbs aren't quite connected to my brain. My stomach is so empty it groans, but I daren't eat anything – huge waves of nausea keep flowing over me, and I feel like I'm going to chuck up at any minute. After a while, I brave some cornflakes.

"Morning, sleepy head," says Hatty.

"Morning," I say, hardly opening my mouth.

I've brushed my teeth three times already, and my breath still stinks. My tongue feels like a piece of sandpaper that's been used to scrub a toilet.

"You OK?" asks Hatty, scrunching up her face.

"Yeah, just dreading The Visit."

"I know. Me too," she says. "Right, I'm off for a walk. Wanna come?"

"No, thanks," I say, fighting the nausea. "I'm going to do some baking."

"You got the stuff?" she asks, raising an eyebrow. "How?"

"The cook at school."

Hatty taps her forehead with a finger. "Smart thinking," she says. "But not until I get back, you're not."

* * *

I wait for Harriet to return before braving the kitchen. Almost a week has passed since I set the kitchen on fire, and Harriet's doing her best not to interfere, but she keeps making excuses to come into the kitchen.

I prop *Recipes to Make Happiness Bloom* on top of the toaster and prepare all the ingredients. The flapjack recipe promises to bring out rainbows in grey skies and, despite my great evening, I could do with some rainbows right now; I have a banging headache and I'm due at Sarah's this afternoon, but I'm not sure whether she'll be mad at me. Taking out the mixing bowl and wooden spoon, I already feel a little better. By the time I'm melting butter, sugar and honey together, inhaling the rich aromas, my heart feels lighter and I'm hardly thinking about Sarah at all. A twinge of guilt sneaks in as I add the porridge oats – I should at least have spoken to Sarah before I went off with Maddy – but it quickly disappears. The mixture, golden like the barley fields you see on documentaries, draws me in. No wonder Mam sounds so happy in her recipes. Baking really can make the skies blue again. By the time I add the colourful bits, I'm in a dream world. It's like I really could be adding real pieces of rainbow.

It's the old mnemonic that does it. Mam taught me it in primary school – Richard of York Gave Battle in Vain – to help me remember the colours of the rainbow. It's the first concrete sign of a mam I recognize. The mnemonic earned me first prize in a school fundraising quiz. The "colours of the rainbow" was the tiebreaker question and I won a giant box of Belgian chocolates and a ten-pound book voucher. I used the voucher in the sales to get a book each for Mam and me. We read on the sofa, toes touching, chomping on the delicious chocolates for the whole weekend.

"Things weren't always bad," I say aloud, to make it more real. I drop sour cherries into the mixture from a height, watching the fragments glow for an instant as they catch the sun.

When it comes to mixing, I realize I've taken the dream world too far and haven't been paying attention to the measurements. The mixture is thick and difficult to stir so I try blending an extra slab of butter before turning it out onto the greased baking tray and quickly shoving it in the cleaned-out oven. I set the alarm on my mobile for fifteen minutes and sit at the kitchen table, chin in hand.

Time drags and I start thinking about tomorrow's visit to Ashgrove House. I try to keep my attention on baking, but I can't stop my mind from wandering to those echoing corridors, the bright orange walls and fake flowers, the overpowering smell of air freshener. Hatty returns to the kitchen so I snatch up the cookbook and double-check the timings, then stuff it violently into my bag. I'm not ready to share it yet, and I wish she'd just let me get on with things in peace. Settling back in my chair, I wait, arms folded. As soon as Harriet opens her mouth to say something, I jump in before she can.

"Before you start, no I haven't set anything on fire. All right?"

When Harriet doesn't respond, I look up and realize she's been crying. Her eyelids are swollen and her eyelashes look sticky. She glances at the mass of dirty pots and sighs.

"Just make sure you clean that mess up."

I want to ask her what's wrong, but the potential answers scare me. Instead, I say, "I will. I'm not totally useless."

"I never said you were. And don't ever let anyone tell you otherwise."

I expected more lectures, perhaps some tantrums. A slanging match, at least.

"What are you making, anyway?" Harriet sniffs, dabbing at her nose with a tissue.

"Flapjacks. I thought I'd take some round to Sarah's later."

Harriet nods, a distant look in her eyes that reminds me of Mam. Panic flutters in my stomach. I've never seen my sister like this.

"There's some for you, too. They'll be ready in… five minutes."

"Thanks."

Harriet pours herself a glass of cold water. She downs it in one go, pours another, and joins me at the kitchen table. It's months since we sat here together; we usually eat in our rooms or in front of the TV.

Last time, we'd been discussing what we'd do if Mam went into residential care again. Visits to Alcoholics Anonymous and outreach support had failed and we knew what was coming. When the social worker started hinting, we weighed up our options: either I went into care or Harriet took a year out of uni. Harriet cried back then as well. I should be grateful, really, that she's looking over my shoulder. At least she cares.

"So, what's going on with all this cooking, then?" asks Harriet.

I shrug. I'm more interested in what's wrong with her, but I don't know how to ask. She's in charge. Things feel different since she starting playing Mam, despite all the "sisters together" chats. I consider sharing the cookbook with her to see if it brings us closer again, but it's nice to have something that's just mine.

"I like it, that's all."

"Mam used to bake, you know."

My mouth falls open. Hatty's never mentioned this before and I can't remember Mam baking. Ever.

"Mam doesn't eat, never mind cook!"

"I'm serious!"

"What did she make?"

"Cakes, mostly. I used to love the smell. It was like..." She sniffs at the air.

"Like mine?"

"Actually, yes."

I smile to myself as I wipe the side down.

"Did you help her?"

"I was too young. She had a friend, Rosa, who used to come over and bake with her. There was talk of opening a café at one point."

"What sort of café?"

"A cake café, I guess."

The recipe book; it must have been for the café! It all falls into place. It's not just a book of cakes and biscuits, it's a book of Mam's dreams.

"I was only a kid," continues Harriet. "So I was more interested in my toys, but I would listen to them fooling around as they worked. When you came along, they used to sit you next to the counter in your high chair. You didn't make a peep. It was like you were taking it all in. Maybe that's why you're a natural?"

I beam with pride. I know it's sad, but I can't help it. But then I think of what I missed out on and the smile disappears. Why couldn't Dad have stuck around longer, so I'd have some nice memories too?

"So what happened?" I say, trying to keep my voice steady.

"I don't know for definite... Rosa just stopped coming. Not long after that, we moved here. But it wasn't always bad."

"I wouldn't know."

"Don't say that! There are people much worse off than us. At least we've got each other, right?"

I pull a face, but really I'm surprised how comforting her words feel. As the warm smell of melting honey fills the kitchen, I close my eyes and try to imagine Mam and Dad here too.

"Hmm, that smells so good," says Harriet, reaching over and giving me a gentle shove. "Better than last time, hey?"

Despite my embarrassment, I manage to keep my temper.

"I cleaned the oven while you were out."

Harriet exaggerates wiping her brow in relief, then gives me this weird, intense stare.

"Listen, Liv, you'll get outta here too, you know. Just hold in there. OK?"

I nod, confused. It's Harriet that's crying. Harriet that's falling apart. But what does she mean by *too*? Is she leaving again? Has she finally given up on me?

"Hatty, are you all right?"

The words come out shaky and slow. Before Harriet can answer, the alarm on my phone sounds, making us both jump.

"Saved by the bell," says Harriet, smiling sadly. "Don't worry, I'm not going anywhere, if that's what you're thinking. I'm just tired. Stuff's getting on top of me."

"Like me, you mean?"

"No, not you. Mam, late assignments… that stupid job interview. I'm missing my mates and trying to deal with stuff on my own. But forget it. Let's try these flapjacks instead!"

As soon as she finishes speaking, Harriet's hand shoots out and grabs a steaming biscuit. I copy and we giggle loudly as we shove hot chunks of flapjack into our mouths like pigs.

Chapter Twelve

Through the Ocean, Guiding a Calf

The sun is shining low and bright as I reach Sarah's house. Armed with carefully wrapped flapjacks, I ring the doorbell several times in quick succession, my heart thumping. Even though Sarah's mum says I can just walk in, I can't bring myself to do it. Mam would go nuts if she found out I was walking straight into other people's houses – it'd make "a show" of her.

"Hi Liv, come in! Sarah's waiting in the living room," says Mrs Butler, opening the door just enough to be visible.

Her greeting tumbles out clumsily, only half of her face smiling.

She suffered a stroke whilst giving birth to Sarah – that's why Sarah's an only child – and she hasn't regained full use of her left side.

It was the stroke that made Mrs Butler agoraphobic, which means she's too afraid to step outside her own front door. When it started, she was scared that people would laugh, and then it grew into this massive phobia. At first it seemed weird, but I'm used to it now. I often wonder what she'd do if there was a fire.

"Thanks, Mrs Butler."

"I've told you, call me Fran!"

"OK, Mrs Butler."

Being on first name terms would also make a show of Mam. Another big no-no. Another thing to worry about.

Sarah's laid flat on her stomach, head resting on her hands, eyes glued to the TV.

On the screen, a huge blue whale makes its way through the ocean, guiding a calf. The calf is so graceful it seems weightless, even though it probably weighs a couple of tons. I flop on the floor next to Sarah.

"Hi," I say a bit too loudly, my nerves getting the better of me.

"Isn't it lovely? That something so b-big can be so gentle?" she says.

Her tone of voice is fine, but the stutter shows she's upset.

I decide I'll make it up to her – the flapjacks are a start.

"You'd expect it to kill the calf or something, being that massive," I say.

Sarah turns around, eyes wide.

"Would you kill your baby if you were a blue whale? That'd be the ultimate betrayal."

I know the challenge is more about me than it is the whales, but I don't bite.

Cringing, I point at the screen, where a pack of killer whales flank the calf.

"I wouldn't need to."

We watch as the mother whale tries her best to guide her offspring, but the pack is stronger. It's like Maddy's gang when they spot Sarah. I don't say that though – especially since I went off with them.

"That's disgusting," says Sarah, blocking her eyes from the television.

"It's nature," I say, eyes glued.

The killer whales succeed at separating the calf from its mother. Thrown around by the hunting pack, bashed and bruised, the calf eventually tires and drowns.

"How can anything be so cruel?" asks Sarah, as the camera switches to a killer whale's graceful retreat.

A hot, steaming mug of chocolate arrives just in time – before things have a chance to get too heated.

"Thanks, Mrs Butler," I say sweetly.

Mrs Butler's the best mam in the world, and you can't help feeling chilled out around her – she has this calming effect. I always feel at home here, and my worries melt away as I relax into the familiar surroundings. There's no tension. Everything is consistent. When she walks away, I decide to get my apology over with.

"Sorry about yesterday. I didn't know how to say no to Maddy – you know what she's like."

It's not quite an apology, and not quite true either, but I figure there's nothing wrong with a little white lie now and again to spare your best friend's feelings.

"It's OK," says Sarah, her face relaxing. "I don't blame you for going."

"Thanks – you're the best," I say.

My conscience cleared, I realize the timing is perfect for the flapjacks, and jump up.

"Goodness, my heart!" cries Mrs Butler, jumping as well.

"Sorry! I just remembered that I brought you something."

Fumbling in my bag, my hands turn clumsy and awkward.

I eventually find what I'm looking for and, as I pull out the tangle of paper and Sellotape, I can't help the cheesy grin that spreads across my face. "Here!"

Sarah and her mum glance at each other in wonder as I unravel the complicated wrapping and flatten it into a makeshift plate.

"George, I think you'd better come in here," calls Mrs Butler. "Liv has something special for us."

As Sarah's dad saunters in, I realize there isn't enough for everyone.

Me and Hatty got carried away earlier, so there are only three flapjacks left – and one of those is mine. Sarah's dad usually works on Saturdays, so I hadn't expected him to be home.

The flapjacks are delish and, although I want one – I mean, really, really want one, more than anything – I hold the biscuits out in full view.

"See, one for each of you."

For some reason, the flapjacks no longer look as mighty as before.

They're a bit dark at the edges, too pale in the centre, and not at all straight like the ones you see in the shops. They look a bit dry and shrivelled. I feel my face flush. How could I bring something so inferior to the Butlers'? As the three of them peer down at my outstretched hand, I fight the urge to bolt.

"They look delicious," says Mrs Butler, just at the right time.

"I'll get some plates," says Sarah, bounding off to the kitchen.

I wait, my body tense. I can't believe I'm getting the jitters over some daft flapjacks, but I can't peel my eyes away as they each take a biscuit and lift it to their mouths.

Mr Butler winces as he bites into his.

"Are they too tough?" I ask.

"Nope," he replies, crunching loudly. "I've been having trouble with my tooth. I can eat it very well on the other side."

And he can. It seems they're OK after all. I watch, breath held, as Sarah and her parents munch and chomp their way through.

At first, I worry they're just being kind, but it soon begins to sink in that they really are enjoying my gift.

"Where did you buy them?" asks Mr Butler, shoving the last chunk into his mouth.

"I made them myself."

"They're really good. You've a real talent, there," says Mrs Butler.

Her face crinkles into a proud grin and she reaches out to pat my arm. Without meaning to, I pull away. I wonder if Mam will look at me like that one day.

"Now I know what you were up to with Mrs Snelling! These are seriously good, Liv," says Sarah. "I didn't know you could cook!"

Beaming, I turn back to the TV, hot chocolate in hand.

"It's nothing. You just need the right recipe."

Eccles Cake, Like Your Granny Made

They say that the older you are, the wiser you get; well, here's a recipe from a wise, wise woman, aged just twenty-seven. Make them and see – then feel free to call me Granny Bloom!

INGREDIENTS

500 g / 1 lb 2 oz puff pastry (you can cheat this time)
25 g / 1 oz yummy melted butter
Pinch of freshly ground nutmeg
55g / 2 oz candied peel
115 g / 4 oz caster sugar
225 g / 8 oz plump and juicy currants

HOW TO MAKE THE MAGIC HAPPEN

1. Pre-heat oven to 220 °C / 425 °F / Gas mark 7.
2. In a saucepan, mix the sugar and butter, and cook over a medium heat until it's melted into liquid gold.
3. Take off the heat, add currants, candied peel and nutmeg. Watch the currants swell and get a whiff of those smells!
4. On a lightly floured surface, roll the pastry thinly and cut into rounds – approx. ¼ in./½ cm thickness and 4 in./10 cm diameter – but don't worry too much, no one's watching!
5. Place a small spoonful of delicious filling into the centre of each pastry circle – be careful not to overfill.

It's tempting, but resist – otherwise they'll burst open and burn.

6. Dampen the edges of the pastry with a little cold water and draw the edges together over the fruit, pinching to seal.

7. Turn the bundle of love over and press gently with a rolling pin to flatten the cakes. Snip a little "V" for "Victory" in the top with scissors.

8. Place on a greased baking tray, brush with water and sprinkle with a little extra sugar – go on, spoil yourself!

9. Bake in the oven for 15 minutes or until golden round the edges. Place on a wire rack and allow to cool. Travel back to simpler, happier times with every bite.

Chapter Thirteen

You're a Right Fat Pig

The next morning, I slouch next to Harriet in the visitor waiting room. We haven't spoken a word since we arrived and, from the look on Harriet's face, I know she's thinking the same: that she'd rather be anywhere else in the world than here.

I hate this place. With a passion. It's so over-the-top cheery and fake. It's no wonder Mam isn't getting better – places like this make you feel sick. They make you worry about not complying with the norms. It's like they're designed to alienate you, and that's the last thing anyone needs. I also hate the weirdos that wait here – with their shifty glances and blank stares. We don't belong here at all – Mam included. We should be at home, doing normal things as a family. Why can't Mam just pull herself together and quit drinking – how hard can it be?

Every time footsteps sound in the corridor, Harriet glances at the doorway. Each time it's not Mam, she sighs. I can't decide whether the noise signifies relief or disappointment, but it's driving me nuts. I tangle small plaits into my hair, tugging so tightly that my scalp pinches, and I pull my knees up to my chest. Resting my feet on the chair cushions earns a disapproving look from Hatty, but I'm past caring.

"She's obviously not coming," I say, head between knees. "We've been waiting nearly half an hour. We should go."

"You'd like that, wouldn't you?"

"Sure. I could see what I need for the pastries I'm planning for later in the week."

"You and your bloody cooking. Is that all you care about?"

It's like being hit in the face with a slab of fresh liver. I finally find something I really like doing, and all it does is get me into bother.

"Can't you see there are more important things going on – bigger things to worry about?" continues Hatty. "Mum's stuck in here, and all you care about is bloody cake."

I know Harriet's trying to keep her voice quiet so the others can't hear, but it's not working.

"It's her own fault!" I say. "How is sitting around here helping, when she doesn't even want to see us? You're just jealous I've found something I like doing."

Harriet's shoulders slope and her face darkens. I should leave it there, but I can't stop my mouth from running away with itself.

"The only thing you're good at is eating all the cakes. You're a right fat pig."

Instead of retaliating, Harriet lowers her head into her hands and cries. It's a low, deep wail that comes from a very dark place – somewhere even worse than the Recovery Centre waiting room. Stunned, I watch my sister shake with sobs.

"I'm sorry, Hatty – I didn't mean it."

I try putting my arm around her shoulder but Harriet keeps crying. No matter what I try, she stays crumpled, like she no longer has the energy to lift her head. The crowd in the room shuffles, embarrassed by the show of such strong emotion. I feel a hot sting as my face glows all the way to my ears.

"Hatty, Harriet, come on, it's OK. Let's go home. I'll make you something nice."

The other people in the waiting room are really quiet. Harriet's sobs sound magnified in the silence. Heart racing, I rub her back, but other than that, I'm clueless. My sister is growing more alien to me each day.

"Try giving her some space, love," says a kindly voice.

When I look up, a middle-aged lady with tired eyes gives me a warm smile. I follow her advice but give Harriet's knee a gentle squeeze to let her know I'm here if she needs me. She slaps my hand away.

"What's it got to do with you?" snaps Harriet, suddenly lifting her head, revealing blotchy, tear-swollen skin.

"Excuse me," says the lady, averting her gaze. "I was only trying to help."

"It's because of people like you helping that Mam's in this hovel in the first place!" says Harriet, getting to her feet. "So, if you don't mind, I suggest you keep your nose out of other people's business."

I stand too, uncertain what to do next. I've never seen my sister behave this way. Hatty's the one that sorts things out, that stays in control.

A male nurse strides into the room, providing the perfect distraction.

"What's all the commotion?" he asks, trying to assess the situation by scanning the room.

I look to Hatty for an answer. She tosses her hair and wipes her eyes.

"There's no commotion. We're leaving. Tell Mam we said hi. If she even cares."

That's all the answer I need. I link arms with my sister and we march out of the room, heads held high. But we don't get far before a voice calls out.

"Girls. Girls? Where are you going?"

We stop, even though I want to keep going. I want to make her pay for upsetting Hatty like this. But of course I can't – for all her faults, she's our mam. I let go of Hatty's arm so she can wipe her eyes. She blows air upwards over her face, trying to cool it down. I'm the first to turn round, buying Hatty some time.

"We thought you weren't coming," I say.

"I'm sorry – I got carried away watching *Downton Abbey* DVDs and didn't realize the time."

When she pulls a daft pouty face, I feel like leaving again. But Hatty stands by my side and adds, "Well, we're glad you're here now."

Her face brightening, Mam rushes over to us and links our arms.

"Can we play table tennis?" I say.

"I forgot to book the table," says Mam. "But never mind, we'll go to my room. You can tell me all about what you've been up to."

As we walk along the corridor, I lean back a little to check on Hatty. She seems completely fine. You wouldn't know she had a meltdown just minutes ago.

Mam's room looks more homely than last time. She's put some flowers in a vase, and she's been drawing. There are sketches of fruit and birds strewn across her small table. Other than the pictures in the recipe book, I haven't seen her draw for years.

"These are really good, Mam," I say, admiring the detail on a swallow. She's put just enough effort into the feathers.

"Oh, those? It was my counsellor's idea. Said it would be therapeutic. Nowhere near as good as I used to be."

"I wish I could draw like that," says Hatty.

I sit in the seat near the window and continue flicking through the drawings.

"Can I draw you?" asks Mam.

When I look up, her face is beaming towards me.

"Sure," I say, taken aback. "Where shall I sit?"

"You're perfect where you are," says Mam, snatching up her sketchbook and pencil. "The light is just right."

Mam draws standing up. The sound of the lead scratching against the paper is soothing and the sun warms my neck. Hatty has the biggest smile on her face as she stands behind Mam, nodding as the image forms on the page. It's like old times, and I almost forget where we are.

"It looks like you already," says Hatty. "Mam, you should see Liv's drawings. She's getting really good – must get it from you."

"She's a talented girl," says Mam. When my jaw drops she adds, "Liv, don't fidget! It'll go wrong."

The scratching goes on for another ten minutes and I find it harder and harder to stay still. Mam has to remind me a few times, but soon she stops and holds the paper out.

"That's brilliant!" says Harriet. "You've got her eyes just right."

""No, no. It won't do at all," says Mam, staring at the drawing.

"It's great!" says Harriet, throwing me a worried look.

"Can I see?" I ask. "Can I have it?"

"Let Liv see, Mam," tries Harriet.

But Mam's face clouds over as she scrutinizes her work.

"Too much fidgeting. And the eyes… yours are much more beautiful."

Moving to my side, Hatty rests a hand on my shoulder. "It's lovely, Mam, honest," she says. "A perfect likeness."

"Let's have a look," I say, getting to my feet, but before I can see the drawing, Mam rips it into four pieces. The pieces drop to the ground and a single eye stares up at me.

"I'll do another one – a better one," she says. "Only the best for my girls."

I try to smile, but it feels sticky on my face. Suddenly, the orange walls feel overly bright. I make my excuses and go to the loo. When I return, the pieces have been cleared away, the TV's on and it seems Mam has forgotten all about drawing. Hatty gives me an apologetic look as she listens to Mam's recap of what's been happening up to this point on *Downton Abbey*.

Chapter Fourteen

Clues in the Curve of His Shoulders

I try calling Sarah from the landline, but there's no answer, and I've no credit to text. I scroll through my phonebook and realize most of the people in there are either relatives or they aren't even friends any more. It's like Facebook – hundreds of contacts, but none I can actually contact to hang out with in real life.

Hatty is shut up in her room and I decide it's best to leave her alone after this morning's upset. I check the weather, put my lightest jacket on, then head out for a walk to clear my head. Without realizing where I'm going, I end up at the shops. They're closed, except for the chippy, but the place is throbbing with people my age. There's music blasting – some dance stuff I can't stand – and I squint into the distance, trying to decide whether I should join in or avoid it like the plague. Unexpectedly, my knee gives way behind – someone has knocked into it on purpose, making my leg buckle.

"What the—?"

As I spin round, I recognize his deep laugh before I see Jack's face.

"Got ya!"

"Yeah, thanks a lot," I say, any annoyance falling away as soon as I see his smile.

Seeing as I'm facing back towards home, I decide to avoid the crowd. But as I walk off, Jack catches me by the arm.

"Hey! Where do you think you're going?"

He pulls me along towards the others, and I don't fight it. I'd be mad to! I could do with some cheering up and it's not like I'm letting Sarah down this time.

When we reach the crowd, Jack sits on the wall near the chippy, and pats the bricks for me to join him. I find myself admiring his toffee-coloured mop of hair. I like the way it catches the glow from the streetlights in its waves.

"Did you get into bother the other night?" he asks.

"Nah. I got away with it," I say, the smell of hot fat assaulting my nostrils.

"I hope you didn't mind me asking about your dad like that?"

I shake my head.

"It's just… I got the impression I might have upset you."

"Mam and Dad split up when I was two. I don't know much about him. Some people remember things from when they were babies. Not me."

There is a loud sizzle as some fresh chips are lowered into giant vats of oil.

"I'm like you. I don't remember stuff either. Have you ever tried to find him?"

"Not really… unless you count running away when I was five! My sister and I had this big, secret chat about Dad and she told me everything she could remember – everything I wanted to know. Afterwards, I got so obsessed that I packed a bag and headed off across the Rec to try and find him."

Jack bursts out laughing, and gives me a playful shove. I can't help laughing too.

"You're funny," he says, and looks at me for a few seconds longer than I feel comfortable with.

I put my head down and pretend my shoes are more interesting.

"Would you like to meet him?" asks Jack.

"Yeah, but it's not going to happen."

"You could make it happen."

"You sound like my counsellor. I don't think he wants to be found. Anyway, the dad in my head isn't real."

"The one I had in my head wasn't real for a long time either. It was like I'd wrapped him up in this imaginary bubble of what I wanted him to be."

"Me too! A giant rainbow-coloured bubble. When I think about him too much, the bubble bursts and turns a kind of mucky brown – like when you get over-excited mixing paint in Art class. Did you know that if you mix more than three colours together, you always get brown?"

"I didn't know that," says Jack, a smirk on his face.

"It's true. I stopped doing it in Art but not with my dad."

"Do you like Art class?"

"Yeah."

"I saw your drawings last year at the exhibition – they were good."

My face flares. I feel my ears and neck turn hot. Even my arms turn pink. Right on cue, Maddy appears at the other end of the shop parade. It takes a while for her to spot us, so I wave. I don't want her to think I'm sneaking around with Jack – not after her warning.

"Maddy, over here," I call.

Her expression falters for just a moment – a brief, dark cloud settling over it – but then she brightens. Joining us, she's all smiles.

"Fancy seeing you two here," she says. "You're as thick as thieves lately."

She pauses, waiting for an explanation. I'm hoping Jack will offer one of his quips, but instead he rolls his eyes and heads off towards a group of lads a few years older than us, who I don't know. As soon as he's gone, Maddy sits in his spot and swings her feet, lighting a cigarette as the interrogation begins.

"What's going on with you two?" she asks.

"Nothing."

"How come you're always together?"

I laugh. "We've hung out like three times. I hardly know him. It's just a coincidence that you've seen us."

"A rather convenient coincidence, if you ask me."

Maddy takes a deep drag, then blows smoke rings into my face. I don't move. I just sit there and let her do it.

"Did you get that baking thing sorted out?" she asks, taking me by surprise.

"Not really."

"Still struggling to get the stuff you need?"

"Yeah," I say, hardly believing that she's remembered – let alone taken an interest.

"Are you a complete idiot or what?" continues Maddy. "If you want something, take it. That's what my mam and dad always say."

"I can't."

"Why not?"

"It wouldn't be right."

"Who decides what's right and wrong?" Mad Dog takes a drag of her cigarette and blows the smoke out slowly – away from me this time. "Is it right that good people like my brother die young while bastards like my dad get to grow old in a jail cell?" She gulps before continuing. "Or that some people are loaded and others are skint or sleeping on the streets?"

"I guess not."

I daren't catch Mad Dog's eye, but she has a point.

"Nicking stuff isn't always wrong. Robin Hood was a thief and he's a bloody hero."

"True."

We both go quiet. I feel Maddy fidget and I slide away from her a little, in case she accidentally knocks into me and takes offence. After a while, Maddy starts up again. Her voice turns all weird and sly, and she reaches out to my hair and starts plaiting it on one side. She hasn't done this since we were about eight years old.

"So, Jack then... has he mentioned me at all?" she asks, her fingers weaving through my hair.

"In what way?" I ask, knowing full well, but buying time.

"You know. Like, has he said he fancies me?"

"Not in so many words but—"

"But what?" She pauses, then yanks my hair as she begins plaiting again. "He used to call me to hang out and we'd chat about all sorts of stuff. I hardly hear from him now. Any idea why not?"

"No. Sorry. It's not like we're close."

"You looked close enough to me the other night in the cemmy – and tonight, all cosy on the wall. It seems every time I find Jack, you're there. If I'm treading on toes, just tell me…"

"No! Honestly. It's you he fancies," I say.

"But I've seen how he looks at you. I think he fancies you."

"No way," I say, glancing in his direction.

He's busy chatting with his friends. Could Maddy be right – is it possible that Jack fancies me? I look for clues in the curve of his shoulders, the way he laughs. I half expect him to turn towards me, a spark in his eye. A sharp tug on my scalp brings me out of my daydream.

"He fancies you, not me," I say.

"Did he say that?"

Her voice is hopeful – vulnerable, almost.

Before I can answer that no, it's just my perception of events, a look of triumph spreads across her face.

"Of course he'd fancy me more than you."

She lets the plait drop and looks around. Spotting Zadie and a couple of girls I've seen around but don't know, Maddy waves them over. When they join us, Maddy laughs and points at my hair.

"Who does their hair like that these days?" she says, and the girls look at me like I'm an alien. "And who said you could come here, anyway?"

The girls look at each other, then to Maddy, then back to me.

"What?" I say, realizing she means me.

"It's invite only – don't you know?"

"It's the shops!"

"You want to argue with me?"

Shaking my head, I get to my feet and walk away. I don't look back towards Maddy, but I can hear the group of girls giggling along with her.

I sneak a glance at Jack, hoping he'll notice I'm leaving and run after me, so Maddy has to let me stay. He glances up, gives me a wave, and goes back to chatting with his mates.

Walking home, I scuff my shoes along the kerb. Sarah's right – Maddy is a bitch. A Mad Dog. I think of the recipe book, of the cheery voice and lovely treats, and wish I could wrap myself up in its pages. Where is the mam that wrote those recipes, that dreamt those dreams?

Tucked up in bed that night, the conversation with Maddy plays over and over in my head. I reread the next few recipes and I wrestle my brain for alternative options, but can't find any: I've no money and it's too embarrassing to go begging to Mrs Snelling again.

Mad Dog's right.

Stealing is the only way.

Chapter Fifteen

It's the Least I Can Do after Knocking You Flying

I stick my head into the school kitchen and make sure the coast is clear. The industrial ovens and refrigerators catch the sunlight and gleam like monstrous fish scales. My legs tremble and I feel like such a wimp.

"Hello?" I call out.

No reply. School's over and the cooks have finished for the day. They're probably at home now, planning the evening meal for their own families. Something better than the beans on toast I have to look forward to.

I creep past the ovens and serving counters to the dry goods cupboard. Part of me is hoping someone will turn up so I don't have to go through with it. I don't really like stealing, except for the odd essential like eyeliner or lip gloss – but I always take them from big department stores that can afford it. Mrs Snelling was kind to me. Technically, the stuff belongs to the school, so I'm not really thieving from her – but there's a bad taste in my mouth as I yank open the huge metal door of the cupboard. It gives a loud whoosh and a blast of cool air strikes my face. Checking behind me a final time, I take a deep breath and step inside.

The larder is the size of a single-decker bus, sectioned off with interlocking metal shelves. It's filled to the brim with over-sized tins, packets and jars. The spare cooking utensils alone could fill an entire supermarket aisle. Standing in the huge storeroom alone, I realize I've never seen so much food. From tinned tomatoes and dried lentils to soy sauce and custard powder, the supplies look like they're meant for giants, not school kids.

I quickly set to work in the baking section. Pulling out the freezer bags from home, I ladle porridge oats into one, sugar into another, and separate self-raising and plain flour into a bag each. As the bags fill, I stuff them into my rucksack and search again. After stashing what I need, I can't stop. There are so many delicious things available, it would be a crime not to take them. Licking my lips, I nick golden syrup, almond slivers, sticky angelica and strawberry-flavoured chocolate chips. I can't help tasting some of them.

"Oh my god," I whisper, as a strawberry chocolate chip melts on my tongue. "That's divine."

When my rucksack is stuffed, I force a wooden spoon into a gap and zip it up. I'm about to leave when I think I hear a bang. I can't be sure, but it's better to be safe than sorry, so I wait, listening carefully. When there's no more noise, I hoist my rucksack onto my shoulder and peep out.

There's no one around, but a slouchy blue leather handbag is now sitting on the counter. There's a purse peeking out of the top. Maddy's words ring in my ears once more. It's like fate – too good an opportunity to miss. A clunk sounds from the other room. Someone has gone into the noisy, walk-in freezer at the back, so I make a run for it. Starting off on tiptoe, I make it to the ovens without a hitch. Breaking into a jog halfway across the kitchen, I try to take the purse but it's jammed tight. Snatching up the handbag without thinking, I'm out of the door and running down the corridor at top speed, my Converse slapping against the tiled floor more noisily than I'd like. I check behind – no one's following. Yet.

As I reach the exit, I realize I'll have to hide the bag. If anyone spots it, I'll be in big trouble. The alarm will be raised soon enough, and with school not long since over, there'll be plenty of stragglers around. I don't know why I had to be so greedy and complicate things. I guess the purse was too enticing. Surely, anyone in my situation would do the same.

I throw the handbag over my shoulder and position my rucksack on top, but the blue bag keeps slipping down. I have to look like a total loser – putting both rucksack straps on my back – to make sure the handbag is securely wedged. Just as I'm sorted, a shrill cry sounds from the direction of the kitchen. I push open the door and run, full speed, into the schoolyard. As I round the building, I run into something and sprawl to the ground.

"Hey, watch where you're going!" I say, like it's their fault.

Then my throat turns dry. It's Jack. Judging from the way he's wrestling with his huge sports bag, that's what I ran into.

"Hey! You again!" he says. "We'll have to stop bumping into each other like this."

He chucks his bag to the ground and stoops to help me up, his brown eyes full of concern. But getting me up isn't easy. I'm laden down with the baking stuff and can't move much in case the handbag drops out. I can't believe I'm wearing my rucksack like a tourist and, when I'm finally up and sorted, I'm so embarrassed I can't think of anything to say. I just stand there, mouth open.

"Seriously, are you OK?" he asks.

"Of course," I snap.

I hate the way my voice sounds. Jack's only being friendly – it's not his fault Maddy's jealous or that I've got a stolen bag digging into my back.

"Are you heading home? Box Lane, right? That's not far from me. I was going to hang out with the gang for a while, but I could walk back with you instead. It's the least I can do after knocking you flying, right?"

There is something lovely about the way he says "right" at the end of his sentences. I look into his eyes and notice how thick and pretty his lashes are. Then a cough sounds from behind him. As Jack turns and steps aside, there she is: Mad Dog, smiling sweetly. She gives me an angry glare before tossing her hair over her shoulder and tilting her head coyly.

"Jack, are you ready?" she asks.

"I'm just gonna go home, if that's all right with you."

The words sound more like a statement than a question.

"But the guys are gonna get some cider from Ali's off-licence and head to the park. Macca said we could give some to his dog – get it wasted again. It'll be a laugh."

Maddy's eyes sparkle beneath her heavy mascara. Probably MAC, not crappy Rimmel like I wear.

"She can come if you like?" adds Maddy.

I cross my fingers, hoping he turns her down. I don't want to be in the firing line, and I have a bag to hide.

"Nah. You go ahead. I'm wrecked after footie, and I've got homework to do."

Maddy saunters over to Jack and gives him a long, suggestive kiss on his cheek. Then she wraps her arms around him and gives him a hard squeeze. He doesn't exactly join in, but he doesn't resist either. I glance behind me as though searching for something, so I don't look like a perv. When I look back, Maddy pulls away and snorts.

"All work and no play makes Jack a dull boy," she teases.

She winks and blows him a kiss. He seems to like it – I can't help wondering why he can't see she's just being a bitch. Maddy swaggers off towards her friends. Behind Jack's back, she shoots me an evil glare and runs her finger across her throat. I quickly look away, but it's pointless. I'm out of favour. And I'm going to pay. I decide to wait for Maddy to leave, in case I make a wrong move and set her off, but the door behind me crashes open and reality hits.

"Sorry, Jack – I have to go!"

Running as fast as I can, I hurtle out of the school gates and across the Rec, the wind burning my eyes and throat as I gasp for breath. Feet and heart pounding, I hope that no one sees me legging it across the field, that no one meets Jack and starts asking questions. It's bad enough that I bashed into him wearing my rucksack geek-style and then ran off for no reason. Jack must already think I'm a total loser. But a thief? Even though he'd never be interested in me, I'd die if Jack knew what I'd done.

* * *

As soon as I'm home, I shout hello as I run upstairs, whack on Johnny Cash full blast, and then kneel on my bedroom floor. Blocking my door in case Harriet tries to come in, I rifle through the bag. I dance in time to Johnny, checking one compartment at a time. It really sucks when I open the driving licence and Mrs Snelling's happy face smiles out – I hadn't even considered it would belong to her. Hadn't considered who it would belong to at all. I stop dancing and continue my search. I find cherry lip-salve, tissues, keys and a few utility bills. The purse has exactly £91.80 in it, along with a graduation photo of some guy with ginger hair. Probably Mrs Snelling's son, judging by the hair.

I should be ecstatic – I've never had so much money, and can buy loads of ingredients now – but deep down, I feel like a right scumbag. I'm no better than the smackhead in the news last week, who clobbered an old lady over the head for a few measly quid. Mrs Snelling helped me when I needed it. If only the bag had belonged to someone else.

After returning all of its contents to their correct compartments, I throw the bag into my wardrobe and bury it underneath a heap of clothes. I slouch back against the door – why did I have to listen to Maddy? What have I done?

Chapter Sixteen

In Full Swing, Marching Up and Down

"Hey, sorry I m-missed you after school, Liv. I'd have waited longer if I could, but you kn-know how Mam worries. What happened to you, anyway?"

Sarah looks at me suspiciously – she thinks I sneaked off again.

"I wasn't sure about the homework, so I stayed back to ask about it."

It's amazing how fast lies can come out of my mouth sometimes. Sarah raises an eyebrow but I'm ready for her. I roll my eyes dramatically.

"I know, since when did I care? Hatty's on my case."

"You look knackered."

"Thanks! Glad I can count on you for moral support."

It's enough to stop the questions. If I could tell Sarah about the bag, she'd know what to do. But I know how much she hates stealing, and I still haven't made it up to her properly for ditching her for Mad Dog. I hardly slept a wink last night, worrying – but Sarah can't bail me out this time.

"Let's get school over with. Another day of imprisonment and torture!" I say.

"It's not *that* bad."

I give Sarah my best "have you got two heads" look.

"We've got Careers Studies after registration class," she says. "We'll see more of Chris today!"

"You're obsessed. It's embarrassing," I say, turning my face away in case I blush. I wish Jack was in Careers Studies too.

We giggle the rest of the way to school. When we get there, it's like a disturbed ant nest. Thousands of pupils in burgundy uniforms swamp the corridors. Our usually calm registration teacher, Mrs Pearl, flaps and fusses as she redirects us to the Main Hall. A whole-school assembly has been called.

"I wonder what's up with her," says Sarah. "Must be something bad."

I shrug, dragging my feet, as we follow the others.

Even though it's full, the hall is deadly silent. We find a pair of empty chairs with our registration group and sit down. After a while, the whispering starts. Everyone's looking at each other, wondering what's going on. What's happened? Has someone died? But as soon as the head teacher, Mr Morrelly, walks in, everyone shuts up – apart from some moron at the back, who isn't paying attention. He'll get it later.

Mr Morrelly paces at the front of the hall. He's in full swing – marching up and down, with his arms clasped behind his back.

"Someone's in for it," whispers a lad a few rows behind us.

I glance at Sarah to see if she's figured out what's happening yet, but she's busy concentrating on the front of the hall.

Mr Morrelly clears his throat.

"I'm afraid I have some grave news. As a school, we've experienced something terrible. Something shocking."

A whisper ripples around the room.

"Quiet!" calls Mr Morrelly, waiting for silence before continuing in his baritone. "I'm afraid our beloved cook, Mrs Snelling, has been the victim of a terrible crime. Her ankle is broken."

I can't help gasping. I slap my hand over my mouth to hide the noise, but Sarah has already heard. "Oh my god," she mouths. I feel sweat bead on my forehead as I mouth "I know" back.

Surely this isn't anything to do with me.

"Her injury is the result of a terrible theft," continues Mr Morrelly, raising his voice to shush us. "Yesterday, at approximately four o'clock, Mrs Snelling returned to the kitchen to check on something for today's lunch. And some spiteful person – possibly a recipient of that lunch later today – took advantage, and used the opportunity to steal her handbag."

A weird noise – a mixture of shock, admiration and disgust – erupts from the others. I shudder and start to burn up. The heat racing through my body makes me feel sick, so I lean forward and take deep breaths to try and make the nausea go away.

"We are hoping, of course, that this awful attack was not carried out by an Egerton Park pupil. That it was an outside job. Who would want to belong to a school where pupils behave that way? Who'd feel safe coming here if it turns out to be one of our own?"

A loud murmur travels around the room as he lays it on thick. Sarah glances at me, wide eyed and open mouthed. She could never contemplate doing something like that. Why can't I be more like her?

I bunch my fist and dig my nails into the palm of my hand, shoving my arms between my legs so

Sarah can't see. Old Mozzer makes it sound like it was some evil, preplanned attack – something Mad Dog's dad would be involved in. I feel like shouting, *I didn't hurt her – it was nothing to do with the bag!* But thankfully, I'm not that stupid. I sit quietly, listening hard. I want to make sure no one knows I was involved.

"We would be grateful," continues Mr Morrelly, "for any information leading to the resolution of this crime. Mrs Snelling has generously requested that we be lenient to any pupil that steps forward. She has asked for the police not to be involved." Old Mozzer shakes his head slowly, his face turned to the floor. "She has even offered a cash reward to anyone who brings in evidence that leads to her bag being recovered. The bag contains something very precious, something irreplaceable. What a shame for something like this to happen to someone so kind."

An electrified chatter shoots through the pupils. My stomach churns and gurgles loudly, like it's trying to give me away.

"Of course, if the perpetrator does *not* own up, and is *found out*..." Mr Morrelly's arm bolts out. His extended index finger seems to point at every one of us. We all shrink back like we're conjoined, a string of paper dolls. "There will be dire consequences. We're talking police, suspension – possible exclusion."

Pausing, hands clasped behind his back, Mr Morrelly lets the flame that he's ignited work its way around the room. From Year Seven up to Year Twelve, there are whispers, sniggers and accusing stares. Everywhere, kids plot with their friends against their enemies, preparing lists of suspects. I imagine myself to be invisible and it's working. Until Jack's warm, brown eyes search me out. I quickly look away.

"Attention!" calls Mr Morrelly, satisfied that the message has spread sufficiently. "Thankfully, I also have some good news for you. Something positive has come out of this – something we can all be proud of."

The room silences. I exchange confused glances with Sarah, digging my nails deeper into my palm.

"Jack Whitman, would you come out to the front, please?"

Again: an excited rumble from the pupils. I hold my breath as Jack shuffles to the front, glowing puce. When he reaches Mr Morrelly, the head teacher grasps Jack's hand and shakes it hard, like he's an adult.

"This young man heard Mrs Snelling's cries and came to her rescue. Then he had the foresight and kindness to make sure she was as comfortable as possible before contacting the emergency services and alerting me. Can we have a round of applause, please?"

For some weird reason, as the clapping begins, I feel really proud. Relaxing my fists and resting my hands on my knees, I sit up straight. But then I think about Mad Dog's throat-slitting gesture and slump back. And what if Jack puts two and two together and mentions my name? As I slide lower in my seat, I run my fingertips over my palm, searching out the half-moon imprints.

"As a reward," continues Mr Morrelly. "I have decided to allow Jack's registration group to choose their own end of year trip. Mrs Pearl, see to it that the destination is chosen democratically."

This time only our class explodes with cheers. The rest of the school stays quiet – probably jealous. Sarah shoves me delightedly but I can't muster the same enthusiasm. All of a sudden, I'm leaning forward, grasping my stomach as sharp, stabbing pains attack my gut.

"What's wrong?" asks Sarah.

It hurts too much to answer.

"Your mam's been playing up again?"

I nod, feeling rotten for lying again, but I want her to leave me alone. Shame courses through my body and, when Sarah starts rubbing my arm encouragingly, I swear I'm going to throw up. I close my eyes and swallow hard.

"Quiet, please!" calls Mr Morrelly, his smile switching to a serious stare. "I'd like to finish by saying, I hope more of you will take a leaf out of this young man's book. Assembly dismissed."

As we file out of the hall, I feel Jack's eyes following me. *Does he know?*

I put my head down and escape, hoping to be invisible in the crowd. But it doesn't take long for Sarah to find me.

"Who would do something like that? And to poor Mrs Snelling?" she asks. "They must have issues."

"What if they didn't know the bag belonged to Mrs Snelling?"

"It obviously belonged to someone. Would you have taken it?"

My jaw clenches and I avoid her eye.

"No… But maybe they were desperate."

"Still no excuse for stealing."

"They might realize what they've done and bring it back?" I say.

"Yeah right. They'll be in a heap of trouble anyway, so what would be the point?"

Sarah's words stick in my head all day, playing over and over, like when a speck of dust gets trapped on one of Mam's records. Scritch, scritch, scritch.

Chapter Seventeen

Screwing Up Her Nose Like I'm Diseased

Arriving home, I check the bag. It's still hidden – in the exact spot that I left it. After assembly today, I feel anxious touching it, like the bag might suddenly yell out or trigger some secret alarm at the school or something. But Sarah is right – there's no way for me to sneak the bag back now everyone knows it's missing, and I'll only get in trouble anyway – so I decide to put its contents to good use instead.

I sneak out to the shops for some pastry, leaving Harriet caught up in her uni work. My hands tremble every time my fingers brush the stolen £20 note in my pocket. I can't stop thinking about a short story we read in English. A thief steals a valuable artefact from a museum, not knowing that it's been dusted with a special powder that glows under UV light. The police trace the thief as a suspect. He denies everything, but the case is sealed as soon as the UV lights come out. Each time I touch the note in my pocket, it's like I can feel something dusting my skin.

As I wander down the food aisles, I begin to feel better. The hum of the chest freezers drowns out my guilty thoughts as I hunt around the frozen goods for puff pastry.

"Liv!"

I look up to see Jack waving at me from across the freezer. He's with an elegant, expensive-looking lady. She gives me a brief, disapproving glance before heading towards the deli section, nose upturned. I'm guessing it's Jack's mam and my first thought is, *I can't imagine a woman like this being beaten up by a drunk*. Jack mutters something, the woman nods, and then I realize: he's heading my way.

I quickly smooth my eyebrows and fluff up my hair, wishing I'd made more effort. I'm not wearing any makeup, and I haven't run a brush through my hair since lunchtime. My skinny jeans and striped T-shirt look fine, but how can I look Jack in the eye without mascara? No wonder Jack's mam looked down her nose at me.

"How are ya, Liv? What you up to?"

I hardly dare to look up, but it's difficult to make a freezer seem that interesting.

"Just getting a few bits of shopping. For baking. You know?"

Inside, I want to curl up and die. Why would Jack want to know about baking? What a stupid thing to say.

"Mum doesn't have stuff like that in the house. She's always on diets."

"Like my sister, Harriet. Only she's always on a see-food diet."

Despite the lame joke, Jack laughs.

"Well, if I saw your food, I'm sure I'd eat it," he says.

As we both grin at each other like idiots, Jack's mam appears.

"Aren't you going to introduce me to your friend?" she says, her voice clipped and unfriendly.

Jack looks half nervous, half relieved.

"Mum, this is Liv. She's in my year at school."

"Pleased to meet you," I say, offering my hand.

The gesture feels stupid and I'm painfully aware that my palm is ice-cold from poking around in the freezers. Mrs Whitman accepts my hand limply, without making eye contact. When our hands separate, I watch Jack's mum wipe hers on a tissue, screwing up her nose like I'm diseased. Without acknowledging me any further, she signals to Jack with a nod of the head that it's time to leave. Jack looks horrified.

"Sorry, Liv, I've got to go. Enjoy the baking!"

I lean back into the freezer, select the pastry I need and head straight for the till, feeling like I've died a little inside. I grab a Coke and some prawn cocktail crisps – blue cheese and onion are out of bounds – hoping they'll make me feel better. As I hand over the money, I expect my fingertips to glow.

* * *

"What are you making for us this time?" asks Harriet.

I continue melting the butter and sugar over a low heat. I can tell from Hatty's eyes that she's forgiven – but not forgotten – my cruel remarks about her weight. I should feel bad and apologize, but as Harriet peers into the saucepan hungrily, all I can think is… at last, I'm finally good at something!

"Don't look so smug, Delia Smith!" says Harriet, sucking in the smells. "Seriously, though – what is it?"

"Eccles cakes."

"What are they?"

"Dunno. Pastry, currant-y things. Like Granny makes, apparently."

Harriet nods, even though neither one of us knows what that's like. Mam grew up in foster care. She was given up for adoption, but it never happened. No one chose her. Mam spent her childhood going from one children's home or foster house to the next.

Spying the pre-made pastry, Harriet points, mock horror on her face.

"Hey, sis, you're cheating!" she cries, and ruffles my hair in the way that winds me up. But I decide to make allowances today.

"It's not cheating. It's what the cookbook says to use."

"Sorry, bad joke. Where's this recipe book that's got you so fired up anyway?"

I stop, mid stir.

"It's over there. From school. Home Ec."

"You don't do Home Ec," says Harriet, narrowing her eyes. "You took Art instead."

She picks up the polka-dotted book, turning it over in her hands. Before she can peek inside, I snatch it out of her grasp.

"Liv, what are you up to?"

"Nothing! I need the recipe – just in case. Don't get your knickers in such a twist. Just because I don't do Home Ec – that doesn't mean I can't borrow a book!"

"True. But there's no need to overreact. It's just—"

"What?"

"Nothing. Forget it, Liv."

"No, go on!" I insist.

I lift the saucepan off the heat and throw the currants, candied peel and nutmeg into the liquid gold as dramatically as I can, forgetting to inhale the scents as the recipe suggested. I'm too busy waiting for my sister to dig herself into a great big hole.

"You didn't steal it, did you?"

My body turns rigid and the muscles in my arm ache as I stir. I think of the look on Sarah's face when Mr Morrelly told the school about the theft. I imagine watching Mrs Snelling fall and seeing Jack run to her rescue. And, worst of all, I think about getting rewarded for it as part of Jack's registration class.

"I'm not judging you," continues Hatty. "At least you're interested in something. I just—"

"Just what? You tell me to be responsible – then when I am, you accuse me of stealing."

"I take it back. Sorry. I want us to be straight with each other, like sisters should be."

I don't know whether to laugh or tell her where to go. Where was Hatty when things started getting really bad last year? The time Mam "accidentally" put her hand through the glass table, the time she locked herself in the bathroom and threatened to kill herself. My first period, my first bra – where was Hatty's sisterly concern then?

"I'm sick of this. You're always on my back," I mutter.

"I just want it to be like the old days, before all this crap happened."

"Then start acting like my sister and not my mam." I churn the mixture and my stomach churns with it. "You're such a control freak."

"If you do well, you can get out of here…"

"What? Run away like you? Is that what you want? Some of us are happy to stay where we are."

"If you stay here you'll end up miserable. You've got to see different things, meet new people. The world doesn't have to be like this."

Harriet's voice grows squeaky and her eyes fill with tears. It's so pathetic.

"If that's what you think, you're dumber than you look. No one from here gets out. You can try, but look at Mam... She left and then came back."

"See? It was coming back here that did it! She should have stayed in London – even without Dad. She was happy there, Liv. I just want what's best for you."

Sticking my hands into the flour bag, I sprinkle the surface. The powder looks so light and airy.

"So that's why you left? Ran away so I had to cope on my own?"

"I didn't run away, Liv. I went to university to better myself."

She puts her hand on my shoulder, but I shrug it away.

"So you're better than us now, are you?"

"I didn't mean that! I want to improve things for us. You understand that, right?"

"No. I don't understand," I say, as snottily as I can. "I don't see how you being selfish benefits anyone but you. You're as bad as Mam. Now, if you don't mind, I've got to concentrate. I've never rolled pastry before, and it's meant to be difficult. Even when cheating."

Harriet opens her mouth to say something, but instead backs away, her eyes on me the whole time. I pretend I don't notice and persevere with the pastry – pressing, shaping and rolling it to the required thinness.

"Is there anything else I can help you with?" I ask.

Shaking her head, Harriet leaves me to it. Hands covered in flour, I stare at the empty space my sister leaves behind. Then I open the recipe book, clear my throat and continue with the Eccles cakes.

Chapter Eighteen

Trying to Decipher its Special Code

A few days later, there's a nasty surprise waiting for me at my front gate when I return home from school. The words "WATCH OUT SLUT" are scrawled in chalk on the pavement. The local kids often tease Mam – trying to get her to chase after them when she's drunk, but they've never done anything like this before. There's no one around, so I scuff the message out with my foot. The chalk powders the concrete like spilt icing sugar.

"Bloody kids," I say aloud, just in case there's someone hiding nearby. "Next time, I'll cut off their hands!"

Inside, Harriet is on the sofa, studying a piece of paper intently. She's spilt tea down her unflattering grey T-shirt and hasn't bothered to change.

"Liv, come listen to this. It's a letter from the Social Services."

"Oh crap..." I rush over to snatch the letter and read it myself.

"Liv!" Harriet leans away, clears her throat and reads aloud.

Monday 17th June 2014

Dear Miss Harriet Bloom,

We acknowledge that you have been the guardian of Miss Olivia Bloom since 16th May 2013, and would like to inform you that a review of your current circumstances is now due.

Your social worker, Mrs Harvey, will visit you at your home address of 19 Box Lane on Friday 5th July 2014 at 2 o'clock. Please ensure that you are available for this meeting, as it will directly affect the future status of your guardianship.

If there are any problems that affect your ability to attend, or if there are any pressing matters you wish to discuss prior to the appointment, please contact us at your earliest convenience, so that suitable alternative arrangements can be made.

Kind regards,
Mrs Walker, Secretary

When Harriet lowers the letter, her hands are shaking. "Liv, that's less than three weeks away."

"Any pressing matters?" I hit the arm of the sofa with my fist. "I'd like to know why they can't keep their noses out of our bloody business!"

"I know – I agree, but we have to be compliant," says Harriet.

"Be what?"

"Do what they say, go along with it."

"It's our life, not theirs. You're almost twenty-one. Surely they can't tell you what to do?"

I watch as Harriet tries her best to pluck a solution out of the air. When her face settles into a blank expression, I realize there isn't one.

"I'm afraid they can. They have the law on their side. But I don't want them to take you away from me. Look what happened last time."

"What can we do?" I ask, realizing I've been scratching at my neck. Although my skin burns, I can't stop.

"I'm not really sure." Harriet stares at the letter without reading it. "I guess we just have to keep our noses clean. Stay out of trouble. Make sure this place is spotless for their visit."

"You mean *I* have to stay out of trouble."

I join her on the sofa, thinking about the bag – and how to get rid of it.

"No, I mean *we*," says Harriet "Both of us. I still have assignments that should have been handed in. What if they check up on that?"

"Why would they care about dumb assignments?"

"Because assignments aren't dumb. They show that I'm responsible – responsible enough to look after you. If I fall too far behind, they might think I can't cope."

We both fall silent, lost in our own thoughts. I can't get the scene at Ashgrove House out of my mind. What if Hatty *can't* cope?

"I'll make them some biscuits or something," I say.

Harriet snorts. "I don't think we need to go that far... we want them to go away again. Once they get a taste of your cooking, they'll move in."

I smile at the compliment. Maybe stealing the ingredients and spending the stolen money isn't such a bad thing after all. But then I picture Mrs Snelling's jolly face and the big bag of stuff she gave me when I needed it, and any positive feelings melt away.

"Anyway," continues Harriet. "You'll be in school – or, at least, you'd better be!"

"I will. Promise. But I can bake the night before. Show them I'm interested in something. You could say that you got me into it, that you wrote the recipe book?"

The words tumble out of my mouth before my brain kicks in. Laughing, Harriet sits back and folds her arms.

"Why would they think I've written a recipe book? It'd be a good reason for not finishing assignments – but seriously… I think all that sugar's gone to your head!"

"Wait and I'll show you."

It's a spur of the moment decision, but if *Recipes to Make Happiness Bloom* can help our cause and keep us together, I'm willing to share. I fetch the cookbook from my room – avoiding even the briefest of glances at the wardrobe where Mrs Snelling's bag is hidden – and thrust it into Harriet's hands.

"See for yourself."

Harriet tucks a lock of hair behind her ears. "What am I looking for, exactly?"

"Open it!"

Doing as I ask, Harriet looks from the book to me. "I've never seen anything like it… did you write it?"

"No."

"The handwriting looks familiar," says Harriet, studying it carefully.

"It's Mam's. Look at the message on the inside cover. I think you'll find it interesting."

Harriet peeks inside, then freezes. Her voice turns serious as she reads aloud.

"To the love of my life, Abigail 'Happiness' Bloom. May we have many adventures together. Yours always, Max. Christmas 2000."

Her eyes glint, but then her face falls. "Liv, where did you get this?"

"It's not important."

"Tell me. Right now."

"OK, chill out. It was in Mam's pillowcase."

"You went through Mam's things?"

"I was bored."

"So? You think that makes it OK to go through people's personal things?"

I can hardly breathe with the weight of Harriet's eyes on me. I finger the edges of the cookbook, waiting for the eruptions.

Instead, Harriet sits back and says in a quiet voice, "Is that what this is all about?"

"What?"

"You acting up lately?"

"I dunno what you mean," I say, meaning it.

"Seeing the message from Dad – did it stir things up again?"

I keep my eyes on the recipe book and shrug. I clench my jaw and feel the veins on my forehead throb. How do I explain that most things are about Dad when you think about it? If I hadn't driven him away, Mam wouldn't drink and there'd be no stealing, no making a mess of everything. And I wouldn't have to find out about Mam through a stupid cookbook. She'd be right here.

"Do you want to ask me stuff? It's been a while."

"Are you sure?"

Surely she's winding me up. After the time I tried to run away, Harriet decided it was best not to talk too much about him. "Too much" – meaning ever.

"Quick, before I change my mind!" says Harriet.

"OK. What was he like?"

"Dark hair—"

"No, I mean, as a dad."

I twiddle my own hair round my finger, wondering whether it's the same texture as his.

"He was always fooling and joking."

"Not like Mam."

"Liv… if you're going to keep interrupting—"

"I won't. I'll stop. Sorry! Go on…"

"He plagued Mam and her friend, Rosa, in the kitchen – sneaking their cakes when they weren't looking. Rosa had a beautiful little baby girl called Amber, about the same age as you. He used to put you in your bouncy chairs, side by side, and tickle you both till you could hardly breathe for giggling. Sometimes, he'd sit you on his lap and sing rock-a-bye baby, opening his knees like he was going to drop you. I always panicked and tried to catch you. It was part of the game."

"He sounds fun," I say, wondering why she never told me this before.

"Once, Mam had to go away somewhere and Rosa and Amber came to stay. Rosa and Dad baked a whole tray of cakes just for me. I ate them all and got really sick and had to go to bed early."

"Did Mam go nuts?"

"I didn't tell her. Dad said it probably wasn't a good idea. Said it would get everyone in trouble, so we probably shouldn't even mention Rosa was there at all. So I kept quiet. It was only years later I realized he was having an affair."

"You should have told her!" I say.

"Would you have realized something like that when you were six? I knew there was something wrong, but didn't really know what. Mam was happy back then, and I didn't want to upset things."

"She never got cross? Or drunk?" I ask, finding it hard to believe.

"Maybe a glass of wine with Dad or Rosa over dinner. She certainly didn't smoke. There were mood swings, but they were rare. It was after they split up that she started getting angry. Sometimes you'd get scared, so I'd turn Mam's records up a little bit."

"Maybe that's why I like Johnny now? It's all your fault!"

"Maybe it is," laughs Harriet, before falling silent. After a while, she adds, "Anyway, if I'd mentioned it, Dad would have gone off with Rosa even sooner."

For the first time ever, I understand why Dad left. Why Mam is still so gutted. She lost the two people closest to her at the same time, and was left stuck with us.

"Mam's friend went off with Dad? What a cow! But all this time, she's been blaming me. If *I'd* been better behaved…"

"She's not coping – she's just looking for a scapegoat and—"

"I'm it? I've been hearing it since I was a kid, Hatty. A little kid!"

"Oh Liv, sorry – I shouldn't have said anything—"

"You should have told me before! Maybe then I wouldn't have spent my whole life feeling bad about something I didn't do. You say you want to be a proper sister but you treat me like a baby."

Harriet chews on her lip, staring at the floor like she wants it to suck her in.

"Sorry," she says.

A heavy silence fills the room. I mull the situation over in my head: how come I'm always on the receiving end? What gives Mam the right to pick on me all the time? It's pathetic. I'll never be like Mam. I'll never let the wrong person take the blame. Taking a deep breath, I consider the situation properly. None of this is Hatty's fault. I'll have this out with Mam later, once the Social Services visit is over.

"Hatty? Don't be mad at me for the cookbook…"

"I'm not. Not really. It's only a cookbook. But why would she hide it?" Harriet taps the recipe book with her index finger. "Did you check it for Dad's address?"

"Every page."

We both stare at the cookbook, as though trying to decipher its special code.

"Why was it under her pillow?" says Harriet, thinking out loud.

"She'll have got all maudlin about Dad with drink inside her. There were bottles around the place too."

Harriet gives a knowing nod.

"Did you ever hear anyone call Mam 'Happiness Bloom'?" I ask.

Harriet shakes her head slowly. "No. Abigail doesn't even sound anything like Happiness."

"I know. And I wonder what happened to Rosa."

"Dunno. We never heard any more once Dad ran off with her."

"I'd never do anything like that to a best mate! Can you imagine? I'd be lost without Sarah."

A faraway look crosses Harriet's face and I realize what I've said.

"Do you miss your friends?"

"Yes. But it's OK."

I know it's not. All of Hatty's mates are in Edinburgh and she's stuck here with me. The friends she had here have all moved away. I make a mental note to try and spend a bit more time with her when I'm home, instead of in my room.

"You'll be back there soon," I say, trying to keep the doubt out of my voice.

"Don't worry about it," says Harriet, overly cheerily. "You're more important. You know that, right?"

I angle my body away from hers. "Watch the mushy stuff, sis!"

We burst into giggles.

"OK, no more mushy stuff. But listen – Mam wanted to keep this secret, so we'd better not mention it to her. Promise me you won't, even though you're mad at her? Even if you lose your temper?"

I nod, knowing full well I probably won't keep my promise.

Butterfly Cupcakes

Butterflies are a symbol of rebirth, happiness and regeneration in Native American mythology – and it's believed that certain butterflies and moths are visiting ancestral spirits. So, take heed of some ancient wisdom and come fly with me – high up in the sky above your woes and worries. You can thank the spirits later.

INGREDIENTS

175 g/6 ¼ oz self-raising flour
115 g/4 oz caster sugar
115 g/4 oz soft butter, chopped into small cubes
2 big fat eggs
50 ml/1 ½ fl oz creamy milk
1 tsp baking powder

FOR THE BUTTER CREAM ICING

150 g/5 ¼ oz softened golden butter
½ tsp sweet vanilla extract
275 g/10 oz sifted icing sugar

HOW TO MAKE THE MAGIC HAPPEN

1. Preheat the oven to 180 °C/350 °F/Gas mark 4 and line a 12-cake baking tray with paper cases.

2. Combine all the dry ingredients in a large bowl. Make a decent-sized well in the centre of the bowl. Break the eggs into the well, make a wish and add the butter. Beat the ingredients together (an electric mixer is faster, but less fun!) until combined. Pour in half the milk and beat again until the mixture is light and creamy. You can add splashes of the rest of the milk if you need to – but stop as soon as the dough looks gorgeous.

3. Dollop the batter into the paper cases and bake in the oven for 15–20 minutes. You know they're ready when they're firm and light brown on top. Let the cupcakes stand for a minute before moving to a wire rack to cool. When the cakes are cool, cut a circular lid out of the top and set aside (these will be your wings).

4. It's time for the icing! Beat the butter and vanilla extract in a bowl until light and fluffy as air. Add the icing sugar a little at a time, until it is all added and the mixture is smooth and silky. Separate the icing into a few different bowls and add a dab of food colouring to each.

5. Spoon the icing onto the cupcakes. You can mix the icing colours if you like – look at some beautiful butter-flies for inspiration and let your creativity fly! Now, slice each top in half and stick into the butter cream icing to add your wings.

For an extra cute touch, add a few candied violet or rose petals as decoration. Or serve on leaf-shaped plates. It's your time to shine.

Chapter Nineteen

Is This a Trick?

As soon as I wake, I take out the recipe book and trace the inscription lightly with my fingertips. After revealing the cookbook to my sister, it feels even more special. Harriet seems to like what I make, and she likes that I have an interest. Maybe it will spark something in Mam when she comes home too? It might even bring us all closer. The idea puts a spring in my stride and, while I'm on a roll, I decide to tell Sarah about the other night with Mad Dog as we walk to school.

"You'd better watch yourself," says Sarah. "I'm telling you, Liv – I know you think she's OK, but she's two faced. Mad Dog's dangerous."

"She's acting weird and I don't know how to take her – but dangerous? That's a bit far-fetched."

I don't mention the way she drew her finger across her throat. Absent-mindedly, Sarah strokes the bruise on her arm – it has spread now it's healing, turning brown and yellowish in colour.

"I don't know why you keep hanging out with her anyway," says Sarah.

I chew my lip, deciding whether to tell her about Jack.

"What?" asks Sarah, picking up on my hesitation. "Go on – out with it!"

"It's... well... I've been hanging out with Jack more than her."

Eyes widening, Sarah demands every gritty detail – and although there isn't much to tell, she's suitably impressed.

"I think he fancies you," she says.

And even though the idea is crazy, the day flies by. Nothing can spoil it. Not even double Maths all afternoon.

"Watch out, Sarah," I say as we leave Maths class. "Mad Dog's near the exit."

Sarah's body tenses as she readies herself for the inevitable. "You mean your b-best mate. Can't you put another word in for me?"

"You're not funny."

"I still can't decide whether you're brave or stupid hanging out with her."

"She's honestly not that bad," I say, trying to ignore the image of Mad Dog drawing her finger across her throat. "She's not too different from when we were kids. I think it's just show."

"It's official. You've finally lost it."

"She'll get bored of picking on you and move on – you'll see."

"Fingers crossed," says Sarah, taking a deep breath. "Here goes nothing."

As soon as we step out onto the playground, the gang flocks towards us. Within moments, they have us surrounded – but instead of singling out Sarah, they turn to face me.

"We've been making a list of people who've pissed us off lately, and guess what – you're on it," says Maddy, poking me in the chest and shoving me off balance. Then she turns to Sarah and offers a handshake. "Congratulations. You're off the list."

Neither of us budges. Fear roots us to the spot and we're thinking the same thing – is this a trick? She's not a bestie like Sarah, but Maddy's still a mate, and I've been getting on fine with the others. Sure, she's been territorial over Jack, but I thought we were friendly enough for it to not really matter. Evidently I was wrong.

"What are you gawping at me like that for?" Maddy asks Sarah. "It's good news for you. But your friend here – well, she's a small sacrifice for getting into our good books, don't you think?"

Sarah takes a small, tentative side-step, flinching as Maddy sticks out her arm. I wince too, but Maddy simply cups it around Sarah's shoulders and pulls her round to face me.

"You see," continues Maddy, chewing loudly on her gum, "we've decided that you've had enough. You've responded well to our lessons, but your friend – *ex*-friend – here, has been sticking her neck out a bit too much for our liking. Thinks she's better than everyone else. So now, it's time for us to teach *the slut* a lesson."

Sarah doesn't move – and neither do I – as it all falls into place. The chalked message on my path: I should have known. Mad Dog's been looking for something to use as a weapon against me, and I walked right into the trap by talking to Jack. How could I be so stupid?

"Do… do you m-mind me asking… what sh-she's done?"

"Yes, I mind. But you're our friend now. Part of the gang." Maddy pats Sarah with her free hand, like she's a pet dog. "We reviewed the criteria for enemies. And we..." She gestures towards Emma, Zadie and Lorna, who quickly nod assent. "We decided we're not interested in people with annoying habits any more."

At mention of it, Sarah's face tenses and her lip quivers.

"Sorry, Sarah, but that stutter of yours is rather annoying."

Sarah tries to formulate a reply, but the stutter leaves her unable to speak. The gang falls about in fits until Mad Dog silences them with a glare.

"Shut up. We're not after *her* any more." The girls sober their faces and try to look sympathetic. Mad Dog slaps Sarah's back. "See, that's much better, isn't it? I told you, you're OK now."

Sarah fakes a thin, cautious smile.

"We've been studying *Animal Farm* in English. It's a great book, you should read it – teaches you a lot about people. So now we're concentrating on people who think they're better than us. People who go around trying to steal other people's blokes. People who are really pigs. Like her."

Maddy leans towards me and snorts twice, loudly. When I flinch, everyone laughs – except for Sarah.

"Don't you agree, Sarah?" asks Maddy.

"Well, I-I-I'm—"

Mad Dog takes this as a good sign.

"See, pig, your friend agrees with us." She steps up to my face and grunts again. "Go on, your turn. Squeal, pig."

I pause, hoping she's joking. Hoping she'll start laughing, like she did that night at the shops, and say she doesn't really mean it. Instead, Maddy checks behind her to make sure no one's watching, then she grabs my arm. Reluctantly, I make a small noise, hating myself for being such a coward.

"Now, say after me, Comrade – I am a ginger pig and I deserve everything I get."

Typical. My hair is the only feature I like about myself, and now it's getting me into bother. Maddy twists my arm tighter and my elbow starts to burn.

"I-I-I'm—" I stutter, finding it difficult to speak with the pain.

"Ha!" roars Mad Dog. "I-it's c-c-catching. Maybe you're in the clear, Sarah?"

The gang stifles giggles as their leader winks. I chance a glance at my best friend. Her stutter is in full flow. A strange gagging noise sounds in her throat. The harder she tries to control it, the worse it gets, and tears well in her eyes.

"Ha! I guess even I can be wrong sometimes," says Mad Dog.

The gang let out a few small guffaws, keeping a close eye on Mad Dog's expression. I wish I could vanish. Or spin myself into a safe little chrysalis like the Native American butterflies mentioned in the cupcake recipe. Then I would break free, fly high above the Egerton estates and everyone in them, leaving my troubles behind for good.

An excruciating pain suddenly jolts me out of my daydream, as Maddy kicks my shin.

"What the hell is wrong with you? Say it! I'm a ginger pig and I deserve everything I get."

I meet Sarah's eyes, before repeating the words slowly. "Again! Louder!"

I mumble the words a second time. I might be a coward, but I don't want *everyone* to know it.

The gang chuckles. Emma cups her hand over her mouth. It magnifies her amusement rather than hiding it, and some passing kids look in our direction.

"Shush," says Maddy. "We don't want to attract attention."

Emma continues to grin, but quietens. Sarah was right all along – Maddy's the leader, not the follower. When she's certain no outsiders are watching, Mad Dog yanks my hair and I cry out in pain.

"Listen to how the ginger slut squeals! Now snort, loudly – for everyone to hear. Show them what a disgusting little ginger pig you are."

As I perform a series of loud grunts, the group laughs – all except for Sarah.

A small crowd of boys gathers, and a couple of the younger lads start joining in, hissing "Ginger pig! Ginger pig!" So much for not attracting attention! Egged on by the support, Maddy pulls a pair of scissors from out of her pocket. They're small but sharp – the ones used in Art class for cutting card. She lets go of my hair as she waves the scissors in the air for everyone to see.

"The only way to cure a ginger pig is to cut off its hair!" says Maddy, as a grand finale.

Emma and the small crowd of boys gasp, but the other girls don't react. It seems this was planned.

There's only one thing for it. I turn and leg it as fast as I can towards the fence behind the smokers' corner.

Chapter Twenty

I Didn't Know Pigs Could Cry!

By the time I've cleared the fence, three of them have already caught up: Mad Dog, Emma and Zadie. Emma looks uncertain, hanging back behind the others. After a moment, Lorna arrives. She's a strong girl – one of the school's top athletes, with biceps to rival the boys' – and she's dragging Sarah behind her. I try to catch Sarah's eye to plead "don't do this", even though I know Sarah has no choice. Sarah averts her eyes and stares at the ground.

"Go on, Sarah, make the first cut," says Mad Dog.

Lorna shoves Sarah forwards, forcing the art scissors into her hands. Sarah freezes, mouth agape.

"I said go on. Unless you want the same treatment."

Our eyes meet. Sarah's face pales and her eyes fog over as she steps forward, visibly trying to blank out what is happening.

"Hurry up – we haven't got all day!" says Zadie, arms crossed and foot tapping.

Gently, Sarah teases out a small lock of hair and mouths "sorry" as she cuts. I give a single slow blink to show I understand. It also helps me to hold back the tears.

"Is that it? That's hardly teaching the ginger pig a lesson! More!" cries Lorna.

Lorna's not even looking at me. Her eyes are on Mad Dog, making sure she's saying the right thing.

Sarah takes another, larger chunk of hair, and snips again. It falls to the ground in wisps, like smoke. I hold my breath, hoping that's enough, but I doubt Sarah's half-hearted efforts will satisfy the gang. Mad Dog straightens to her full height, a triumphant look on her face.

"OK girls, scissors out!" she orders.

To my horror, every one of them except Emma has a pair of scissors hidden. They round on me and start grabbing at my hair, pulling and twisting and cutting. I flinch and cry out. There's no way you can act hard with scissors so close to your face. I try to protect my head with my arms, but it's no use. Someone pushes me to the ground, pulling my arms behind my back, so I shove my face into the dirt for protection. It smells of mud and grass and fear. When there's a pause, I glance up to see Sarah's shoes turn and run. Those times I abandoned Sarah – I had no idea how lonely it felt. I want to run too, but I stay put. I wish the ground would open up and swallow me whole. I'm pressed so tightly to it, I imagine it almost possible.

The crowd of boys arrives on the scene, along with a few girls. Maddy no longer seems to care about attracting attention. She seems to be enjoying being in the limelight.

"Remember, comrades, your resolution must never falter. No argument must lead you astray," Mad Dog calls out, quoting from *Animal Farm*. "Keep going till I tell you to stop!"

As instructed, the girls start cutting again, growing more feverish in their efforts as the seconds – which seem like hours – tick by. My hair tumbles to the ground in chunks. The scissors snag again and again, and it feels like I'm being torn apart by giant birds. I wonder if the torture will ever end. As hot tears drip down my face, I feel wet mud smear my cheeks.

"I didn't know pigs could cry!" yells Mad Dog.

Zadie stops, seemingly moved by the tears, but Maddy and Lorna keep going.

"I think you should stop now," says Emma in a weak voice.

"Yeah, she's had enough," adds Zadie.

A few of the onlookers wander off, but some stay to watch as Maddy sticks the boot in for good measure. Winded, I cough and splutter, holding my stomach. Over the embarrassing sounds I'm making, I hear a voice call out, "Oi! Pack it in!"

Mad Dog makes a strange whimpering sound and backs away, Lorna quickly following. When I catch my breath and dare to peek, I see Jack, his eyes sparkling with fire.

"What the *hell* do you think you're doing?" he says. "Get away, all of you!"

The crowd disperses. Only Maddy and her friends stand their ground.

"We're teaching the pig a lesson. Animals need to be reminded how to behave now and again," says Lorna, looking to Maddy for backup.

Only Maddy's face is flushed bright red and she's lost for words, unable to look Jack in the eye. Her scissors hang limply by her side as he stares at her icily.

"The only animals I see here are you lot." He snatches the scissors from Maddy and snips them a few times in mid air. "Maybe you need a reminder too?"

My heart is pumping so fast it feels like it'll burst out of my chest. No one has ever stuck up for me like this.

"Jack, it's just a misunderstanding," blurts out Maddy. "There's no need for us to fall out."

She smoothes her hair and pulls a sweet smile.

"A misunderstanding? Are you nuts? No wonder people call you Mad Dog behind your back."

Maddy's face crumples, but she composes herself quickly.

"That's just people being mean. I haven't done anything to…"

But she can't even finish her sentence. The evidence is clear. She's been found out.

"I can't believe I always defended you," says Jack, shaking his head. "I should have listened… Come on, Liv."

As he helps me to my feet, Maddy looks from Jack to me and screws her face into a scowl.

"You can't be serious…" she says.

She lunges at me, but Jack reaches out and snips the scissors in her direction, catching a few stray ends. The blonde strands whirl on the breeze, feather-like. Sweat glistens on Maddy's cheeks, dampening her hair so it sticks to her face. Her mascara has smudged, and a small trickle of black runs from the edge of one eye. I think – *not so attractive now, are we?* – but I'm careful not to be caught looking.

"I'll get you for this, Jack Whitman. When my father hears about it, he'll—"

"What?" asks Jack.

"He'll see that you get hurt. *Real* hurt."

Jack just shakes his head pityingly and wraps his arm around my shoulder to lead me away.

Mad Dog's eyes glass over. The corners of her lips quiver and she looks close to tears, but manages to hold it together. I'd feel sorry for her if she hadn't just tried to scalp me.

"Don't think this is finished," she says, and spits at me. "You'd better watch your back."

"I'll be watching it for her," says Jack.

My heart is still thumping as Mad Dog and her gang stomp off, quickly disappearing out of view. I reach up to my scalp to check the damage and can't help gasping. There are clumps of hair sticking out all over and a glob of Mad Dog's spit coats my fingers. I burst into tears – snot running down my face and everything. Jack tightens his grip around me, and helps me away from the scene.

"It's 19 Box Lane, right? Come on, I'll take you home."

I wonder whether he'd been this kind to Mrs Snelling the day that she'd fallen, and the thought makes me sob even more. My head is spinning, so I have to lean on Jack for support. I notice a string of snot has lodged itself on his jacket and discreetly wipe it away.

When we reach my front door, Jack insists on coming inside.

"I'm not leaving you until I know you're OK."

"I'll be fine. Harriet will look after me."

"Let's check she's in first."

Rather than fussing on the doorstep, I decide it's a good idea to let him in. I'm not giving Pauline the opportunity to grass me up to Mam. But as I try to turn my key in the lock, it jams – there's a key on the other side. I knock loudly on the door, dreading Harriet's reaction. There's no answer, so I knock again. The door swings open a moment later, but it isn't Harriet. It's Mam.

"Sorry about that, sweetie, I didn't mean to lock you out," she drawls. She has a burnt-out cigarette stub dangling between two fingers and she's wasted. I'm too ashamed to look at Jack. "I've run away from the circus. I'm home for good!"

If she notices my tear-stained face or scarecrow haircut, she doesn't say anything. She sways in the doorway, her eyes glazed and slightly wonky. Then, just when I think it can't get any worse, she latches onto Jack.

"Ooh, hello handsome," she says, and tries to grab his bum.

I drag her away just in time. She keeps turning back, blowing kisses to Jack and giggling. I wrestle her into the living room and yank the door shut, holding it firm against her pathetic attempts to tug it open from the other side.

"Quick – upstairs," I say.

Jack doesn't need telling twice.

Chapter Twenty-One

The Monstrosity Staring Back at Me

"She'll have a sore head when she wakes up," whispers Jack, even though Mam's well out of earshot.

"She'll probably start drinking before the hangover kicks in."

Why did Mam have to show me up in front of Jack, of all people? And where the hell is Hatty? I don't even want to know what Jack thinks. So long as he doesn't feel sorry for me – I couldn't bear that. It's bad enough he has to clean me up because Mam's out cold.

I wince as Jack reaches for the comb, dips it into luke-warm water and carefully pulls it through my hair to try and give it some sort of style. It was Jack's idea – an attempt to soften the blow, so I know I must look a state. My sore scalp is another clear indicator.

"Ouch!"

"Sorry. Do you want to take a break?"

"No, ignore me. No matter how much noise I make, keep going. Until it looks half decent."

"I'm not sure I'm helping much… I don't think I'd make it as a hairdresser. But I'll be as gentle as I can."

"Thanks. Ouch! Sorry…"

"This is one sorry room!" jokes Jack, and we laugh.

The noise sounds odd. Out of place. Wrong.

"That's the best I can do," says Jack, stepping back. "I'd recommend a trip to the hairdressers as soon as you can."

"*Now* can I see?" I ask.

"Only if you're sure you can handle it."

"I'm as ready as I'll ever be," I say.

But I'm wrong. Nothing could have prepared me for the monstrosity staring back at me from the mirror.

It looks as bad as it felt. There are longish bits dangling over my ears and the back is reasonably untouched, but the front is a mess with tufts sticking up here and there. I'll never go out in public again. I wouldn't be seen dead with a mullet.

"What am I going to do?"

"Lay low for a few days. Get it all cut short," suggests Jack.

"I'll look like a boy."

"You have a nice face so you'll pull it off. It'll grow back quickly."

Did I hear him right? A nice face? Not pretty or beautiful – but at least it's a start. I avert my eyes from his gaze in case he can see too deeply inside me.

"What if they attack me again? It'll be even worse next time…"

Jack stays silent. He focuses on drying his hands, taking extra care with the grooves between each finger. When he looks up, his lips and jaw are tight, defining his cheekbones and emphasizing his eyes.

"I meant what I said earlier. I'll watch your back."

I search out his eyes to see if he's telling the truth, and lose myself in their warmth. Then I remember that it was talking to Jack that got me into this mess in the first place. I'll be in even deeper trouble now. I take a step back, creating some distance between us.

"Are you OK?" asks Jack, following me.

When I don't reply, he tilts my face up towards his. He smells spicy, warm. I can't move. Is he going to kiss me? I hope he tastes as nice as he smells. A yelp of surprise from downstairs interrupts us.

"Finally, Hatty's back! She must have found Mam."

I run to the door but can't make myself go through it.

"Come on," says Jack, gently. "There's no point putting it off. She'll have to see you eventually."

Trembling, I follow Jack downstairs. Harriet dashes into the passageway, jittery and breathless.

"Liv, did you know Mam was home? Why didn't you…?" She stops when she sees the state of me. "What the hell happened to you? Liv?"

Her reaction is too much and I dissolve into sobs. Again. Tears cascade down my cheeks and my shoulders shake. I want to stop acting like a baby – at least while Jack is here – but however much I try, I can't control the emotion. I sense Jack's presence behind me, can tell he's explaining things to my sister, but his words are a blur.

"We'll phone the police," says Harriet. "Let them deal with this."

"No," I gasp. "We can't."

"Why not? It's assault."

"Please, Hatty… not the police. If we involve them, they'll call the Social Services and take me away. I'm OK. Hatty, please!"

Harriet nods reluctantly. She looks much older than she is.

"How about Mr Morrelly?" offers Jack.

Chapter Twenty-One

I throw him a look of disbelief.

"Good idea," says Harriet, tight lipped. "We'll go to the head teacher. He'll know how best to deal with it. They can't get away with this – bloody animals."

"No! They'll get me even worse then."

"Your sister's right," says Jack, looking at me calmly. "They can't get away with it. We have to go to Mr Morrelly and tell him what's happened."

"And then what? A slap on the wrist? They'll kill me!"

Harriet snorts. "They won't kill you. They won't touch you."

"You'll be OK," says Jack.

"Really? Where was Old Mozzer today? It's not safe at school. Mad Dog rules that place. You should know. You're one of her best mates."

Jack winces. "Not any more."

But I'm too mixed up to listen – anger, shame, embarrassment and fear rage inside me.

"Why are *you* helping *me* anyway? Where were you when Sarah was getting bullied? Oh yeah, drinking in the cemetery with Mad Dog, not saying a word."

"Your friend Sarah? Maddy was bullying her?"

"Don't pretend you didn't know," I snap.

Jack shakes his head. "I had no idea. But you knew – and you were there too, remember?"

"Get out!" I yell, not even trying to wipe away my tears any more.

"You're upset," interrupts Harriet. "There's no need to take it out on your friend."

"He's not my friend. He's one of them. And just as bad as they are. I'm not going to Old Mozzer and I don't need your help, Jack. Got it?"

Eyes downcast, Jack nods. "Got it."

Without saying another word, he pushes past us and out of the door, closing it softly behind him.

"Jack, she didn't mean it," Harriet calls after him.

I put my head in my hands and groan. I squeeze my nails into my scalp, allowing the pain to distract from my thoughts, dissolve them into white fuzz.

"Oh, Liv – what are we gonna do with you?" says Harriet, trying to pull me into her arms. "It'll be OK, I promise. It'll all be OK."

But I resist because I know it won't. I've been completely humiliated, I'm dead meat when Mad Dog catches up with me, and Jack will never speak to me again.

Chapter Twenty-Two

Something Resembling an Abandoned Nest

I'm shaking as I lower myself into Pauline's hairdressing chair.

"You might have to shave it off," I half-joke, hoping I'm wrong.

But Pauline isn't fazed. She might be a grass, but she's an awesome hairdresser. She lifts a water sprayer and jiggles it so that the water sloshes around inside noisily.

"Are you ready?" she asks.

I nod, crossing my fingers as the lukewarm water mists my hair. It stings when she combs, but I don't cry out. I'm determined not to buckle. Especially not in front of Pauline – even though she's kind enough to help me with my hair, she's still the local gossip.

"You promise not to mention this to Mam?"

"Me? I won't say a word."

"I don't want her getting upset."

"It's OK, you can trust me."

I'm not sure I can, but I need her help.

"How is your mam anyway? She seemed good last time I saw her. Saw a lovely drawing of you."

"She's good," I say. The automatic reply. And I manage to resist asking whether the drawing was ripped up into pieces.

"She'll be home soon, I expect."

"Erm… yeah. I guess so."

My face colours as I think about Mam, probably sparked out by now, next door.

"Don't sound so pleased about it!" chuckles Pauline. As she continues running the comb through my hair, it feels like I'm being scalped. "I guess you've got other stuff on your mind right now. Don't worry, we'll get you looking tip-top in no time." Her doughy face creases with concentration. "And don't be worrying about those animals. They've had enough headspace. Things'll get better."

Staring into the mirror, I'm not so sure. Mad Dog and her gang have done a proper job on me. Now that my hair's had time to settle, it looks a bit better, but my glossy locks have been replaced by something resembling an abandoned nest.

"A pixie cut is the only way to go. What do you think?" asks Pauline.

"You're the expert."

Pauline lifts her scissors and snips at the air. As chunks of hair fall, I realize I'm gripping the arms of the chair, my knuckles turning white with the effort. It's like it's happening all over again. I can't get the sound of the scissors and Mad Dog's orders out of my head. Pauline is too busy concentrating to notice: time and again she leans in close before stepping back to take a look and snip another few locks. I can't face watching in the mirror. I close my eyes and count slow, deep breaths. After what seems like hours, I hear the clink of metal against glass as Pauline lays the scissors down and rests her hands on my shoulders.

"It's all over. Take a look," she says.

Forcing my eyelids open, I gasp. Pauline has used longer bits to cover the most damaged areas and the result is a ruffled pixie cut – there's no sign of a mullet. Surprisingly, it even suits my face. If the face staring back at me wasn't my own, I'd say it looked quite lovely. *Better than just nice. Jack Whitman.*

"Pop back next door and see what your sister thinks," says Pauline, brushing me down and removing the protective gown.

I take my time, growing into my new look with every step closer to the front door. Harriet must have been hiding behind the curtains, waiting, because as soon as I step inside she rushes into the hallway, squealing with relief.

"Liv, it looks great! It really suits you!" She lifts her hand to ruffle my hair and I flinch. "Sorry, I didn't mean to scare you…" She bites her lip, then smiles. "I know it happened under horrible circumstances – but you look amazing!"

"Thanks."

I should probably accept the compliment more enthusiastically, but my bones ache, my scalp hurts and I've a headache like you wouldn't believe. I just want to stretch out and listen to some Johnny.

"Can I make you some dinner?" asks Harriet.

"No thanks, I think I'll just go up. Have an early night."

"You should eat something."

"I'll have a glass of milk. And one of those cupcakes I made."

As Harriet follows me into the kitchen, she says, "Your hair is very Emma Watson."

I check her face to see whether she's joking, seeing as Emma is one of my icons. I'm feeling pretty good, when I realize something is missing. Glancing at the sofa, there's a dent in the cushions where Mam should be sleeping.

"Is she in bed?" I ask.

"No, but it's OK. She went for a walk to clear her head."

"You're joking – you let her go out? You know what'll happen!"

Harriet rubs her palms down her hips, turning her back to the sofa.

"She was really, really sorry, Liv – and she promised… she promised she'd come straight back."

Harriet actually sounds convinced.

"How long ago was that?" When my sister checks her watch and refuses to reply, I lose it. "Hatty, you're an idiot!"

"I told her about the Social Services visit. She understands that she has to go back to the Centre. She even said she wanted to."

"Then what's she doing here in the first place? She'll say anything when she wants more booze. Hatty, how could you be so stupid?"

"There's no need for that."

"It's a fact and you know it. Once again, it's all about her." I point at my hair. "No one gives a toss about me."

"I know you've been through hell, but acting like a spoilt brat won't help," says Harriet.

I know I'm being a tad childish, but how else am I meant to react? Mam will let us down like she always does, and I'm the one that will suffer. Hatty will run back to Edinburgh and I'll go into care. Hatty's safe, no matter what. In fact, it would probably be better for her if I did get put away. Just like her stupid friend Robin suggested.

"Look, don't worry. She'll come back. We'll have supper and then we'll get her back to Ashgrove House."

"How?"

"I'll ask Pauline if I can borrow her car."

"You don't even have your licence."

"The provisional is enough. Pauline always says yes – and she doesn't have to know why."

"Will they take Mam back?" I ask.

"They will, I'm sure," says Harriet, sounding anything but.

Memories of my brief stay in foster care flash through my mind, and my heart feels ripped in two. I fight really hard to keep a lid on my feelings. I'm not a kid any more. I've got to show Hatty I can deal with stuff sensibly, so she'll want to stick around.

"I think they've got to take her back," continues Hatty. "Anyway, she'll be sober by then. We'll come up with a story. It'll be fine."

But the vein pulsing in Harriet's temple betrays her fear.

"I'm coming with you. To make sure it goes smoothly," I say.

"I don't see why not," she says. "You've got as much right as anyone to be there."

"That's right," I say.

I realize she's trusting me and treating me like an adult, so I shut up. Better to end on a high than embarrass myself, like I did arguing with Jack. I tell myself not to go there and pretend to stare out of the window instead.

"Well, now that's all sorted, I don't know about you, but I'm starving," says Harriet. "I vote pizza for dinner."

Suddenly, a glass of milk and a cupcake doesn't seem that appealing. I check the freezer and shake my head.

"The pizza's my treat," says Hatty. "After the day we've had we deserve it. I can use a bit of my emergency money."

For the first time since I was attacked, I smile – genuinely. It's good to know I still can.

"Can I have pepperoni and jalapenos, with extra cheese?"

* * *

It's almost midnight and Harriet is pacing the living room like a trapped zoo animal. "Where the hell is she?" she mutters frantically.

"I told you!" My stuffed belly starts churning. So much for an early night. "I told you she wouldn't come back."

"Don't sound so bloody pleased with yourself," snaps Harriet. "You're not the only one this affects. We have the Social Services coming soon."

"I know that! It's all you go on about."

I ice my final few cupcakes, then place them carefully in an airtight container, too nauseated to even try one.

"Well at least I'm not obsessed with a stupid bloody cookbook!"

Glaring right at her, I let my anger fly. "It's better than being obsessed with being fat!" With Harriet rendered temporarily speechless, I go in for the attack. "If you hadn't been such an idiot, letting Mam out, we wouldn't be in this mess."

"What was I meant to do? She's an adult. She has to make her own choices."

Chapter Twenty-Two

"She might be an adult, but she acts stupid. Just like you!"

We round on each, our faces close and angry. Harriet is the first to back down.

"We should be working together, not against each other," she says. "Right now, we're all we've got. We have to make it work."

"Yeah – all down to us again."

"Look, Liv, you might not like it, but she's the only mam we're ever going to have."

"If that's what you can call her. Sometimes, I think we'd be better off without her."

As the words slip out, Harriet's face tightens.

"You'd better get that nasty little butt of yours out of my face, right now. Otherwise, I won't be held accountable for my actions."

Harriet shoves me in the chest. It's not that hard, but it winds me. I start coughing and spluttering – adding a little extra drama for good measure – but she's too angry to care. She shoves me again.

"Hatty, calm down!"

I rarely see this side of Hatty – and I don't like it one bit.

"Maybe I should listen to my friend and send you into care after all. Maybe then you might wake up a bit."

I glare at her, my arms crossed. Let's see her get out of this one.

Her arms droop at her sides, and she runs a hand through her hair, trying to find the words to apologize.

"Liv. Sorry, I didn't mean it."

As she reaches out, I dash from the room. Behind me, I hear Harriet whimpering another apology. Hugging my arms around myself, I stomp up to my bedroom and slam the door. Hatty might have taken back her words, but what if they're still lodged in her heart? What if she's sending me away?

Chapter Twenty-Three

Like Jekyll and Hyde on Spirits

In the early hours of the morning, I hear the front door slamming into its frame. I curl up, foetus-like, and pretend to be asleep as Mam's footsteps climb the stairs. It's like she's never been away.

I can tell by the heavy thumps that Mam's been drinking spirits. Spirits always tip her over the edge, making her playful one minute and nasty the next.

"Liv. Oh, Liv!" calls Mam.

I sink down into my quilt. Why can't she bother Hatty for a change?

"Liv, sweetheart. Come and play!"

Play? I'm really in trouble. Mam lumbers along the corridor. It sounds like she's wading through quicksand, not treading our crappy threadbare carpet.

"O-liv-i-a!"

Mam's footsteps stop outside the door. I squeeze my eyes so tightly closed that the blackness behind my lids turns green.

"Are you awake, honey?" calls Mam, pushing the door open.

Of course I'm awake! How could anyone sleep through such a racket? But I keep quiet, hoping Mam will fall for my trick. I stay as limp and still as possible. There's enough light from the corridor to be visible if Mam can still focus. Probably not, but I can't chance it.

"Come on, love, wake up! Let's have some fun. Everyone else runs out on me, but not you, Liv. I can depend on you, can't I?"

Her fingernails scrape the doorframe as she clings on. "Olivia!"

I'm not going to get away with pretending to be asleep for much longer, so I pull my best act. Turning over, muttering and murmuring, I adopt my most convincing angelic face. It's meant to make Mam think "aww, how sweet" and go away, but I realize my mistake as she lunges for the bed. She lands heavy and clumsy, her skinny body weighed down by drink.

"That's it, Liv – wake up!"

I pretend to turn again, sinking deeper under the covers. Frustrated, Mam shakes me roughly, knocking my sore head. Behind my eyelids, the darkness explodes into green and red lights, sparkling like broken stars.

"I said *wake up*! You're just like the rest of them, spoiling my fun. Who decided life has to be so bloody miserable? Wake UP!"

Losing patience, Mam starts tapping me on the head. It's not hard, but after being jumped recently, it really hurts. Between taps, I hear footsteps on the landing.

"Get off her!" cries Harriet. "I said *get off*!"

Harriet pulls Mam away, giving me enough time to jump to my feet. I keep my distance, following Hatty's lead. She holds Mam's hand and switches to a soothing tone of voice.

"Come and lie down, Mam – you'll feel better after some sleep," she says gently, indicating with a look that I should wait a while before helping.

As soon as Mam responds to Harriet and is coaxed out of the room, I go to my sister's aid. We loop our arms through hers, one on either side, and carry her to bed. Mam will already have forgotten about waking me – she's like Jekyll and Hyde on spirits – but I squeeze her arm a bit too tightly anyway. It's a lame shot at revenge but it makes me feel slightly better.

As we carry her the last few steps, we whisper the stuff she likes to hear – daft promises and baby talk – to lure her into bed. Flopping on her side, Mam groans.

"You're good girls," she slurs. "I'm sorry. I'm so, so sorry."

We drag her further up the mattress and cover her up, working together fluently without saying a word. Mam's eyes sink down and, within seconds, her breathing relaxes. We leave, pulling the door closed quietly. Neither of us walks away. We both stand there, silent and listening.

"Is it always going to be like this?" I ask.

My sister just sighs and reaches out to my fringe. When she pulls away, there's a perfect white feather in her palm.

"Where the hell did that come from?" I ask.

"Beats me. Shall we make a wish like we used to?"

It's a silly, childhood game, but I agree anyway. Harriet holds out the feather and I cup my hand over hers. We close our eyes, make our private wishes, and only open our eyes when we're ready to seal our fates. Harriet blows the feather into the air and I count. One. Two. Three. The feather is still floating.

"Looks like our wishes will come true," says Hatty, and I giggle, despite myself.

Smiling, Harriet nods towards Mam's door. "We'll give it an hour to make sure she's asleep and then we'll drive her back to the Centre."

"What?" I can't believe Hatty can be so thick sometimes. How she got into uni, I'll never know. "That idea sounded fine earlier but now... It's far too late and she's wasted. They'll never have her back. Not at this time, in her condition. It's a *Recovery* Centre, remember?"

"Exactly," interrupts Hatty. "They're under obligation to look after her if she's in their care. They shouldn't have let her escape in the first place. They'll be delighted to see her back. It'll prevent any embarrassment over their own carelessness."

"So what are we going to do? Just dump her there?" I ask.

Harriet looks at me a little guiltily. "Not dump... But we'll leave her at the door and let them find her."

"Fine, but don't blame me when it all goes wrong."

I don't wait for a reply. I march down the corridor to my bedroom, head held high, but as soon as I'm alone I let the pretence drop. Will Mam ever be back to her old self – the woman full of dreams and recipes? Because that's the mam I wished for on the feather. Not this clapped-out mess we have to put up with.

Chapter Twenty-Four

Blood Is Thicker than Water

"Ssh!" whispers Harriet as we get closer to the turrets and chimneys of Ashgrove House. "Don't make too much noise!"

"I can't help it!" I grunt, lifting one of Mam's legs higher in the air. "She's heavy!"

"It's not much further. We're almost there."

Between us, we clear the driveway and reach the steps leading up to the Recovery Centre's front entrance.

The grey stone building looms over us, stark and severe as an angry face. Mam's none the wiser; she has managed to sleep her way through the whole journey, snoring her head off. We carefully lie her down at the base of the steps and take a well-earned breather. There's no sign of life indoors. Most of the lights are off and everything is still. The place feels empty and abandoned. I lean forward to catch my breath.

"What'll we do with her when we get up there?" I ask, between pants.

"I... don't know," says Harriet, looking alarmed. "I guess we'll leave her at the door and, by the time she's discovered, she'll have sobered up. It's not that long till breakfast!"

"What? We can't just leave her there! She'll die of cold! What if we ring the bell — hand her over in person?"

Harriet cocks her head, deep in thought.

"We can't force her to go inside," she says after a while. "It has to seem like she's going back of her own accord. If we ring the bell and hand her over plastered, they'll know it's not her own choice."

We look down at Mam's sorry, slumped body. I can smell the booze on her from here.

"But we've come this far," I say. "We can't give up now. If the authorities get a whiff of this before their visit…"

My sister strokes Mam's face, and I wonder how she can be so nice under the circumstances.

"We could always leave her on the top step, knock and leg it, then call from the car to say that she turned up but is now missing," suggests Harriet. "We could ask whether she's back — make out we just want to make sure she arrived without getting waylaid."

"Do you think that'll work?"

"We'll be able to watch from the car to make sure she's safe and stays put. They won't see us — it's dark, so we've got the advantage. Once she's inside, we can head home."

"I don't know… What if they say something about ringing from a mobile? What if they try to call the home phone and we're not there? If the Social Services find out…"

"I've already put the landline on redirect," says Harriet, waving her mobile phone in the air. "And this is a private number, so it won't show up when we call."

I look from Mam to Hatty to Ashgrove House. My heads feels cold with my newly cut hair, and I'm shattered. I just want to get this over with and climb into bed.

Grabbing Mam's legs, I stifle a yawn. Harriet follows suit and together we lift the drunken blob up the steps. I jump when a detector light comes on, almost dropping Mam. Hatty steadies herself and takes the extra weight.

"It's OK," I whisper, regaining my balance. "Keep going."

We struggle up the final few steps and lean Mam against the wall. Harriet pulls her coat around Mam as tightly as it'll go and zips it up to her chin. I'd never even thought of it.

When we're happy that Mam's OK, Harriet starts jogging back towards Pauline's car. Only when she's far enough away do I ring the bell and sprint after her. Safely crouched behind the parked Renault, we watch.

Mam has somehow climbed to her feet. The sensor light clicks on and she stumbles.

"Girls?"

"She's probably scared – we should go get her," I say, making a move in Mam's direction.

But Hatty catches me by the wrist. "No. She's got to do this. We've got her this far. The rest is up to her."

The door of the centre opens and a nurse rushes out to help Mam up. Mam lashes out.

"She's confused. We've got to help her," I repeat.

"No."

"But if we don't, she'll get into more trouble, and then we'll be separated."

"Don't you see? That's the problem... We say she has to get better, but then we keep bailing her out. Mam has to do this alone. It's for her own good."

Picking up her mobile, Hatty dials the Recovery Centre and clears her throat while she waits for them to pick up.

Finally, they answer.

"Hello, this is Harriet Bloom, daughter of Ms Abigail Bloom."

A pause.

"Yes, that's right. I'm calling to make sure that my mother arrived safely. She turned up briefly today to visit us and then headed back to the centre. She should have arrived around eight-ish – but I had a missed call from her an hour ago..." She wiggles her eyebrows at me. "I was wondering if you could confirm that she was with you... Yes, if you could check, that would be great."

The front door of the centre opens wide and two nurses chat to Mam, probably trying to explain where she is.

She's stopped flailing but still isn't cooperating, so they lift her and half carry, half drag her inside. My sister's face turns stony.

"Hello, yes, I'm still here. She arrived safe and sound? Good. I hope you don't mind me phoning at this hour – it's just that we worry if we get late calls... What's that?"

Harriet winces as the reply comes through. Then she thanks the person on the other end and hangs up.

"What is it?" I ask.

Harriet chews on her bottom lip, guilt all over her face. "They say she's distressed. They're putting her under sedation."

"But she hates that," I say.

"I know," replies Harriet, climbing into the passenger seat quietly. "But now she's in professional hands."

"So professional they let her leave?"

It's an awful drive home. Harriet only speaks once, to say I should have the day off school – after the bullying and so little sleep, I'll need the day to recover. Other than that, she doesn't speak a word.

When we get home, I hunt out the tub of cupcakes and click open the sides. The scent of vanilla icing wafts out as the lid comes off. Harriet's not even slightly tempted.

As I take a bite, the creamy sweetness dissolving on my tongue, I catch a glimpse of my new self in the kitchen window. I'm grateful Hatty has said I can have the day off tomorrow. Everyone will be looking and asking questions about my hair. The teachers will be interrogating people to find the whereabouts of Mrs Snelling's bag.

And then there's Jack. Sighing, I take another bite. The cupcake may not have helped me to rise above my worries, but it sure tastes good. Hatty watches me, her hands wrapped around a cup of tea. It might be late, but we're too hyped-up to consider sleeping.

"Do you think Mam will forgive us?" asks Hatty, eventually.

"She won't even remember. Anyway, that's not Mam. It's a monster that's taken over."

"Don't you dare call Mam a monster."

I almost laugh. Even now, after everything, Harriet can't help sticking up for Mam. I guess that's why they say blood is thicker than water.

"Stop worrying," I say. "You said yourself – Mam won't get better if we keep correcting her mistakes. We did the right thing. It's for her own good."

"I don't know what the right thing *is* any more, Liv. I'm sick of thinking – for me and everyone else. I'm sick of everything. And everyone. I wish it'd all just go away."

I can't believe what I'm hearing. My own sister has turned against me.

"Maybe I will!" I say.

Hatty rolls her eyes. "Not you! Actually, do you know what? I am just *sick* of your self-pity. So, good!"

"Fine then!"

I flee the room and slam the door. Harriet follows me upstairs a few moments later, and I hear a loud rustling noise from her room. It sounds suspiciously like she's packing. My heart thumps in my chest as I strain my ears. Have I pushed things too far this time?

Leaning against my bedroom door, I slide into a crouching position and scratch at my neck. All that advice from Hatty – about getting out of Egerton and doing something good with my life – it was just talk. Harriet doesn't give a monkey's. Deep down, she just wants rid of me.

I climb into bed and hide under the pillow, hoping with all my heart that my sister is still there when I wake up.

Raspberry Fool

A simple but delightful dish, this is good for calming the nerves and soothing your soul – or that of a friend in need. Make with love and give with kindness. Especially good for when your own misdemeanours have left you shamefaced…

INGREDIENTS

170 g/6 oz raspberries
2 tbsp powdery icing sugar
150 ml/5 fl oz yummy double cream,
whipped into soft mountain peaks

DECORATION

½ tbsp chopped lavender flowers
4 raspberries
sprig of fresh, invigorating mint

HOW TO MAKE THE MAGIC HAPPEN

1. Crush the raspberries in a bowl with a fork. Add the icing sugar and mix well. Fold two thirds of the sugared raspberry mixture into the whipped cream until it's delightfully smooth and pink. Set the remaining mixture aside.
2. Spoon the sugared raspberry mixture into the bottom of two serving glasses and gently layer the raspberry cream on top.

3. Sprinkle the raspberry fool with chopped lavender flowers, then garnish with raspberries and mint.

For an extra-special touch, serve with my "Lovers' Lemon and Choc-Chip Shortbread".

Chapter Twenty-Five

Mint and Chopped Lavender Flowers

Light pokes under the curtains. Unable to get back to sleep, I creep across the hall and quietly open Hatty's door. She's fast asleep – her hair sprawled across her face and pillow. Breathing a sigh of relief, I close the door and return to my room. But there's no way I'm getting back to sleep. The argument with Jack pops into my head and eats away at me. What will I say to him next time I see him? It's Mam I'm annoyed at, and Maddy – so why did I have to go and fall out with him?

I go downstairs, hoping to leave my worries behind. Hatty will join me soon, and maybe we'll go for a walk or something. But hours pass, and I'm completely alone and bored beyond belief. I flick through every TV channel, which lasts all of five minutes – we can't afford Sky any more and the Internet was cut off months ago – and I read an old edition of *Marie Claire* that Harriet has left lying around. With Sarah at school, there's nothing else to do. There's always a new recipe to try, but I don't feel like pushing things. Even listening to *Unearthed* on repeat on Harriet's old MP3 player doesn't improve my mood. It's a bad day when Johnny doesn't cut it.

A cold shiver sweeps through me as I realize that school will soon close for summer. Everyone else loves the summer holidays, but I hate them. What's good about six long, dreary weeks with nothing to do? Apart from Art class, school is rubbish – but having nothing to do is worse. It's not like the weather's great – and even if it was, we've no money to go anywhere or do anything. Whitby might as well be on the other side of the world these days. Sarah and her dad usually go camping in the Lake District for at least a fortnight and I'm never allowed to go, even though they have a spare tent. Mam always makes excuses: I'm not old enough, I can't be trusted. With Mam gone, there's no way I'll be allowed to go this year either – Hatty will need me, or I'll have to study to improve my grades. Why does everything have to be so boring?

If only I could go back to being a kid, to a time when Mam might still be nicknamed "Happiness" by her friends, to a time when she wasn't consumed by drink. I do remember days when Mam was cheery and bright, making fun plans. Like on our day out in Whitby: I breathed steam on the train windows so we could all play Hangman, and Mam pointed out all the animals in the fields as they sped by. The day was bright but chilly and our noses turned postbox red within minutes of stepping into the fresh Whitby air. We jumped waves and, to warm up, huddled together on the beach around bags of hot chips. Sand gritted our teeth as we ate, but that didn't matter. Sometimes I can still hear the gulls calling overhead, making their weird laughing sounds. It's so clear, it's like they're right here with me. But I can't remember the last time I heard an actual gull. Or Mam laugh. Can't remember what her laughter sounds like.

"Stop being such a baby, Liv!" I chide, trying to fill the silence. "You're fourteen now. Stop pining for a mum that doesn't exist."

The words sound good but my heart doesn't listen. Picking up *Recipes to Make Happiness Bloom*, I flick through the pages, but they don't offer any comfort. The gentle fluttering of pages, their magical recipes; it only reminds me of how things should be. The next recipe is "Raspberry Fool".

"How appropriate," I say to myself, out loud.

Sometimes, when we were kids, Mam would get wasted day after day; she'd spark out at random times and the house would be so still, I'd get scared. Hatty would tell me we were going on adventures, leading me around the house to hide in strange places. We'd poke about in drawers and wardrobes, looking for treasure or stray coins we could spend on sweets on our way to school. We would try on things we shouldn't – like Mam's best dresses – while Mam snored on top of her bed. When we were finished with our adventures, we'd hide the evidence and cover Mam up with sheets. She often had no clothes on and I'd stare at the silver pregnancy stretch marks on her stomach. They rippled like patterns in sand. She always looked so fragile then, and we'd be especially delicate with her, knowing that we caused the scars. Sometimes, we'd give her extra covers to compensate.

I reread the recipe book's inscription aloud. Then I close my eyes and try to picture Dad. I imagine soft, caramel hair, a floppy fringe. I picture warm brown eyes – he is kind, good looking and gentle. Then I realize I've made my dad look like Jack. What a freak. That has to be some kind of illness.

Sadness swells inside me and I decide there's only one thing for it. I've nothing to lose by making a few treats. There are some raspberry fools begging to be eaten. They promise to calm nerves and soothe souls – isn't that what we need? It would be a good peace offering for Hatty.

Despite the guilt, I take a bit of money and race to the shops to get what I need. I can't buy lavender flowers, but I collect some on my way back, from a garden from the posher end of the estate. I collect mint too – I Googled them at school to make sure they wouldn't poison us. As I crush raspberries and whip the cream, I start to feel a bit better. But soon my thoughts turn to the stolen bag. I know I should return it, but I've never had so much money before – and where else will I get the stuff I need? Mrs Butler looked so proud of me when I gave her the flapjacks, and even Hatty approves. It's rare for me to do something that makes people smile.

I mix some of the cream and all of the sugared fruit into dreamy pink folds. When it's the colour of marshmallows I pause, wracking my brains for a solution. I have to come up with something before it sends me nuts like Mam.

I decide to spend the money, but return the bag. My options are: I could keep it hidden until the whole sorry mess blows over, then ditch it in some waste ground. There's plenty nearby, so I could probably get away with ditching it now. But I guess I should make sure the bag is returned to Mrs Snelling. After all, it contains something important that she wants back. Despite several searches, I haven't found anything that looks particularly important. The bills are probably paid by Direct Debit and the keys and driving licence can be replaced. Maybe Old Mozzer was just trying to make the culprit feel bad? If so, it's working.

It's a week since the assembly, and the handbag is taking over my life. I check it's still there every time I come in or out of my room, and I've even started putting my own washing away so Harriet doesn't find it. Every glimpse of the bag makes me shudder. The more I try and ignore it, the worse it gets. I've no idea why I took the stupid thing. No recipes – even Mam's – are worth this much stress. Why couldn't I have left it behind?

Concluding that it's Mam's fault, really – I shouldn't have to steal, normal kids get help from their parents – I layer the pink cream and sugared raspberries into four glasses I've set aside.

A noise upstairs signals to me that Hatty is awake. I go to call her, but she beats me to it, her footsteps padding down the stairs. Quickly, I add the last layer to the final glass, then top all four with raspberries, mint and chopped lavender flowers. A calming, fresh perfume rises from the toppings. Harriet soon arrives – her eyes are red and swollen, but I don't want to embarrass her, so I make a point of pushing one of the desserts straight in front of her.

"For you," I say. "Raspberry fool."

Still trying to avoid eye contact with my sister, I put two of the desserts in the fridge and set about washing up, letting the suds cover my forearms with rainbow bubbles.

"You make some amazing stuff," says Harriet. "Maybe you could give me lessons some time?"

"I'd like that," I say, even though I doubt I would. It'd only disintegrate into arguments when Hatty tried to take over.

A long silence edges its way in. Eventually, I take the lead.

"Hey, I'm sorry about last night, Hatty. I didn't mean to argue."

I dry and put away the pots I've washed, and hand her a teaspoon. We stare at the pretty desserts, the sweet scent of lavender wafting around the kitchen.

"It's not your fault," says Harriet sadly. She reaches out to scoop some cream. "We're just stressed out. I guess it's time I faced facts – I might never go back to Edinburgh. I should have listened to you. It doesn't matter whether I go to uni or not – I'll never amount to anything."

"Don't say that!" I say.

"This is amazing," says Harriet, taking a big spoonful and giving a long, slow groan of appreciation.

I try a spoon of my own and follow suit.

"You're right, this *is* good!" I say it too quickly – like I'm showing off – and my face burns up. "I mean, for a first attempt, it's not bad."

Harriet chuckles.

"Have you heard from Jack at all?"

"No, why would I?"

Harriet shrugs, continuing to spoon mounds of the raspberry dessert into her mouth.

"I thought you liked him."

"'As a friend' like him, or 'as a boyfriend' like him?" I ask.

"You tell me."

The problem is I can't, because I don't know. Or I'm not yet ready to admit it. Thankfully, Hatty lets the discussion drop. But then she has to go and spoil things.

"You know… you'll have to go back to school tomorrow."

"Can't I wait until after the weekend?"

"I know you're worried about those bullies, but we can't chance it. With the Social Services visiting soon, the quicker you get back and face up to them, the better."

Losing my appetite, I push my dessert away. My jaw tightens with anger and it feels like my insides are made of ice.

"How would that be better?" I ask.

"Trust me, Liv. It just would."

"What makes you so sure? Why don't you sort out your own life before butting into mine?"

As soon as the words are out, I wish I could spoon them back into my cruel mouth. Harriet pushes back her chair and leaves the room without saying a word. I go back to eating my fool. It sticks to the roof of my mouth and cements my teeth together. Pity it couldn't do that sooner.

Chapter Twenty-Six

An Outcast for Eternity

The first day back at school passes too slowly. I try harder than ever to melt into the background, but with my drastic new hairstyle, it's not easy. Some smirk, others snigger and more still pretend to see through me. Sarah sticks by my side as much as possible, but she's quiet, afraid of being turned on again. As if the reaction from the pupils isn't bad enough, Mrs Pearl makes a point of saying how nice I look.

"Very like that girl from the Harry Potter films," she says, to a chorus of sniggers, before making a fuss about the school trip. "I want each of you to put one – and only one – suggestion forward anonymously in this box, which I'll leave at the front of the classroom," explains Mrs Pearl. "At the end of this session, I'll add the suggestions to a chart. Over the next few days, tick the ones you're interested in. The three most popular will go through to a final round, and next week, you can elect your final choice in a voting ballot."

An excited hum breaks out.

"I've too many ideas," groans Sarah. "How am I going to choose just one?"

I busy myself with organizing my rucksack to avoid the conversation. Everyone in the room seems excited except for me. I sneak a peek at Jack, and accidentally catch his eye. When I offer a weak smile, he looks away. My mood takes an even steeper dive as Mrs Pearl finishes her arrangements with a grand finale.

"The trip will be even better when the thief owns up," she says, peering at everyone in turn. "Mrs Snelling is recovering nicely and will be back to work soon. I hope the perpetrator gets their dues before she returns."

I'm sure Mrs Pearl's eyes linger on me for a moment longer than everyone else. I put my head down and pretend to concentrate on the task in hand, certain the day can't get any worse.

But I'm wrong.

During last lesson, Sarah is in French while I'm in Art. We have to choose partners for portrait-drawing, and no one will work with me – even when Mr Vaughn, the Art teacher, insists. I'm forced to work with the teacher, and he decides to act all cool, like he's my best friend. The rest of the class can't resist pointing and whispering. As if I'm not the butt of enough jokes already.

"What's wrong, Liv?" asks Mr Vaughn, looking between my face and his drawing board, his arm moving vigorously as he sketches. "Why won't anyone work with you?"

"She's upset the wrong person, that's why!" shouts Trinnie Fox.

She's my biggest rival in Art class and a bit of a troublemaker – if she knows Mad Dog did this, then you can be certain the whole school knows.

"This is a private conversation, Trinnie!" calls Mr Vaughn over his shoulder, smiling like it's OK really. Trinnie grins and continues with her work. I can see the concentration on her face as she tries to make her drawing better than mine. Mr Vaughn points his pencil at me.

"If you need to talk…"

I shake my head, like I've got it all under control, and try to concentrate on varying the pressure of my 5B pencil. But my mind is a jumble of worries and it shows on the page. I can't get the teacher's eyes the same size, his ears are too high and the tones are all wrong. The finished portrait is awkward and distorted. Like a bad Picasso. When we display our drawings like we always do at the end of class, mine's the worst by far. One of the lads points at my efforts and starts mocking it.

"I'm glad she didn't draw me."

The rest of the class crowds around my crap artwork. One by one they burst into laughter. It's that bad, I can't even be bothered trying to defend it. Instead, I copy Mam. Ripping it in half, then half again, I dump my drawing in the bin. Mr Vaughn peers into the bin, raises his eyebrows, but doesn't say a word. No one else mentions it either.

When I check out my own portrait, my stomach knots with excitement. Is that really how I look? Mr Vaughn has made me look like a fifties film star – Audrey Hepburn, eat your heart out! Not that it matters – I'm still the school leper.

By the time the final school bell rings, I'm near breaking point. Thankfully, Sarah is waiting outside.

"So – what are you going to suggest for the school trip?" she asks excitedly, as we head for home.

I notice the purple shadows under her eyes have lessened. Being dropped by the bullies is doing her good. I, on the other hand, feel drained.

"Dunno. I'll just go along with what everyone else wants."

"It's a toss-up between the British Museum in London and the Pitt Rivers Museum in Oxford for me. I've read about them so many times and they sound amazing. I think I'll go for the British Museum. No! Pitt Rivers – they have shrunken heads and Samurai armour and everything. What do you think?"

I can't help groaning. "Trust you to choose something sensible!"

"Have you got any better ideas?"

"Alton Towers or Disneyland Paris?" Places I've always dreamt of visiting but would never be able to afford – but I don't really have the right to suggest anything. "No, you're right, Pitt Rivers sounds good."

"What's up? You never give in so easily. You can tell me it's none of my business…"

"It's none of your business," I cut in, smiling, knowing full well that Sarah won't let this one go.

"You can't let those bullies get to you. They won't be on the trip and it'll be good to be away from them for the day."

Trust Sarah to think the best of things, to think the best of me. "It's not just them…"

I open my mouth to confide in her about the bag, but then I think better of it – what if I lose her? After chasing Jack away, and most of the school gossiping about me, I can't risk telling her. The timing has to be right.

"Let me guess… is it something to do with Jack?" asks Sarah.

I lose my cool and gasp. If Sarah and Jack start talking, they'll figure out I'm the thief for sure. I'll be an outcast for eternity.

"Ooh I'm right... Come on, tell me! How are things going? I've seen the way you two glance at each other across the room," says Sarah, pulling a sickly, adoring face that makes my throat clench.

"There's nothing to tell," I say, trying to end the conversation.

"He fancies you."

"Hates my guts more like."

"How do you work that out, Sherlock? Is there something wrong with your eyes? He's always avoiding you, then watching you when you're not looking. It's a sure sign..."

"Of how much he hates me. He's avoiding me because I threw him out of our house."

Sarah's eyes threaten to pop out of her head. "Jack Whitman was in *your* house and you *threw him out*?"

She fakes a swoon, pretending to fall to the ground in a faint. Checking the street behind her is clear, Sarah lowers her voice to a whisper.

"Is that why Mad Dog's after you?"

"Probably. That night we missed each other after school I bumped into Jack..."

"The night Mrs Snelling's bag was stolen?"

"Yeah... He should have been hanging out with Maddy but changed his mind. Then he intervened the other day after you ran off... told them to stop and walked me home."

Sarah winces at the reminder, but quickly gathers herself. "He saved you – a real-life knight in shining armour."

"I don't think Maddy sees it quite like that."

"So what? Just cos she fancies him – it doesn't mean she owns him. He's obviously not interested in her." Sarah gives a knowing smile. "And you know what that means, don't you?"

"It means she won't stop until she's killed me. Great. I'm screwed."

An uncomfortable silence edges its way between us. Sarah's lost her mind. There's no way Jack would be interested in me over Mad Dog. She might be a bitch, but she's experienced. That's what boys want.

As we venture out onto the open field, I check behind me every few steps, in case we're being followed. Sarah tries to make me feel better by chatting.

"So, how did today go?" she asks.

I give her my best "are you kidding me?" look.

"That bad?"

"Let's see… everyone sniggering at my hair, avoiding me like the plague, and me being in constant fear for my life – it was great! Best day ever!"

"It's not like we were ever popular."

The way she says it, I can't help laughing.

"I know, but people wouldn't even stand next to me in the dinner queue. You saw them – they were actually pushing others in front of them to get away from me."

"Yeah, that sucked all right. But at least you got your dinner while it was hot. And if Maddy keeps being so blatant, maybe she'll get her comeuppance."

I know Sarah is doing her best, so I smile.

"As for your hair," continues Sarah. "They're just jealous because it's gorgeous on you. You've got a nice face so you can carry it off."

I take a sharp breath, my head spinning. That's what Jack said, before we'd been disturbed by Hatty. Before I threw him out. I think of how he smelt – warm and spicy – and how he'd leaned in towards me…

"Liv?"

Sarah is holding me by the shoulder, staring into my face.

"Liv, can you hear me?"

"What? Yeah."

"Did you get checked out at the docs?"

"No need. I'm fine." I pull away and try to stomp ahead, even though the ground swells and sways, magnified one minute, distant the next.

"Are you sure? The gang – they could have done some real damage… we should get you checked out."

"I'm fine! Just because your parents call the doctor over every little thing, doesn't mean I have to," I snap, immediately wishing I hadn't.

There's something clearly wrong with me. Why do I keep pushing people away?

An awful thought shoots through me like a thunderbolt: *I'm turning out like Mam.*

Chapter Twenty-Seven

Attached by an Invisible Thread

I watch as the note travels along the dinner queue, skipping us out, and feel nausea rise each time someone reads it and giggles. No prizes for guessing who it's about, but I can't stick up for myself – one word from me and it'll get back to Maddy – so I keep my head down and try to pretend I haven't noticed. When it goes quiet, I don't need to look up to know that Maddy's here. It's like the moment before a storm when the birds stop singing and seek shelter. Only, there's nowhere for me to hide.

"Let's get out of her way," I say, sensing Sarah tense beside me.

Not long after we're seated, Maddy arrives at our table, flanked by Lorna and Zadie. They slam their plates down and settle themselves for lunch.

"So, ginger pig, what's on the menu today?" asks Maddy.

She reaches over with her fork and stabs at my plate, lifting off a huge slab of meat pie.

"Mmm – meat pie. Exactly what I was going to choose – but then I noticed that's what you picked. So I chose the sausages. Knew you wouldn't mind sharing."

Zadie giggles.

"Here. Take it," I say, pushing the plate towards Mad Dog. "I've lost my appetite."

I don't know where it comes from. I guess I've just had enough. Sarah stops eating and holds her fork mid-air. Mad Dog looks momentarily confused while Lorna and Zadie eye each other nervously. Recovering, Mad Dog leans in.

"Tough, are we?" She grabs me by the shoulder, pressing her thumb against my throat just enough to restrict my breathing. "I decide what happens around here, not you."

As Mad Dog tightens her grip, I struggle for air. A cough from Lorna signals Mozzer's arrival and Maddy releases me at just the right moment. Eyes narrowed, she watches as the head teacher does his rounds, waiting until a shout from the other side of the room diverts his attention so she can lean right up close to my face. The other girls lean forward too, as though attached by an invisible thread.

"You're going to get it, ginger pig. The other day – that was nothing. I'll get you properly – when you least expect it."

Recovering my breath, I rest my hand on my chest and avert my gaze. I distract myself by thinking about the peanut-butter fudge recipe that's waiting for me at home. Maddy wedges herself between me and Sarah, motioning with her head for Sarah to leave. Stalling, Sarah tries to catch my eye, but I purposely avoid her gaze.

"It's OK – go," I say, hanging my head as I listen to Sarah's footsteps fade.

Mad Dog reaches under the table and grabs my wrist. She digs her nails in deep as Old Mozzer approaches.

"Everything all right, girls?" he asks.

"Yes, Mr Morrelly," says Maddy, in a sickly-sweet voice.

My wrist is burning now where Maddy has her claws dug in, but I'm determined not to flinch.

"Olivia? Are you all right?"

"Yes, sir," I say, trying to keep my face from screwing up with pain.

"Good, good."

The head teacher strides off, arms clasped behind his back. As soon as he's out of earshot, Mad Dog lets go.

"See? We run this place now, not him. When it comes to thieves, we're in charge."

I feel my thoughts spin out of control. She knows.

"Think you can steal Jack from me, ginger pig?" Mad Dog continues. "You'd better watch your back."

Relieved it isn't the bag we're talking about, I fight the smile that threatens to spread across my face. Maddy stands, the other girls following. As a parting insult, she unscrews the salt pot and pours it all over my lunch. "Jack might say he likes your hair, but it's only cos he feels sorry for you. It looks like shit."

Now she has my interest. Jack likes my hair?

They're only gone a couple of seconds when a gentle hand lands on my shoulder, making me spin round.

"Mrs Snelling! What are you doing back?"

Despite the cast on her foot, she looks as jolly as ever.

"Well now, that's a nice greeting!" hollers Mrs Snelling. "If you must know, I thought I'd stop by and see how things were going. I'll be back at work next week, and wanted to make sure the place was running smoothly." She points at my ruined dinner. "It's a good job I did! Come with me."

Gobsmacked, I slowly rise and follow Mrs Snelling, aware of eyes turning my way. Not wanting to give them any satisfaction, I refuse to react. I act like this is completely normal and focus on Mrs Snelling's back as she leads the way, limping past row upon row of lunch tables. If only she'd move a bit quicker.

In the kitchen, Mrs Snelling puts a replacement meal in front of me.

"Meat pie, wasn't it?"

Around us, the other cooks continue to serve up lunches, remove hot trays from the oven, replace empty containers on the counter and stack dishes as high as the ceiling. Although I've lost my appetite, I suck in the scents of gravy, custard and baked apples. I see Mad Dog's scowling face in the distance, but she can't see me. Digging into the pie, I chew a small mouthful. It tastes better than before.

"Don't you worry about the likes of her. Another few years and you'll never have to see her ever again."

Another few years? I nearly choke on a lump of pastry.

"Get through school and you can get out of here – keep away from those sorts. It's them that give this area a bad name."

I nod, wondering why Mrs Snelling has to be so nice. If only she knew the truth.

"So, how's the cooking going?"

"Good," I reply, pleased to change the subject. "I've made flapjacks, Eccles cakes and shortbread. And tomorrow I'm making fudge."

Mrs Snelling's eyes grow as round as cake tins. "And they've all worked first time?"

"More or less. The shortbread burned but everything else was fine."

"A little tip with the shortbread... did you put it in the fridge?"

I rest my fork on my plate and shake my head.

"Leave it to sit in the fridge for half an hour before baking. It improves the texture."

"I'll try that next time," I say.

I'll try anything to make life a bit better.

"I also wanted to ask you something," continues Mrs Snelling. "I hope you don't mind. It's about the robbery."

Fear freezes the blood in my veins. Looking up, I try to relax my facial muscles. "Sure, go ahead."

"I hear you're friends with that Jack boy – the one who helped me."

Mrs Snelling visibly shudders, remembering the incident, and my mouth turns dry as chalk.

"Yes. Well – kind of."

"Do you know him well enough to know whether he'd be capable of it?"

I drop my fork with a clatter.

"Of what?"

"Well, Mr Snelling's been onto me. Says it seems a bit coincidental that Jack happened to be there. And I do remember he had a rather large bag with him. Do you think he could have been involved? Helping me was a cover-up?"

Shaking my head emphatically, I clear my throat. I can't let Jack get blamed for something I did.

"No way – I mean, Jack wouldn't do that. He's a good guy. He stuck up for me when I needed it," I say, wishing I could go back in time and put everything right.

Mrs Snelling heaves a relieved sigh.

"Good – that's what I thought. Please don't repeat what I said. It's just a silly idea that Mr Snelling got into his head, and it started niggling away at me. Stupid really. You won't tell anyone, will you?"

Chapter Twenty-Seven

I shake my head, disgusted with myself. I should come clean. But I can't.

"Thanks, dear. I knew you were a nice girl, someone I could count on. I don't care about the bag or the money – there wasn't much in there anyways – but my purse held an important photo."

"A photo?" I picture the ginger lad with the big smile.

"Our son, Simon, was killed in a car crash four years ago, and I always carried our favourite photo – the one from his graduation – with me. I know it probably sounds silly to a young girl like you, but it felt like a bit of his memory was lost when that photo was stolen."

Avoiding Mrs Snelling's gaze, I gulp down the lump that has settled in my throat.

"Mr Snelling always warned me not to carry it around. He said I'd lose it. I guess it's the last we'll see of it now. I'll never hear the end of it."

Turning away, Mrs Snelling reaches for a big helping of rhubarb crumble and custard. She sets the bowl down with tear-moistened eyes.

"Thanks, Liv, you've been very kind to a sentimental old fool. Now promise you won't say a word about what I said? I'd feel terrible if it got out!"

Nodding, I force a tiny spoonful of pudding into my mouth. It feels like boulders as I swallow.

Peanut-Butter Fudge Chunks

Sweets for my sweet, sugar for my honey... A delicious fudge never fails to bring your sweetheart closer to you. If you've had a bitter row, sugar him up with this. If you're all loved-up, make him melt with this crunchy, nutty delight. Trust me – have I lied to you yet?

INGREDIENTS

340 g/12 oz chocolate chips – as sweet as you like
340 g/12 oz crunchy peanut butter
415 ml/14 fl oz sweetened condensed milk

HOW TO MAKE THE MAGIC HAPPEN

1. Line a square pan (approx 8 in.) with waxed or parchment paper.
2. In a bowl placed over a pan of boiling water, melt the chocolate chips and peanut butter until they turn into gooey goodness.
3. Stir well to make sure there are no lumps – we want the only crunch to be the peanuts.
4. Add the milk and continue stirring until it's smooth and golden.
5. Pour the mixture into the pan and refrigerate until chilled (make it at least 2 hours, if you can. I know – it's tempting!).
6. When set, place fudge on a cutting board, remove waxed paper and cut into around forty delicious fudge squares.

Tip: Don't worry about making the fudge squares perfect. After all, imperfections are a part of life. That's what makes those we love special.

Chapter Twenty-Eight

Placing It Carefully on the
Spring-Loaded Donkey

As soon as I'm home, I race upstairs to my room. Pulling the bag out of my wardrobe, not even bothering to be careful, I rip it open and yank out the wallet. Gently opening the clasp, I search inside, feeling like anything but the kind girl Mrs Snelling believes me to be. As I pull the photo out for a closer look, Harriet's voice floats up the stairs.

"Liv, your tea's ready."

"I'll be right down."

The lad smiling up at me is a bit older than Harriet. He's wearing a mortarboard and has bright red hair and a smattering of freckles on his pale skin. He doesn't resemble Mrs Snelling much, apart from the hair and the infectious grin. I guess he looks more like his dad.

"Liv! Your food is on the table. It's getting cold."

"I said I'd be right down."

I try to imagine how Mrs Snelling must feel, but I can't. I've never known anyone who has died. Dad isn't around, but he's not dead. As far as I know, he's out there somewhere, living his life. A life without us. I try to ignore what that means – that our dad doesn't want to know us. I guess he doesn't realize how bad things are with Mam. Or maybe he does and it doesn't make any difference.

Focusing back on the photo, I can't believe that this person is dead. I try to imagine what it would be like if Mam or Harriet died. What would I do? Probably carry a photo with me, just like Mrs Snelling.

Simon's eyes seem to stare at me accusingly, so I carefully return his picture to the purse and make a decision. I'll sneak the photo back to Mrs Snelling and put things right without getting caught. But how?

"Liv! For God's sake will you come and GET YOUR TEA!"

"I'm COMING!"

Racing down the stairs, I run straight into Harriet. She's flustered and cross.

"I have better things to do than make tea for an ungrateful brat," she snaps.

"Fine. Let me make my own tea then." I sit down at the table in front of a plate of sausages, potato waffles and beans. "I'm a better cook than you anyway. You only make frozen muck."

As I pick up my fork, smug look firmly in place, Harriet snatches my plate away.

"Right. If that's how you feel!"

She marches to the bin, stamps on the pedal to open it and pours my food away. Then she lets the lid slam shut, slings the plate into the sink and stomps off. It happens so fast, I can't even think of a smart comment.

"I'm fed up of you, you little cow," she calls after her.

"Not as fed up as I am," I shout back.

Hardly an impressive comeback, but at least it's something. Starving, but determined not to give Hatty the satisfaction of knowing it, I decide that dinner's overrated and it won't kill me to miss it. She'll be sorry when I end up dying of anorexia. Jack too. I stamp up the stairs and play Johnny as loudly as the record player will allow, imagining a long, slow, dramatic death. I'm halfway through planning my obituary when my anger abates and I decide the whole thing would require far too much effort. Especially when there's a heap of recipes still to try.

Laid on my bed, listening to *Personal Jesus*, my mind races. How am I going to put things right? I can't go on like this. Guilt sucks. It destroys your life. My mind wanders back to Harriet's advice: "*You'll get outta here one day too, you know. Just hold in there.*"

What if Hatty is wrong? What if hanging on means I'm trapped in the Egertons for ever? If only after returning the bag I could leave the estate – take some time out. But where would I go?

My mind goes crazy, thinking up possibilities. Whitby, Oxford, Disneyland Paris, London… if only I knew where my dad was. Then I could visit him. Like Jack said, I could make it happen. Imagine how happy he'd be – reunited with his long-lost daughter. It's all I can think of for the rest of the night. As I drift off to sleep, stomach rumbling, my made-up image of his face is the last thing I see.

* * *

That night, I dream of breaking glass and loud sirens. Long streaks of laser beams blast the sky like a pyrotechnic show and the whirr of a helicopter's propellers fill the thick night air.

There is a search party out. It's looking for me.

I run upstairs to the safety of my room. Harriet's bedroom door swings open and my sister sways in the doorway, her hair replaced by writhing snakes. They squirm and coil.

"You sssteal… you sssteal…" they hiss, preparing to strike.

I take a sharp breath in and edge my way past just in time. Slamming the bedroom door behind me, I rest against it, breathing hard. Inside, gentle music plays, birds sing and sunbeams pattern the floor like lace. My carpet is littered with retro toys I liked as a kid: Ladybird books, Operation, Buckaroo. As I pick up the plastic saddle, placing it carefully on the spring-loaded donkey, a voice calls from the wardrobe.

"Liv, sweetheart, are you there?" It's Mam. The sweet, light-hearted voice of a Mam I barely remember. A Mam that could be nicknamed "Happiness". "Come and see the surprise I have for you."

Uncertain why I'm scared, I edge towards the wardrobe. As I swing the door open, the room turns dark and cold.

"Thief, thief, thief."

The chant starts off quietly, growing gradually louder. The voice is gravelly and angry. It's coming from somewhere beneath my clothes.

"Thief, thief, thief."

I try to say something but can't. Searching my face with my hand, I discover my mouth has gone. *It wasn't my fault*, I want to call out. *I didn't mean to do it*. The chant continues, growing louder still. I have to make it stop.

Stepping into the wardrobe, I search through the rubble of clothes. As jeans, skirts and polo shirts fly beyond me, the voice grows deafening.

"Thief, thief, thief."

Pain shoots through my jaw as I try to talk without a mouth. I shove more clothes out of the way and realize I'm crying. Then I find it.

The Blue Handbag.

It has eyes and teeth.

Dancing up and down on the spot, the handbag screams out its accusation. I try to wedge my hand over its mouth but it bites down hard, drawing blood.

The helicopter whirr grows closer. Light beams from sniper guns settle on my chest. I scream.

On waking – sweating and shivering, my legs entangled in the quilt – I lie as still as I can and let the darkness wash over me. Wiping my teary cheeks dry with the back of my hand, I wait until my heartbeat calms and the fear abates.

When I feel brave enough, I sit up and check around me, happy to see my floor littered with vinyl sleeves, Harriet's cast-off magazines and *Recipes to Make Happiness Bloom*. Rubbing my eyes, I check the time.

4.30 a.m.

It's going to be a long night.

My mind turns into a jumble of questions. What can I do with the bag? Should I tell Sarah? Will Jack ever speak to me again? Will I ever meet my dad – and when will Mam come home? I try to figure out some answers – even one would do – but I end up giving myself a headache instead. Thank God it's Saturday and I'll be visiting Sarah's. Only a few more hours to go.

I distract myself by practising my kissing technique – first on the pillow, then on the back of my hand. I manage to get my teeth out of the way of my lips, but I have no idea what to do with my tongue. It strays in all the wrong places, looking for somewhere to go. Maybe I should be grateful I'm too ugly to kiss? Thinking I'm relaxed enough to sleep, I snuggle down into my quilt and try to drift off. But every time I drop off, I jump awake, certain I can hear the handbag hopping around chanting Thief! Thief! Thief!

Instead of fighting it, I decide to get up and make the peanut-butter fudge. Only when it's cooled and divided up into portions – some to share with Mam, some for Sarah – do I dare go back to sleep.

* * *

Crawling out of bed and rubbing my eyes, I approach the wardrobe with caution. As I shovel down into the mound of clothes, my heart races. Even though I know Harriet will be busy making breakfast, I can't help checking over my shoulder.

When I see the stupid blue bag, I flip and start kicking stuff around. I can't take it any more. I have to figure out how to return it without getting caught.

Checking the time, I quickly pull on my green and black stripy tights, short black skirt and khaki Converse. Walking always helps me think, and Sarah's is a good half hour away. Smoothing some wax into my hair, I grab Sarah's fudge and head out, pausing only to double-check my hair in the mirror. Just in case I bump into someone along the way.

Chapter Twenty-Nine

Did I Say Something Funny?

"I was thinking... if you want to make it up with Jack..." Sarah rolls onto her side and leans her head on her hand.

"There's not much to make up, is there? We hardly know each other," I say.

"So? You want to talk to him again, right?"

"Yeah. Of course – he stuck up for me."

"I bet that's not the only reason – but anyway, I've got the perfect plan... Why don't you impress him with your cooking?" Sarah dips her hand into the airtight container and pulls out a huge piece of fudge. She chews loudly, smacking her lips. "He won't be able to resist."

"What? That's the most ridiculous thing I've ever heard! It's going to take more than sweets to impress someone like him."

"*Like him*? He's not a god, you know! And it's not a stupid idea. Think about it. They say that the way to a man's heart is through his stomach."

"That's nonsense. Who's 'they', anyway?"

Sarah shrugs, raises an eyebrow and chomps on the fudge. "My mum, for one. She says that Dad doesn't communicate with words – he uses his belly instead."

I have to smile. Her dad's always the first to sit at the table and he clears the leftovers from everyone else's plates. He even sneaks your food while you're still eating if you don't keep an eye out, and he's as thin as a whippet.

"For your information, I don't *want* to get to Jack's heart," I say.

I don't know how I expect to convince Sarah when I'm not convinced myself.

"So, if he tried to kiss you, you'd tell him to get lost." Her question almost winds me.

"Yes. I'd tell him to get lost."

"Liar."

"I'm not in the same league, Sarah. This isn't a fairytale." We both laugh awkwardly.

"So, what *do* you want?" asks Sarah.

"I dunno… friendship. To thank him for helping me."

My heart pounds so loudly, I'm worried Sarah might hear it. Friendship would be OK, but it would be nice if Jack were something more. The way he leaned in… Then I think about my straying tongue, and dismiss the idea instantly. Until I get that thing under control, there's no way I'm kissing anyone.

"Hmm. Just good friends," says Sarah, in a loved-up voice.

"Stop it!" I plead.

Sarah stops, but not for long. After a millisecond, she starts up again.

"Seriously, though. It could work. Think about it: you need to distract the class from Maddy's nonsense – she thinks she's a big deal since everyone found out she attacked you – and you need to patch things up with Jack. You could do it in one go by baking. Something for everyone to share."

"But I'm not good enough… what if no one likes it? That'd make things even worse."

"How could it make things worse? Liv, you're brilliant. Taste this and tell me it's not divine."

I roll some fudge around my mouth. I have to admit, it's good. Better than the pre-packaged stuff you buy. My fudge is creamy and melt-in-the-mouth.

"You honestly think it would work?"

"Yep."

"I can't just bring in a bag of goodies and expect everyone to dive in. Mad Dog's got them wrapped around her finger."

"Bring it on a Monday morning," suggests Sarah. "Mrs Pearl always asks if there's anything we'd like to share about our weekend. She's all hippy like that—"

"I want you all to have a voice, feel like you're equals—" I mimic.

"Exactly! It's fool-proof."

"I dunno…"

"You'll win Jack over."

Sarah grins, knowing she has me hooked.

"I guess it's not such a bad idea…" I say.

"It's a great idea."

"But what should I bake?"

"Something Jack likes. Find out his favourite."

"How do I do that when he's not talking to me – and the whole class thinks I'm a leper?"

"That's a problem. Maybe we could ask Maddy?" Sarah offers with a roguish expression.

"That's not even funny," I say.

"Sorry… maybe I could find out?"

"How? What are you gonna do – march up to Jack and ask him? You've hardly spoken two words to him outside of lessons!"

"No, but I have an inside weapon: Dad."

I almost spit out my fudge. "What's your dad got to do with this?"

"He knows Jack's mum. They're on the Neighbourhood Watch committee together."

"Don't you dare! The last thing I want is your parents knowing about this!"

"They don't have to know why. I could tell Dad I need to know for a project and that I'm too embarrassed to ask. He's a soft touch." She lowers her voice to a whisper. "He's been looking after Mum since for ever, don't forget. He'll find out – no questions asked. Then all you have to do is make it and bring it in."

I lean back, popping another piece of fudge in my mouth.

"Fine," I say. "I'm in."

"You are? Liv, this is going to work, I promise you!"

We squeal and hug, not noticing Mrs Butler's arrival.

"What are you two all excited about?" she asks.

"Nothing," we reply in unison, then fall about giggling. Mrs Butler shakes her head and smiles.

"It doesn't look like nothing to me."

Mr Butler sticks his head round the door. "What's the commotion?" Before anyone can reply, he notices the container on the floor. "Ooh, fudge – don't mind if I do!" he says, taking the biggest chunk and shoving it in his mouth.

This time, we collapse. I hold my stomach, which hurts so much from laughing. Sarah whispers, "I think I'm going to pee myself," and that makes us worse.

Mr Butler stares at us, reduced to a puddle of giggles on the floor.

"Did I say something funny?" he asks.

Chapter Thirty

A Glimpse of How Things Used to Be

It's a week since I had the fight with Jack. We're completely avoiding each other and I can't think of anything other than how great it would be if Sarah's plan worked – especially the "more than friends" bit. I've decided to concentrate all my energy on our plan – I need to pull out all the stops to put things right. So the last thing I want to do is visit Mam, but we have no choice.

"She probably won't even turn up," I say, as we sit at the back of the bus. I tuck my legs up against the seat in front of me, knowing it will wind Hatty up.

"Liv, you can't say that."

"I just did. It's true, isn't it?"

"You can't think that way. We've got to treat it like a new opportunity every time. Anyway, she'll love the fudge you've brought her."

"The fudge she won't get because she won't turn up."

Harriet lets the matter drop. She knows something's up and would probably listen if I opened up to her, but every time I decide to try and be nice, her words play over and over in my head: *"I'm sick of everything. And everyone. I wish it'd all just go away."*

The journey seems to take much longer than usual. The bus stops in every town and village and it's difficult not to lose my rag. I keep quiet so I don't take things out on my sister. After a while, Harriet gives me a nudge.

"The only way Mam will get better is if we give her the support she needs," she says.

I nod, though I'm not sure how I can help Mam when I can't even help myself. To avoid any further conversation, I turn to the window and check out my reflection. I'm getting used to my hair, and I actually quite like it. My black eyeliner makes me look older, but I'm still plain and boring. Why I ever imagined Jack might be interested in kissing me, I don't know.

To try and take my mind off things, I watch the world flash by. There's nothing better than laughing at other people when you're fed up with yourself. I see a lady in red, spiky heels wobbling along the pavement. Then, a round, red-faced man jogging clumsily, clutching his chest like he's having a heart attack. I chuckle as a small, curly-haired girl trips and bawls – until her dad scoops her up, hugging her close and whispering in her ear. So much for laughing. I can't take my eyes off them as he dusts her down and dries her tears. My hand splayed against the glass, I watch as they grow smaller, fading into the distance until they're invisible. Then I sit back and close my eyes.

When we finally arrive at Ashgrove House, my feet feel leaden as I climb the steps. It was much more fun sneaking around at night. It takes every morsel of energy and courage to keep going. My instincts scream at me to turn round, but one glance at Harriet's determined face forces me through the door.

As we walk up to Reception, Harriet adopts her best smile, and I do the same. Wearing our masks, we sign in and turn towards the waiting room. But before we can sit down, Mam arrives, smiling and bright skinned. Her eyes sparkle golden-green and her greying hair is freshly washed, swishing in waves around her shoulders. I run my fingers through my own hair nervously.

"Oh no – you cut your beautiful hair!" cries Mam, before hugging each of us in turn.

I glance at Harriet. Doesn't Mam remember seeing my hair – does she even remember running away? Harriet looks just as confused, but Mam doesn't seem to notice.

"But why so sad?" continues Mam. "I love it! Don't ruin that cute face with a frown. C'mon, I've reserved the table tennis."

I can't help smiling. To think I was considering turning back. Harriet links Mam's arm and I grab the other. We trot down the corridor.

"Liv's brought something for you," says Harriet, winking behind Mam's back.

"A surprise? You know how much I love surprises!"

The ping-pong table stands in the sunniest spot in the games room. Before we start playing, I hand over the slabs of fudge. As she peers in, Mam gives a squeal of delight.

"Is this what I think it is?"

"Peanut-butter fudge," offers Harriet, before I get a chance.

Trying not to sulk about it, I worry I haven't brought enough. I shouldn't have shared it with the Butlers. Why does everything have to be so complicated? Why isn't there a recipe for how to do the right thing?

"It's years since I've had this!" says Mam, taking a small nibble and chewing slowly. "It's divine – thank you. This calls for a proper celebration. Go get us some drinks from the canteen. Three cream sodas, like old times!" She fishes in her pocket and hands me a five-pound note.

"I'd prefer a Diet Coke," says Harriet.

I hold my breath. Has Hatty gone mad? She should know better than to challenge Mam. But Mam raises an eyebrow, says something about Hatty not needing "diet" anything, then changes the order.

"Make that two cream sodas and a Diet Coke," she says. "And ask to borrow a knife so we can cut this up equally. We'll mind the table!"

I race towards the canteen as fast as I can. My echoing footsteps remind me of running away from the kitchen that day, and no matter how fast I move, I can't outrun the guilt.

As I round the corner into the canteen, a pained screech sounds from somewhere down the corridor, followed by a loud clatter. Like something being thrown at the wall. I quickly select the drinks and rush to the counter to pay. The tall, spindly lady behind the till smiles gently.

"Don't let the noise frighten you," she says. "It's all part of the healing process."

What does she know? She's just a crappy canteen assistant.

"Are you visiting someone special?"

I shrug, wishing the woman would hurry up and hand over the change. I want to get back to Mam as quickly as possible. The lady smiles sympathetically.

"Have a lovely visit," she says, finally handing over some coins.

I feel a violent rush of shame sweep through me. How could anyone enjoy a visit here? It's a place for losers and degenerates. Everyone knows that. Turning, I stop in my tracks, my heart flipping like an acrobat.

Maddy is wiping splatters of dark red sauce from her yellow T-shirt, her blond hair falling into her face as she bends over, trying to clean herself up. I guess her mam must have lost the plot again.

"Are you all right, dear?" the woman behind the counter asks.

Before I can sneak away, Mad Dog looks up. It looks like she's been crying. Tears line her cheeks in tiny streams, mixing with her foundation and powder. And her mascara is smudged across her face. If she weren't so scary, I'd tell her.

It takes a moment for Maddy to recognize me. When she does, her eyes darken and her lips curl.

"What are you looking at, ginger pig? You might think you're great wearing makeup but you're still ugly."

The lady behind the counter tuts and mumbles something under her breath. Maddy shoots her an evil look. Saying nothing, I put my head down and rush past as quickly as I can. As soon as I turn the corner, I run, trying not to shake the cans too much. When I get back to the games room, Mam and Harriet are leaning on the table, deep in conversation. I hand the drinks over, my heart thumping.

"What's up?" I ask.

"Harriet was just telling me about your cooking... Liv, I'm so proud of you!"

Mam pulls me close and I melt into the hug.

"Are you OK?" mouths Harriet, draining her can. She motions with her hand that my face looks weird. I touch my left ear – something I haven't done in years, and Hatty snorts Diet Coke out of her nose.

"Now where's that knife?" asks Mam, letting go.

"Oh. I forgot it." I look nervously towards the door.

"I don't want fudge anyway, Mam," says Harriet quickly, still trying to dry her face with the back of her hand.

"Me neither," I say.

"You're just being kind," smiles Mam. "But losers, weepers, and all that!" She bites off a huge chunk and gobbles it down.

We all chuckle and my heart swells with pride. Mam is proud of me.

"This brings back so many memories," says Mam, a faraway look in her eyes.

"Like what?" I ask, almost too quickly.

"Old dreams. Silly old dreams that once seemed so real. Summery picnics, chips on the beach – do you remember that trip to Whitby?"

"The one where we jumped waves?"

"And our noses got all red from the wind?" adds Harriet.

"That's the one! Those were the days. This takes me back – thanks, Liv."

I puff myself up, tall and confident, feeling like I've grown an inch or two.

"It's nothing," I say

"Nothing?" says Mam, shoving another chunk into her mouth. "It's amazing. It's just like…"

As Mam pauses, I exchange a nervous glance with my sister.

"Go on," urges Harriet.

Mam's eyes mist over.

"I was going to say, it reminds me of one I used to make. I wanted to open a café once, you know? With my friend, Rosa – remember her, Hatty? We were going to bake all our own cakes and serve tea in mismatched china cups."

"You still could," I say.

"I had all my own recipes – there was one for peanut-butter fudge, just like this."

I gesture with my eyes that we should tell Mam about the cookbook, but Harriet shakes her head.

"Are you two OK?" asks Mam, eyeing us suspiciously.

"We're fine," says Harriet.

"What happened? To the café idea?" I ask.

Mum's eyes cloud over and shadows pass over her face. I ignore the "you've-done-it-now" look from Harriet, and wait.

"It was just make-believe. Let's have a game. Shall we play Round Robin? You two go first and I'll play the winner."

I open my mouth to ask Mam more questions, but Harriet nudges me to be quiet. I get it – admitting about the recipe book means admitting I went through Mam's private belongings. And asking too many questions only dredges up the past – including Dad's affair. Harriet wants to preserve Mam's good mood, just as much as I do.

"Deal," we shout in unison, picking up our bats.

Mum watches as we battle it out over the net.

"Yay! I win!" I shout, as I score the match point.

"Looks like you're on, Mam," says Harriet, offering the bat.

I watch Mam position herself in the sun, bat poised and her thumb raised, signalling she's ready. There's a huge grin on her face and I notice the sparkle has returned to Harriet's eyes too. It's a glimpse of how things used to be – how they could be again. I feel my own mouth stretch wide, turning into a smile big enough to swallow up the entire beautiful scene.

Rocky Road

Because life isn't always straightforward, you need a few treats to remind you that there's still goodness in the world. Make when you're worried, give with love and enjoy with a happy heart.

INGREDIENTS

400 g/14¼ oz milk chocolate chunks
8 bars of chocolate-covered Turkish Delight
1 large packet of big, fluffy marshmallows (pink and white)
100 g/3½ oz blanched almonds

HOW TO MAKE THE MAGIC HAPPEN

1. Grab a loaf tin and line with cling film, letting a bit hang over the top all the way around.
2. Chop the Turkish Delight into eight pieces per bar. Smash up the almonds and use scissors to cut the marshmallows into chunky pieces.
3. Melt the chocolate in a bowl over a saucepan of simmering water, stirring all the time to prevent burning (this will keep it heavenly). When melted and velvety smooth, add all the yummy bits.
4. Stir well to make the chunky delights spread evenly. Transfer it all to a loaf tin and smooth with a spatula.

5. Cover with cling film and put in the fridge for at least 4 hours, or until it has set. Cut into slices (be careful – a heavy knife is best) and serve. Don't forget to eat some yourself to make that heart happy, and watch your troubles melt away with every bite.

Chapter Thirty-One

The Frosty Air Lifts Like Fog in the Rain

When Sarah phones me the next day to tell me that Rocky Road is Jack's favourite, I can't believe my luck. The recipe is waiting for me on page thirty-three, and it sounds amazing. Before I can chicken out, I throw myself into baking.

The following morning, as soon as the register's been taken, Mrs Pearl asks her usual question. I'm crapping myself, but I clear my throat and put up my hand. Sarah's encouraging smile helps.

"I have something to share," I say. My face is hot and clammy, and I'm as jittery as a bag of frogs as everyone turns to look at me. I know what they're thinking – they're thinking, what's she got to share that could possibly interest us?

"Good! Go ahead," says Mrs Pearl, looking mildly surprised. Leaning back in her chair and folding her arms, she smiles. "I'm sure we'd all love to hear it."

The class erupts in loud whispers. Purposely avoiding everyone's gaze, I try to stay focused. If I catch Jack's eye, I'll back out. As Mrs Pearl calls order, my heart races and blood thumps in my ears. Almost ready to combust, I wait for the murmuring to stop.

"Go ahead – I think we're all listening now," says Mrs Pearl, throwing an approving glance towards Jack.

"Well, I've... kind of... been baking." My voice is so shaky, I sound like I'm on a bumpy bus. Sarah beams at me. I try to concentrate on that, rather than the sniggers. "I've brought some in for everyone to try."

The class falls silent.

I rifle through my rucksack and slam a giant tin of Rocky Road on the desk. When I remove the lid, several people lean in to take a look, making noises of approval.

"Why don't you hand them out?" suggests Mrs Pearl. "They look delicious."

She climbs out of her chair and takes a good-sized chunk. No one else moves. Only Sarah takes a piece. I feel sweat beading on my upper lip as I sink lower in my seat and wait. Just as I'm about to replace the lid, I hear chair legs scrape behind me. I guess it's Jack coming to my rescue, so I flash my best smile. But I needn't have bothered. It's Valerie Jeckyll, the tall, gangly girl with lots of freckles from Sarah's running group. Sarah's best friend when I'm not around.

"Looks good," she says. The class watches as Valerie bites into a chunk and smacks her lips. "Tastes even better. God, this is amazing!" She gobbles it down, licking her fingers afterwards.

"No one else?" asks Mrs Pearl.

"Here, I'll try one," calls a voice from the back.

Slowly, the tin passes from person to person. They each take a slice and nod approval. The frosty air lifts like fog in the rain, and I feel my shoulders relaxing.

My heart flutters as the tin makes its way to Jack. I made several batches until it was perfect and I only burned one lot – daydreaming about the moment he'd taste it and instantly realize how sorry I am. My hands tremble as the tin inches closer and closer. I try not to get too carried away, but I visualize his gorgeous smile as he tastes my food – just like he talked about that day in the supermarket.

But once again, I'm proved a complete moron.

When the tin reaches Jack, he shakes his head, refusing to even acknowledge the Rocky Road I made especially for him. What was it the recipe said? Make when you're worried, give with love and enjoy with a happy heart. Where's my promised reward?

My hopes sink to deeper depths of despair. I never knew you could hurt this bad when you wanted to say sorry but no one would listen. I see the recipe book for what it is: a pile of nonsense. Just like Mam's café idea. Chasing a stupid dream – isn't that all I'm doing? As far as I'm concerned, Jack's reaction says it all. There are no dreams in Egerton and no happy hearts.

Ignoring Sarah's attempts to look encouraging, I stare at my desk. The positive reactions from the others are wiped out by Jack's cold response. Why wouldn't he try some – is he really still that angry with me? Unless he's realized I was running from the dinner hall that day. Unless he knows I'm the thief. I sink as low in my chair as I can manage without sliding off.

The rest of that morning's class passes in a cloud of gloom. When Valerie comes up at the end and asks for more, I'm all fake smiles and fake laughs. As I get the tin from my bag again, Sarah dashes past and winks.

"I'll see you after running," she says, hurrying by. Valerie thanks me and dashes off to catch up to Sarah. I sigh, wishing Sarah hadn't left me alone, when I hear a noise behind me.

Chapter Thirty-One

There's someone still here. I cross my fingers – please let it be Jack.

My heartbeat quickens as I hurriedly try to replace the lid. I hear footsteps and swing round.

"Jack!" I say, trying to make my voice sound as normal as possible.

He stays quiet. Shuffles from foot to foot. He looks so incredibly handsome, it freezes my tongue and we both stand there, awkward. Opening his mouth to say something, Jack quickly changes his mind and pushes past me without saying a word.

I spin on my heels, wanting to call him back, but I find myself tongue-tied. What could I say anyway? Shaking, I return to packing my things, listening to Jack's footsteps fade. Then I crumple into my chair, put my head on the desk and hit it once with each fist.

Chapter Thirty-Two

Sharp as a Carving Knife

"Liv, there's someone here to see you."

Harriet's voice rings out loud and clear over my music. I stop mid dance and pause – the only person that ever comes to see me is Sarah, and she's at her grandma's for the night.

"Liv!"

"I'm coming!"

I check my hair in the mirror before running downstairs to the front door. When I get there, I feel my bones turn to jelly.

It's Jack.

"I hope you don't mind me coming round..." he says.

I glance nervously at Harriet. She winks covertly as she shoves past, gently nudging me in the ribs.

"I'll leave you two to it," she says, disappearing off into the living room.

"If I've caught you at a bad time, I can go..."

He looks amazing in blue. I'm trying to check him out, without being too obvious, when I notice the package in his hand. I quickly look away. It can't be for me.

"No, stay! It's just... I thought you weren't talking to me..."

I realize I'm rubbing one leg with the other like a stork, and stare at the floor, as if it's covered in the most interesting carpet ever. He even has great taste in shoes – scuffed blue and brown Adidas.

"This is for you," he says, thrusting the package into my hands, taking me by surprise.

The package tumbles to the ground and I wince as it hits the floor with a loud clunk.

"Are you going to ask him in or what?" shouts Harriet.

I should have known she'd be eavesdropping. Scooping up the gift, I hold the door wide so Jack can come in. He towers over me as I close the door quietly.

"About earlier, I was just… I didn't know what to do or say. I heard Maddy's still on your case and I feel awful. It's all my fault."

"It's not your fault. Forget about it," I say. "C'mon up. I was just chilling out."

Together, we slip up the stairs.

When we step into my room, I realize there's underwear all over the floor and it's not even clean. There's junk on every surface: Harriet's cast-off magazines, nail varnish bottles, spilled makeup and even a pair of rolled-up stripy tights – I usually wear them a few times to save on washing powder. But tidying is a great excuse to put off opening the present from Jack. I hate opening presents in front of people. What if you don't like it and it shows on your face? Shovelling everything into drawers the best I can – I don't chance opening the wardrobe – I motion for Jack to sit on the bed.

"Hey, what are you listening to?" he asks, politely ignoring the mess around him.

"Johnny Cash."

I expect him to laugh or pull a face. If only he hadn't caught me listening to Mam's music. On vinyl, of all things. Everyone else has iPods.

"It's awesome," he replies, before jumping up to admire the record player. "Hey, this thing's cool. It's totally vintage. I can't believe it works. I've never seen one in action before."

"I know – sad, aren't I?"

"No, seriously – this is on my wish list. Mum got me an iPod. She thinks I should stay up to date to get on in life. She's been obsessed with self-improvement since Dad left. But if it's not broke, why fix it? An iPod's not going to get them back together..."

"Do you think they'll get back together?"

"Nah. To be honest, I like them better when they're apart. What about your parents?"

"No chance. My dad ran off with Mam's best friend when I was two," I say, as though I'm an authority on the subject. "So Mam moved back here. I wish she'd stayed in London."

"I'm glad she didn't," says Jack, catching my eye.

I turn the music up louder to drown out my embarrassment. Jack jumps up and starts bouncing, pogo-style, in time to "Folsom Prison Blues".

"What else's on your wish list – a trampoline?" I ask, surprising myself.

It feels good to have another friend – if that's what he is.

"I'm not telling you unless you join me," he shouts over the guitar riffs. Then he lurches forward, grabs me by the hands and drags me onto his makeshift dance floor. I brave a little bounce. I swear I'll never wash my hands again.

"That's it!" cries Jack, launching into a mosh. I relax and let myself go a bit. Within minutes, we're in full flow, shaking our heads like lunatics.

"What's going on?" says Harriet, appearing in the doorway.

We stop instantly.

"Sorry, Hatty... we were just..."

"I can see what you were just doing. And you're in big trouble."

I glance at Jack but he doesn't seem bothered. Then I realize: Hatty's joking.

"You're making a mockery of a good song, jumping around like that," she says, chuckling. "I believe it should be more like this."

Without warning, she whacks the volume up full blast and leaps into the centre of the room, bashing out an over-hammed air guitar.

"Awesome!" shouts Jack, joining in.

Soon, we're all jumping around the room, flinging ourselves about. All too soon, the neighbours start banging on the wall in protest. Panting, Harriet flops down next to the record player and turns the volume down.

"I guess the party's over," she says, before disappearing out of the door and closing it quietly behind her.

Jack nods his head towards the wall. "You won't get in trouble, will you?"

Sweat glistens on his forehead. It looks lovely. Otherworldly – like he's an angel or something.

"No – Pauline's on the other side. That's Bob and Jane banging. They're total stoners. They'll forget about it in ten minutes."

Jack chuckles. I can't believe how easy he is to talk to. I can't believe he's here, in my room.

"Mam says they don't have a brain cell left between them. Anyway, Hatty was here with us. And she's the boss."

"She sure is. She's really cool."

"Yeah, she's not bad," I admit. "But sometimes—"

"Sometimes you miss having a mum or dad around?"

I was going to say "sometimes she's a right cow", but under the circumstances, I shrug instead.

"There's nothing wrong with that, Liv. I miss Dad sometimes too. Don't miss the two of them arguing but – you know."

I nod, even though I don't – not really. I know nothing about my dad. Not wanting to sound like a hopeless case, I keep quiet. When Jack points at the present, I wish I'd kept talking.

"Hey, you gonna open that?" he asks.

"Now?"

"Yes, now!"

I pick up the bundle and uncurl the Sellotape from the paper. I want to keep it as perfect as Jack's visit. "I hope it's not broken after I dropped it."

"Don't worry, it won't be."

Nestled in the paper are two cake tins, four smaller tins that are heart-shaped, a whisk and some gingerbread-man cookie cutters.

"It's to say sorry for being such a prat earlier. They're Mum's cast-offs, I'm afraid, but I thought you could put them to good use."

"I dunno what to say..."

Smiling, Jack sits back on the bed as "Ring of Fire" comes on the record player.

Chapter Thirty-Two

"Don't say anything. I'm just pleased you didn't throw them at me."

I gently place the gift back on the dressing table, letting my fingers linger on the tins for a moment before plopping down next to Jack. I'm careful not to accidentally touch him.

"This is a great tune," he says, singing quietly under his breath. "I've always liked it, but didn't know who it was by."

Nodding my head in time, I mouth the lyrics. Then I realize Jack is staring at me, so I stop.

"What?"

"You're lovely," Jack says suddenly.

I light up like a flare. Jack leans forward and, as I shrink back, he catches me by my chin and tilts it upwards. His lips are red and sticky like jam, and I like jam – especially strawberry. Before I can react, he pulls my face towards his and I think, *Yes, this is finally it! The moment when all those practice snogs on mirrors and pillows can be put to good use.* I'm too scared to close my eyes in case I miss the target, so I dive in quick. There's a loud sucking sound as we connect and it's nothing like jam. It's like tongue-wrestling a slug.

Even though it's horrible, I keep going. I've dreamt of this moment so many times, but I never imagined it would be with someone like Jack Whitman. I expected it to be some spotty geek that I'd experiment on and then quickly try to erase the memory. Wanting nothing more than to melt into my first kiss, I try to relax, but I can't switch my brain off. What if I'm doing it all wrong? I try to focus on the movement of my lips and tongue so I don't embarrass myself. Boys at school are always mocking girls after they kiss for the first time. I try to remember all the things I've heard so that I can avoid them. Why is it that, in the throes of passion, all those "101 Kissing Tips" from *Cosmo* and *19* disappear? As for the hours of practising – they don't help one bit. And I'm sure my tongue has got thicker. I tuck it into my cheek, out of the way. It makes things a little better and the kiss improves. Once you get over the wetness, it's actually quite nice.

As Jack rests his hand on the back of my neck, his thumb tracing my jaw-line, shivers run up my spine. The kiss doesn't last anywhere near long enough – and I worry that I messed it up. But as Jack pulls away, he smiles at me. His lips are glistening with the remains of our kiss.

"That was lovely, too," he says, stroking my hair.

Lost for words, I nod. Jack leans in and kisses the tip of my nose. It's so romantic – like something out of a film.

"Cat got your tongue?" he asks.

Smiling, I keep as still and silent as possible, wishing that time would freeze so I could stay in this moment for ever.

"Thanks, Jack."

"For what? I've never been thanked for a kiss before."

"You know – not taking that other business into consideration."

"Your mum? You can't help that. They say you can choose your friends, but you can't choose your family."

"Not that. I mean the bag."

"Bag?"

"You know… when I bumped into you outside school…"

"You couldn't help that either. That sports bag's nearly as big as me. It can take a beating from a runt like you." Jack ruffles my hair and I lean in towards his hand. "I should be the one apologizing – I sent you sprawling!"

"No, I mean…" My brain throbs as I try to find the words I need to say. "I didn't mean to take it, you know. I was just getting some baking stuff and…"

"Baking stuff? Liv, what are you talking about?"

As my words click into place, Jack's smile fades. His brown eyes harden and his brow crumples into a deep frown.

"Mrs Snelling's bag… the accident. That was you? You're joking, right?"

He jumps up, his face contorting as he realizes he's just snogged a cretin.

"I thought you knew! I thought that was why you were avoiding my biscuits in class…"

Jack recoils. "I was avoiding you because I fancied you. And I felt guilty about what Maddy had done. But this… You're just as bad as she is!"

"I'm not! It was an accident."

"You can't accidentally steal a bag."

My vision blurring, I glare at the floor, trying to keep control. Stupid, stupid, stupid. Why did I have to open my big gob and ruin things?

"I can't believe it," Jack says, pacing the room. "I never in my wildest dreams thought… how could you?" He spits the words out, sharp as a carving knife.

I can't think of anything to say to defend myself. Even if I could, it would be pointless. Without another word, Jack storms out of the room. Unable to move my legs to follow, I listen helplessly to his retreat. When the front door slams, tears spill from my eyes as I touch my finger to my lips, tormented by the memory of his mouth pressed against them.

Fruity Custard Pasties

A fun, fruity take on the old Cornish pasty, these taste great, both served warm – with ice cream – or cold, on their own. And what's more, they're portable! Perfect for summery picnics with the ones you love. Chase away the cobwebs with a taste of summer.

INGREDIENTS

200 g/7 oz plain flour, plus some extra dabs for dusting your rolling pin
100 g/3 ½ oz yummy butter
8 tsp cold water
Pinch of salt

FOR THE FILLING

Pinch of cinnamon
Four cooking apples, cored and chopped
(Tip: if you're preparing them early, a squeeze of lemon juice will stop them going brown)
250 ml/8 ½ fl oz water
200 g/7 oz brown sugar
Ready-made custard (we can't be perfect all the time)

HOW TO MAKE THE MAGIC HAPPEN

1. Preheat the oven to 220 °C/425 °F/Gas mark 7.
2. Sift the flour and salt together. Rub in the butter until the mixture looks like breadcrumbs.
3. Add the water and work into a large lump. Set aside.
4. In a pan, bring the apples, cinnamon, water and sugar to the boil and then simmer gently until the apples go soft and gooey. Put aside to cool.
5. On a floured surface, roll that pastry! Make it thin enough to bend, but not so thin that it breaks. Use a round cookie cutter to get as many pasty rounds as you can out of the dough.
6. Place the cases on baking parchment and fill each with a spoonful of custard and a spoonful of fruit mixture.
7. Brush the edge of each round with milk, then gather up the edges and pull together, forming a seam down the middle of the pastry. "Flute" the edge of each seam (this is a fancy term for pinching it together so it doesn't separate when cooking).
8. Make a small hole in the top of each pasty (to prevent Fruity Custardy explosions) and place on a baking tray. Bake for 10 minutes, then turn down to 180 °C/350 °F/Gas mark 4 until the pasties are golden brown, like summer sunlight.
9. Cool on a wire rack, dust with icing sugar – and enjoy.

Warning: don't eat them when they're hot, or they'll burn your mouth. Be patient. Remember – all good things come to those who wait!

Chapter Thirty-Three

It's Time to Come Clean

As I skulk down the stairs, Harriet darts into the passageway.

"Where's Jack?" she asks.

"He's gone."

Slumping on the stairs, I hold my forehead in my hands. "What the hell's wrong with me?"

Harriet places a hand on my shoulder.

"Do you want to talk about it?"

I shake my head. Hatty wouldn't understand. She's way too sensible.

"Can I phone Sarah at her grandma's?"

"Seeing as it's an emergency. But try not to be too long. And if you change your mind... I'm here."

I pick up the receiver and turn my back. The phone seems to ring for ever and I'm just about to give up when Sarah answers the call, breathless.

"Hello?"

"Hi, Sarah, it's me – Liv."

"Hey! Give me a minute to catch my breath." I listen to the heavy panting slowing on the other end. "Sorry, I was trying to knock some time off my 500 metres."

I can picture Sarah running laps in her grandma's garden. I've visited there a few times, but don't like it much. The gaudy living room and bedrooms filled with antiques, the massive garden, complete with fountain and orchard – it's too showy. You daren't breathe, in case you break something.

"Sarah, I've got to talk to you. I've screwed up."

"Shoot."

"Jack came over to give me a present and we kissed and then we had a fight and it's all my fault…"

"Whoa… back up there! You and Jack *kissed*?"

My voice wobbles. "Yes," I manage, feebly.

"Jack Whitman? You kissed Jack Whitman?" I hear her settle herself in the comfy armchair next to her grandma's phone. "I knew he fancied you! Tell me every detail!"

I chuckle, despite myself, and reveal only the nicer bits, privately reliving the delicious feel of his soft lips against mine, and carefully missing out the slug bit.

"That's nuts! What about Mad Dog?"

"We won't have to worry about her," I say, hoping I'm right. "Cos it won't be happening again."

"Why not? He obviously likes you!"

"Not any more. We had a fight. He stormed out."

"It's like something out of *Wuthering Heights*," says Sarah dreamily. "You're Cathy, he's Heathcliff, you had The Kiss…" Sarah says this last bit as though the words start with capital letters. "It's all so romantic! Did you feel any lightning bolts?"

"Are you deaf?" I snap. "We had a fight."

Luckily, Sarah doesn't take any notice.

"Whatever you fought about, it'll blow over. It did once. Why not again?"

"It's not that simple."

Trembling, I fight to still my voice. If I'm going to get out of this mess, it's time to come clean to my best mate. Sarah will understand. She'll help me sort everything out.

"Sarah… there's something I have to tell you."

There is a heavy pause on the other end.

"I'm listening."

"It's not good. It's pretty bad actually…"

"What happened? Did he do something to you?"

"No."

"Are you sure? Jack doesn't seem the type to just… Rumour has it that he's more experienced."

Remembering the warmth of his eyes and the tender way he kissed my nose, I sigh into the receiver. But before I can speak, Sarah's over-active imagination gallops ahead.

"I knew it! He tried to make you go further than you wanted. He's got a bit of a reputation, you know… that's why you threw him out—"

"Sarah, stop! I didn't throw him out – he stormed out. He didn't try—"

"But why else would you be so upset? I thought you'd swap a kidney for a kiss from Jack."

My back pressed against the cold passageway wall, I take in a sharp breath.

"Sarah, you have to listen to me. But before I tell you, you have to promise not to say a word. And not to fall out with me. OK?"

"This sounds serious."

"It is serious. Promise me."

"OK, OK – I promise I'll try. Now, what's wrong? Liv… are you crying?"

Tears roll down my cheeks. Sarah is the only one that truly believes in me, and I'm about to betray her trust. Unable to respond, I sob down the phone.

"Don't worry," says Sarah, resolutely. "I'll think of something. Tell me what happened and we'll fix it."

"OK... the reason that me and Jack argued... the reason he stormed out... it was me who took Mrs Snelling's handbag."

For the first time in my life, I understand why people say silence can be deafening.

"Sarah? Are you still there?"

"I'm s-still here."

Disappointment seeps out of every syllable. I feel my insides curl and wither like an autumn leaf.

"I didn't meant to do it... I was taking some stuff for baking and..."

"You were s-stealing ingredients? Have I eaten any of those ingredients?"

"I just wanted to be good at something!"

"This one's t-too much, even by your standards. M-Mrs Snelling got r-really hurt."

"I know but... I didn't know that was going to happen. What am I going to do?"

"Are you s-sorry?"

"Of course I'm sorry. I'm going to give the bag back."

"With everything still in it?"

"I used some of the money... but there's still loads left."

"Give it back before you take any more. Go to Mr Morrelly, admit what you did and hand it over."

"I can't! The Social Services visit is this Friday."

"You heard him in assembly. They'll be lenient with anyone who owns up."

"School maybe – but not the Social Services. They'll take me away. They'll split us up, Sarah… Me and Harriet, you and me!"

There is a pause on the other end.

"M-maybe that's not such a b-bad thing, Liv. You're out of control."

Then, before I can say anything else, Sarah hangs up.

As the line goes dead, I bang the back of my head against the wall. Gently at first, but then hard enough to hurt. I'm sick of messing things up. Every time I try to put things right, I make them worse.

I replace the receiver as Harriet steps into the hallway. When she sees the state of me, she drops the assignment she's working on and runs my way.

"Liv, are you OK? You look sick."

Before I can answer, everything blurs. I hear Harriet cry out but the sound is muffled. The next thing I know, Hatty's tapping my face and calling my name.

"Liv? Liv, can you hear me?"

"Hatty?"

"I'm here, Liv. I'm here."

As I battle to focus, I hear Harriet crumple into sobs.

"I'm not cut out for all this. I just want life to be normal again," she says.

"Please don't cry, sis," I whisper, the words catching in my dry throat. "Please don't cry any more."

Chapter Thirty-Four

If I'm Already in Trouble, What Do Manners Matter?

The next morning, I'm surprised to find Harriet cling-ing to the telephone receiver, tight lipped. It's not even 8 a.m. I plonk myself on one of the stairs and lean my forehead on the banister slats, trying to figure out who's on the other end and why Harriet looks so worried. Is it the Social Services?

"Yes, I'll definitely be there. And Liv too. I'll make sure of it. Can I ask what this is about?" Harriet pauses, listen-ing intently. "OK, no problem. I'll be there, Mr Morrelly."

Old Mozzer? What's he doing on the phone at this time? As Harriet clicks the receiver into place, she looks up at me, eyes full of worry.

"What have you done now? You promised me you'd stay out of trouble!"

"I have!"

"The visit's in…" Harriet checks her watch, as though it will reveal the answer, while working out the dates in her head. "Four days! We can't afford for anything to go wrong!"

I fidget and groan. It's too early in the morning for hassle and, for once, I have no idea what I've done. Unless Jack or Sarah have grassed me up.

"I don't know what it's about," I say, trying to sound innocent.

Harriet shakes her head and breathes a huge sigh.

"Well, it's something to do with that Jack guy – that's all I know. Get yourself dressed. We have to be there as soon as possible."

"What for?"

"That's what I was hoping *you'd* tell *me*. But I guess I'll find out soon enough. As if I don't have enough to worry about. You're a real pain."

Harriet stomps up the stairs, nudging me out of the way.

Rubbing my forehead between thumb and forefinger, I follow after her, desperately trying to think of a way to stall.

* * *

A film of sweat moistens my hands as I wait in the long, yellow corridor outside Mr Morrelly's office. Avoiding Harriet's frequent disapproving glances, I fiddle with my thumbs. Have Jack or Sarah told on me? I doubt Sarah would betray all those years of friendship. As for Jack, surely the kiss meant something? Both know the situation with Mam. Both know how much I have to lose. But if one of them has opened their mouths, I'm screwed. I'll end up in foster care for sure. I shuffle away from Hatty. Might as well start getting used to the separation now.

The head teacher's door clicks open.

"Olivia, Harriet, please, come in." Mr Morrelly's voice is unexpectedly gentle.

Harriet's first to stand – upright and obedient, a total swot as usual. Not like me: always in trouble. I watch my sister's breezy walk with disdain. Who's she trying to kid? She's just as scared, only better at covering it up.

"Please, girls, sit down."

Mr Morrelly's face looks concerned, but not angry. Harriet chances a sideways peek at me, so I avert my gaze. When we're both seated, Mr Morrelly paces in front of the window for a moment, before settling himself behind his big, oak desk. Leaning in, he places his chin on his interlocked fingers, knuckles white as his face. Harriet's lips pull tight across her teeth in a fake smile. I crossed my fingers, hoping I'll get out of this one unscathed.

"How are you, Olivia?" asked Mr Morrelly.

I hold his gaze.

"I'm good, sir. But I'm sure you didn't ask me here to talk about my health."

I should probably be more respectful – but if I'm already in trouble, what do manners matter? Feeling a sharp stab in my ribs as Harriet lets her elbow slip, I reluctantly zip my lips up tight.

"Well, actually, I have, in a way. We're worried about the company you may be keeping. We've received some serious accusations about a friend of yours, Jack Whitman. We want you to confirm whether they're true."

Old Mozzer's eyebrows form a perfectly straight line across his brow. I'm off the hook, but a queasy feeling rises in my stomach.

"We've had reports that it was Jack who stole Mrs Snelling's handbag, resulting in her serious injury. And your name was mentioned."

"My name?"

"Yes. It was indicated to me that you saw Jack in the vicinity of the dinner hall around the time of the incident. Can you confirm this claim?"

I can't speak. It's like my nightmare has come true and my mouth has disappeared. Why is Jack getting blamed for my actions? First, Mrs Snelling, now Old Mozzer.

Too late, I realize that Harriet and Mr Morrelly mistake my silence for confirmation. Oh Jack, I'm sorry. But if I open my mouth to come clean now, Harriet will hate me. And she's all I have left.

"As you know, Jack was hailed as a hero for assisting Mrs Snelling after her fall," continues Mr Morrelly. "But when someone makes a serious accusation, I have to act on it. I know, Liv, that you two are friends, so if you know anything that might help prove Jack's guilt or innocence…" He pauses and lifts an eyebrow before continuing. "I hope you will do the right thing and share this information with me."

Taking a deep breath, I stay silent. Guilt plucks at my stomach, but it's the best I can do.

"There have also been accusations that Jack is involved in bullying. For a while now, Jack's had a relatively clean slate, but that doesn't mean it isn't a possibility. I am granting you full confidentiality if you decide to provide information."

Feeling Harriet's eyes burn into me, I keep my face down-turned.

"I know that this is an uncomfortable situation for you, Olivia, but I must ask – do you have anything to say?"

Slowly, I shake my head.

"That's what I suspected, but I'll allow you time to reconsider. If you think of anything – anything at all – please report back to me immediately. Now, if you don't mind waiting outside, I'd like a word with your sister."

My skin turns clammy as I leave the room, my eyes fixed firmly on the floor – until I discover a familiar pair of toe-worn blue and brown Adidas. Tracing from the shoes, up over the black trousers and burgundy school jumper, I meet Jack's hard, staring eyes.

My mouth turns dry. I have to warn him! But first, I have to make certain that he won't get me into trouble.

"Jack… please don't tell them."

He shakes his head in disgust. Before I can say anything else – warn him what to expect – the door opens. Jack squares his shoulders, gives me an awful look and steps into the office. Harriet shoots him an angry glare as they pass.

"Poor Mrs Snelling," says Harriet, as she guides me away, arms round my shoulders. "You're well rid of him." She lowers her voice to a whisper. "He's about to get suspended."

I swallow hard. What have I done?

That night Sarah sends me a text:

I CAN'T BELIEVE JACK'S BEEN SUSPENDED COS OF YOU

I try to formulate a reply but fail – what can I say?

Chapter Thirty-Five

The Crust Was Designed
for Dirty Hands

The morning of the Social Services visit arrives.

As I shoulder my school bag, I pause to watch Harriet on her hands and knees, dusting the hallway skirting boards.

"What on earth are you doing?" I ask.

"I'm not having the Social Services say we have a dirty house," replies Harriet, scrubbing away vigorously.

"You're starting to sound like Mam."

Sitting back on her heels, Harriet wipes a red-raw hand across her forehead, shifting stray hairs out of her eyes.

I hope she'll make more of an effort when the Social Services come. She looks a total state.

"You say that like it's a bad thing. Why don't you help yourself to breakfast and get off to school? Leave the visit to me."

Grabbing my summer jacket, I yank the front door open.

"Not hungry. Can't eat on a day like today."

Harriet nods. "I can still feel last night's spag bol. It's sitting like bricks. Just make sure you get a decent lunch."

Pausing for a moment, I drum my fingers on the door-frame. I shouldn't have to go to school. I should see them as well.

"Hatty? I've put the fruit pasties in the breakfast cupboard. Make sure you offer them some?"

"Sure. You never know – they could be the clincher."

"Text me as soon as they've gone," I say, closing the door behind me, already dreading the message I'll receive.

* * *

Just as school finishes, Harriet's text comes through.

MAM'S COMING HOME NEXT WEEK. H XXX

I should be excited, or at least relieved, but the news makes my heart sink. If Mam's coming home, Hatty will go back to uni and I'll have to cope with Mam on my own again.

I shudder, thinking back to the time Mam threatened to kill herself. It took hours of pleading and promises to coax her out of the bathroom.

When I finally succeeded, Mam's arms and wrists were covered in smears of blood where she'd scraped at them with a blunted razor. Bloody drama queen. Everyone knows you have to cut up along the vein, not across. It was a cry for help, my counsellor told me. Even if it wasn't a serious attempt, it was still scary.

I scuff my Converse along the kerb, dreading going home, and I feel something race past me.

It's Sarah. I'd recognize her stick-straight ponytail anywhere.

"Wait!" I call, quickening my pace. "Sarah, I need to talk to you. Mam's coming home!"

But Sarah keeps on speed-walking, bag over her shoulder, refusing to look back. I try running, but I still have trouble catching up to her. By the time we hit the Rec, Sarah's within reach. As I grab her shoulder, she spins round. Her face is bright red and at first I can't tell whether it's from rushing or anger. When she starts stammering, the answer's clear.

"W-why c-can't you just leave me alone? I have to m-meet Jack. And I d-don't want to s-speak to you right now!"

I don't have time to say anything. Sarah turns and sprints. Like – actually runs away from me. There's no way I can catch her. Instead, I watch as my ex-friend grows smaller and smaller in the distance. Jealousy ripples through my veins – why is she meeting Jack? They're not even friends.

Back at home, Harriet is sprawled on the sofa, pretending to read a magazine. The way her eyes dart about the place, I know she isn't really concentrating, so I throw my bag on the floor and join her, resting my legs atop hers.

"So, what happened?" I ask.

"Isn't it great? Mam's coming home!"

Trying to smile, I give a slow, thoughtful nod. I wonder whether I'm going to give myself early wrinkles with all these forced smiles.

"What? You're not thrilled?"

"I am, but... that means..."

"I have to go back some time, Liv." Harriet's voice is gentle, but she can't hide the fact that she's pleased. "At least it's under positive circumstances. You're not going into care."

Wincing, I slouch further into the sofa cushions.

"I know that. But what happened? What did they say?"

Smiling, Harriet recounts the day's events: how the social workers were nice – not at all like we'd feared. How they chatted about our education, Mam's improvements and coping mechanisms, and future hopes for our family.

They also discussed Harriet's clothes, why she chose her Social Anthropology degree, what music I liked – as well as many other seemingly pointless topics that make my head spin.

"What about my pasties? Did you give them some?"

"Yep – and I told them what you told me: that pasties were originally invented for the miners. Meat and potatoes at one end and fruit at the other so the miners could eat their dinner and pudding in one go in the dark."

"Did you tell them that the crust was designed for dirty hands – they left that bit behind?"

"I did. They were very impressed."

"Did they say the pasties were nice?"

"They ate them, so I guess that's compliment enough. They didn't say anything specific."

"No feedback at all? I wasn't sure the filling was sweet enough."

"They made a good dent in them, but they were here about Mam, so we talked mostly about her."

It's a gentle dig and deserved, so I disguise my disappointment with a smile. Without feedback, how am I meant to improve?

"So what about Mam?" I ask.

"They think she's ready."

I lift an eyebrow incredulously.

"Despite running away?"

"I know! I'm as surprised as you. But they've been working with her closely at the Recovery Centre and think she'll make better progress here. They told me off the record, but the official letter should arrive in the next few days."

"They probably just want rid of her cos they're overcrowded. Or she costs too much to keep."

"When did you get so cynical, Liv? Whatever the reason, she's coming home. Aren't you excited?"

My heart is full of dread, but I can't say that, can I?

"Of course I am. It hasn't really sunk in yet, that's all."

"We'll have to throw a party for her. Invite some of her friends. Let her know we care. Maybe you could make a chocolate cake?"

"And some biscuits? Scones?"

"Sure! Whatever you want!"

"Do we have enough money?" I ask, thinking about the hidden bag.

"We'll make it stretch. This is a celebration, after all!"

Harriet nudges me happily. I wish I could share her enthusiasm. I'd be happy too if I was heading off to Edinburgh. How will I cope with Mam on my own? Up to now, my track record is pretty bad. If only I could talk to Sarah – or even Jack. Then things wouldn't feel so bleak. But the truth is, I have no one, and I only have myself to blame.

Flourless Chocolate Cake

A flour-free, squidgy cake that's filled with chocolatey goodness, but lighter on the stomach. So if there's anything weighing your heart or mind down, this will free it up so you can flit around, happy as a butterfly. (Have you ever seen an unhappy butterfly?)

INGREDIENTS

340 g/12 oz chocolate (about 50% cocoa)
180 g/6½ oz sugar
5 tbsp ground almonds
5 tbsp milk
5 tbsp butter
1 tsp baking powder
4 eggs, separated

HOW TO MAKE THE MAGIC HAPPEN

1. Preheat the oven to 180 °C/350 °F/Gas mark 4 and grease a lined square, 9-in. cake tin.
2. Smash the chocolate into pieces, place into a bowl with butter and milk, and melt over a pan of hot water.
3. Take half of the sugar and beat into the egg yolks. Fold in the melted chocolate mixture, then fold in the ground almonds and baking powder.
4. Beat the egg whites until they're frothy, then gradually add the sugar until the mixture makes

tasty mountain peaks, and then fold into the cake mixture.

5. Bake for 40 minutes. You can tell it's cooked by doing the chopstick test: stick a chopstick into the centre. If it comes out clean, it's ready. If it sticks, whack it in the oven for a bit longer!

Note: the cake will sag like a hammock in the centre, but this is normal. No panic required!

Chapter Thirty-Six

Disquiet Spreads over the Room Like Mist

"How are the biscuits coming along, Liv? She'll be home in an hour!" asks Harriet.

"Stop rushing me! They're almost done."

Harriet's been snappy all morning, but I totally get it. I'm acting all calm on the outside – but inside I'm shaking. I'm allowed the day off school to help prepare, but I wish I'd gone to my lessons instead. Every time I start thinking things won't be so bad, Harriet says something that reminds me otherwise.

While I lift the biscuits out of the oven, Harriet sets about making piles of sandwiches: ham, egg mayonnaise and a special one I came up with, coronation chicken – a tasty mix of chicken, yoghurt, curry powder and sultanas. I had it once at a birthday party and tried guessing the ingredients. Thankfully, it turned out exactly how I remembered.

"Looks like you've inherited Mam's skills in that department," says Harriet. "You can cook together to your heart's content when you're rid of me!"

Ignoring the last bit of the comment, I assemble each pile carefully on our best plates, and then cover them with cling film.

"Are you sure this will keep them fresh?" asks Harriet.

"Yes! Stop panicking, will you?"

"I'm not panicking!"

I put my hands on my hips and watch Harriet until she notices and stops, a grin spreading slowly across her face.

"OK, smart-arse, maybe I'm a bit more flustered than usual. It's just… I'm excited, you know? We've been waiting ages for this."

"You mean *you* have. So you can get out of here."

As the complaint slips out, I'm painfully aware of how childish I sound.

"Liv, this isn't about you or me today, it's about Mam. Of course I'm looking forward to returning to uni – I worked hard to get there – but that's not the reason I'm excited, and you know it."

"Sorry."

I continue smoothing the flourless chocolate cake mixture in a large blue mixing bowl. Chocolate is Mam's favourite, so it's easy to pretend I'm engrossed.

"This will take just over half an hour, and then we're set," I say.

"Great work, Liv. Mam'll be stunned." Coming close and raising her hand for a high-five, Harriet continues. "I couldn't have done it without you."

I glance at Harriet's untidy mess of sandwiches and wink.

"I can see that," I say, then slap my hand against hers. "Did you tell everyone five on the dot?"

"Yep. Sarah and her dad, Pauline next door, Bob and Jane from the other side, plus a couple of Mam's friends from the pub."

"The pub? Harriet…"

I don't want to think about Sarah's reaction to the invite. We haven't been on speaking terms for exactly eleven days.

"Don't worry, they've all been warned: no alcohol – before or during. Afterwards is fine, so long as Mam stays here!"

I feel my shoulders slacken. It'll be weird around here without Harriet bossing everyone about. I try to set aside my worries, hoping instead that my sister will settle back into her uni life without any hitches. She deserves that much at least.

When the phone rings, Harriet disappears off into the hallway and returns with a worried expression.

"It's not Mam, is it?" I ask, even though an evil gremlin inside me hopes the Social Services have changed their minds about sending her home.

"No. Sandra from the pub. Her little boy has chicken pox…"

"That's OK, there's plenty more coming. Too many and it might freak Mam out, anyway."

"True. But I don't want her to feel disappointed. You know how much she loves surprises – she'll expect it."

When the phone rings again, Harriet returns looking even more deflated.

"Greta, another one of Mam's pub friends. She can't come either. Said she had a ladies' lunch which included a couple of glasses of wine, so she didn't think it would be appropriate."

"What's wrong with people?" I say, pointing to the food. "What about all this?"

"You always say I'm a fat pig. I'll make a dent in it!"

I turn away. "You know I don't mean it."

"Sorry. Ignore me, Liv. I'm just nervous."

I plate the biscuits and the chocolate cake, avoiding her eye.

"No worries." I say it in a way that makes it clear my mood doesn't match my words.

By quarter past five, only Sarah and her dad, a quiet lady called Rita and Pauline from next door have turned up.

"I can't believe you came!" I whisper to Sarah as she takes a seat.

"Only because Dad made me. Have you owned up yet?" When I shake my head, she adds, "Leave me alone."

Crossing her legs so that she faces away from me, Sarah makes it clear there's no chance of reconciliation. All those years of friendship down the toilet.

When the clock shows twenty-past five, Harriet starts pacing the room. By half past, she's beside herself.

"Sorry, everyone, I can't imagine what's keeping her," she says.

"I'm sure it's just the traffic," says Pauline. "Ashgrove House is a long way from here, and there can be heavy traffic when it hits Egerton roundabout."

"That's true," adds Mr Butler.

"Yeah, thanks for the information," I say. "Cos we've never been there before, so we wouldn't know."

Rita smiles nervously, eyeing the door like she can't wait to leave. I catch the tail end of Sarah's loud sigh and disquiet spreads over the room like mist. My heart thumps in my chest. I know what everyone is thinking, because I'm thinking it too: Mam's gone straight to the pub.

When Mam walks through the door at five thirty-eight, everyone jumps to their feet.

"Surprise!" we all shout in unison.

Scanning the room, Mam's face wavers. Panic punches at my stomach but she gathers her emotions and gives a big, toothy grin. Without even thinking about it, I touch my left ear like we used to when we were kids.

"I never expected this!" says Mam, clearly pleased. "You didn't need to go to any trouble. Thank you so much, Harriet. You never cease to amaze me."

Standing up tall and straight, I can't wait for Harriet to tell Mam that I prepared all the food. I need to get things off to a good start – especially with Sarah here. Maybe then she'll see that I'm not so bad after all and make friends again. I rush to Mam's side, ready for the praise.

"You're welcome, Mam," replies Harriet.

As Harriet and Mam hug tightly, I feel the bottom fall out of my world. Why doesn't Harriet say anything? I catch Sarah's eye. Her expression is devoid of sympathy. It says, *You deserve everything you get.*

For the rest of the afternoon, I keep as busy as possible. I pass plates of food around, make pots of tea and cups of coffee and wash up several times – anything to keep out of the way. The whole time, Harriet and Mam chat like best friends. Like Sarah and I used to. But now I'm completely out of the picture. Mam and Hatty throw the odd glance in my direction, but leave me out. Not once do they ask me to join them. After a while, Harriet comes over, full of fake concern. Well she can shove that where the sun doesn't shine.

"Is everything OK with you and Sarah?" she asks.

"Everything's fine. Why don't you go back to sucking up to Mam?"

Throwing her hands up, Harriet walks away. I watch as she sidles up to Sarah. I can't hear what she says, but I guess it's the same.

"Sure, everything's great," says Sarah, loudly and sarcastically enough for me to hear.

"Anyone for more sandwiches?" I ask.

Later, when everyone has gone, Mam slouches on the sofa and rubs her head.

"Alone at last! That was lovely – but now I finally get a chance to spend some quality time with my two girls."

Harriet immediately leaps onto the sofa and puts her legs up, resting her feet on Mam's lap. I stay washing up.

"Lucky us," I say under my breath.

"Liv, why don't you leave those pots until tomorrow? Let's have a catch-up over some of that gorgeous-looking chocolate cake. I've been dying to hear what you girls have been up to."

Taking a long look at my sister and Mam snuggled on the sofa, I can't bring myself to join them. They look happy enough without me. They don't need me spoiling things. I place two stingy pieces of cake on plates and slam them down in front of them.

"Enjoy. I'm off to bed."

"Aren't you having any, love?" asks Mam.

"I'm tired. I'll make it again some time," I say, heading towards the door.

"Wait – you made this?"

Ignoring Mam, I keep going, hovering on the other side of the door to see whether they talk about me behind my back. There's shuffling as Harriet moves to follow, but Mam stops her. Then they lower their voices to whispers, too quiet for me to hear.

I fight the urge to run back inside and join them, to see whether the cake tastes as good as it looks. Why didn't they come after me? Why won't Sarah let me make it up to her? Silently, I climb the stairs, feeling lonelier than ever before.

Chapter Thirty-Seven

I Have to Tell You Something...
It's Long Overdue

Over the next week, nothing changes. At school, I creep around with my head down. People give me funny looks and fire quizzical glances at each other when Sarah chooses to sit with Valerie Jeckyll instead of me. I bring soggy sandwiches for lunch so I can avoid the dinner hall, and Mr Vaughn is my permanent partner in Art class. I feel guilty every time I see Jack's chair sitting empty in class, and I spend my time running from one lesson to another via weird and wonderful routes, to try and avoid everyone – particularly Mad Dog. At home, I skulk about, avoiding my family, while Hatty and Mam hang out together. The way they chat endlessly and snuggle on the sofa all the time makes me sick. Who are they trying to kid, after all that's happened? It's like they've forgotten I even exist. Well, if they don't care about me, I'm not about to start playing happy families. I'm no longer dreading Harriet's departure. In fact, I can't wait to get rid of her.

A few days before Hatty is due to leave, Mam calls us all together.

"It's been a difficult time for all of us, and I want to thank both of you for making it much easier than I expected," she says.

Harriet pats Mam's leg. I glare at her with disgust.

"Harriet's done such a wonderful job while I've been away, but I'm happy to say that she'll soon be heading back to uni – where she belongs. Before she goes, I've got something I want to tell you girls."

Looking from Mam to each other, we both stiffen.

"Is it bad news?" asks Harriet, her voice barely audible.

"No. But it's important. You'd better sit down."

I go to get a drink of water first. My favourite glass is dirty, so I reach under the sink for washing-up liquid. I stop dead. There are six bottles of whiskey sitting there in the cupboard. She's not even attempting to hide them.

"Mam, what are these?" I say.

"Just a few bottles to test my strength," says Mam. "What better way to know I'm on the mend than by resisting temptation?"

I drain the water, then lower myself into the armchair. Instead of sitting on the sofa with Mam, Harriet perches herself on the chair arm next to me. Mam fiddles with her fingers, visibly shaking. She lights a cigarette, blows the smoke high into the air, then clears her throat.

"It's about... it's your dad," she begins.

"Is he coming home?" I ask.

"Is he dead?" asks Harriet.

Mam shakes her head slowly, takes another drag of her cigarette, then stubs it out – even though there is plenty left. I'm so nervous I feel like grabbing it for a toke, even though I don't smoke.

"No, nothing like that. But I have to tell you something... he's been in contact. I know where he is, and it's about time you did too." She catches my eye and smiles awkwardly. Reaching into her pocket, Mam pulls out an old, crumpled letter. She drops it onto the coffee table, then sits back, rubbing her eyes.

Tentatively, Harriet reaches forward and picks up the envelope, easing out its contents with unsteady hands. Then she reads aloud.

My dearest Abigail, without you and the girls, life is flavourless. If ever you change your mind, come back to me. I've bought a house: 43 Crooms Hill Grove, Greenwich. You and the girls will always have a home with me. You are, as always, my life, my love, my Happiness Bloom. xxx

I stare at the letter, gobsmacked. My eyes stretch wide as saucers and my mouth drops open. I try to speak, but it takes a while for the words to come out. When they do, my voice is high pitched and shaky.

"I thought you said he just got in contact?"

"He has."

"But this letter isn't new – you knew exactly where Dad was all along!"

"Yes. I mean no. I mean—"

"But you told us that you'd no idea where he was!" I continue. "You said he never cared one bit about us, not even enough to make sure we had shoes…"

Instinctively, I jump to my feet, and the rest is a blur – until I'm aware of Harriet grabbing me around the waist, of my arms and legs fighting to get free.

"You made me believe he didn't want anything to do with us – that it was my fault he left!"

"I'm sorry," says Mam. "But I've been talking this over with my counsellor and—"

I think I'm crying, but I can't be sure – and I can't control it anyway.

"You're a vindictive old maggot," I shout, wiping my eyes on the back of my forearm.

Mam lowers her head into her hands. My stomach feels like it's ripping in two.

"Calm down, Liv," Harriet says, but only when she can see I've calmed down a bit anyway. "It's taken a lot for Mam to tell us this. Let's hear her out and work through it together."

"No way! I'm sick of tiptoeing around her," I say, finally breaking free. "I've had enough. If she's coming back for good, we'd better start establishing some rules around here. Rules that suit us, not just her. Like: no more worrying about upsetting her, no more worrying about her drinking. This is our home, our life, too!"

Sitting up, eyes bloodshot and puffy, Mam re-lights her misshapen cigarette and takes long, deep drags. She stares at Hatty imploringly. Harriet picks up the letter, takes me by the hand and leads me to the door.

"We'll be back," she says.

Leaning into each other for support, we leave the room. Behind us, Mam is left chain-smoking.

As soon as we reach Harriet's bedroom, she faces me, staring into my eyes.

"I know you're hurting, but think about it. You've always wanted to meet Dad. Maybe this is your chance?"

"But why did she prevent it, Hatty? What right does she have? Why did she lie?"

Harriet shrugs.

"I don't know, but she's telling us now. Haven't you ever lied to protect someone, Liv?"

To protect myself, actually. I feel my anger shift into something else entirely: shame.

"I don't know what to think," I say. "I've been waiting for this for ever, but now it's here—"

"It'll be all right," promises Hatty. "Wash your face and we'll go back down. Hear Mam out. She's been through hell – she deserves a fair ear."

"What about us?"

"I'm sure if Mam's ready to talk, she'll be prepared to listen."

Rooted to the spot, I run my fingers through my hair and ruffle the back. I imagine it's Jack's hand, not mine.

"Think about it," continues Harriet. "We might be able to make contact. You never know – we might get to see Dad."

Grabbing a notebook, I copy Dad's address, wipe my eyes on my sleeve and give a big sniff.

"What are you waiting for?" I say.

* * *

When we return to the living room, Mam is red eyed on the sofa, dabbing at her nose with toilet paper. As quietly as we can, we listen to her story.

"I wanted to tell you about your dad, take you to him, but it was too painful. And I couldn't cope with you seeing him without me."

"So we missed out because you're selfish," I say.

"I'm so sorry – I didn't mean for this to happen. Time just slipped away. The more time passed, the more difficult it was to tell you. Before I knew it, I didn't even know how to broach the subject. I missed him so much. I still do."

"So why now?" asks Harriet.

"It's the least I can do after what you've been through. I've discussed it with my counsellor… I owe you the truth."

"You only just realized that?" I say.

But then my thoughts turn to the sweet, hopeful voice of the Happiness Bloom recipes and my anger drops away, replaced by a painful yearning to see my dad. What seemed like devastating news half an hour ago now shines with possibility: finally, I might meet him.

"Why don't you just get back with Dad if you miss him so much?" I ask.

"Nice idea, love," says Mam, her face downcast. "But those days are long gone. He wasn't always… honest. And he values money much more than people. But you can't always switch off love."

"It might stop you feeling so lonely," I say.

"If I'd wanted to go back, I would have done years ago. Walked into The Bear Arms or knocked on his door…" She stops abruptly.

"The Bear Arms?" I'm determined not to miss a trick.

"Max owns it. At least, I think he does. He was buying into the business when we split up. The profits were meant to fund the cake business but…"

I wait for the revelation of Dad's affair but Mam's done talking. I'm so sick of all the secrecy – it's exhausting.

"The profits were meant to fund the cake business, but Dad ran off with Rosa," I say, finishing the sentence for her.

Harriet's jaw drops open and Mam's hands shake as she stubs out her cigarette.

"That's not nice," says Mam.

And I'm on my feet again – my body fizzing and my tongue loose.

"You're quite happy to blame me for your breakup, but you can't face the truth. Dad fancied your best friend Rosa and he couldn't stand you or your moods any more."

"Liv, stop!" cries Harriet, jumping up.

I'm unable to control myself. Carried away on a tide of anger, I push myself into Harriet's face.

"What do you care? You're leaving!"

Harriet's eye go wide with fear and I realize I have my fist raised.

"No wonder I bloody drink," says Mam, and storms out of the room.

I crumple, burying my face in my hands. Harriet reaches out and puts her arm around me, even though I don't deserve it. The front door slams.

"I'll stay if you want me to," she says, pain evident in every syllable.

"I-I'm sorry. I didn't mean for Mam – oh god, Hatty. She's only just back! Shall we go after her?"

"No. She's going to have to start dealing with the real world herself."

Inside, my stomach churns. I know there's no way Harriet can stay, and I can't ask it of her. *I* wouldn't stay if I didn't have to.

That's when the idea hits – the solution to all my problems. I'll take Harriet's advice and meet Dad. Only, I'll
go alone. To London. My friends have deserted me and
I can't make Mam get better – but I can avoid the fallout
if I run away. And when Dad welcomes me with open
arms, I'll never have to return to stinking Egerton Park
or Egerton Hill ever again. I'll leave it all behind – the
bag, my mistakes and my crappy life. I'll start a new one!

Harriet is still looking at me with concern so I decide
to play along.

"I'll be all right, Hatty. You go back to uni. I'll be fine.
I promise."

Although I hate the look of relief that spreads over
Harriet's face, it's easy to smile. Mam, Harriet, Sarah,
Jack – I'll show them all.

Chapter Thirty-Eight

My Words Have Pierced Her Heart

"I wish you'd never been born, Olivia Bloom," says Mam.

She sways in my bedroom doorway, whiskey bottle in her hand. I try to focus on what my counsellor, Rachel, says – she doesn't mean it, it's the addiction talking – and resist the urge to scream back.

"You're wrong about Rosa – if you hadn't been such a naughty little child, he wouldn't have gone…"

"Shut up!"

"Typical teenager – think you know everything." Mam's voice is mean and bitter. "But you're in for a shock, young lady. Just you wait and see. Life's nothing but false hearts and broken promises."

I roll my eyes, thinking she can't see. "Don't I know it?"

"Don't roll your eyes at me!"

I try the relaxation breathing Rachel swears by. It doesn't help.

"When you've lived the life I have…"

In two three, *out* two three.

"…Seen what I've seen, *then* you can act all high and mighty. But until then…"

In two three, *out* two three. She doesn't mean it.

"You should be grateful to have a roof over your head and a family. It's more than I ever had."

I rush at her, no longer able to contain my anger. Snatching the bottle out of Mam's hand, I scream into her face.

"Family? You think this is normal? I'm sick of hearing about how bad your childhood was. Mine's just as crap! Get over it!"

Reeling back, Mam puts her hand to her chest as though my words have pierced her heart. I'm not falling for the drama this time.

"As for the life you've lived, every time you touch this stuff…" I lift the half-empty bottle up high. "We suffer too. You're the mam. Act like one!"

Mam's hazel eyes – the exact same shape and shade as my own – fixate on the bottle. Both of her eyes have a hazy film covering them, and there's a turn in her left one. I hate it so much – any chance of compassion completely disappears.

"Are you listening to me?" I wiggle the bottle in the air. "Do I even exist while this is around?"

Taking a step closer, Mam softens her voice and forces a smile.

"Liv, love, give that to me. You'll make it rancid."

"No!"

Stepping onto my bed, I hold the whiskey up high, out of Mam's reach. My legs wobble and I almost lose balance. The bottle dangles precariously as I right myself. Mam gasps in panic. It's pathetic.

"Is this all you care about? I thought things were going to be different this time. I actually hoped you might try."

Jiggling the bottle again, I feel a strange sense of satisfaction as Mam struggles to follow its movements.

"Things'll improve – hand it over. It'll make me feel better in the meantime."

"You want it? Get it!"

It's not like she'll remember once the drink wears off. Desperate, Mam swipes at the air.

"Come on, love, just one little sip?"

"Get it then! Look – it's just here."

"I can't reach it, sweetheart." Mam's voice is soft, but strained – like the final twist of a band securing a pony-tail. Let go – just a little – and it'll all come tumbling out. "Give it to me. You owe me! I brought you into this world. I didn't leave you like your dad."

My knees wobble, threatening to give way. I swallow hard, struggling to keep composure. *In* two three, *out* two three. It's no good. My resolve melts. What's the point in trying to fight? I never win. Lowering my arm, I thrust the bottle into Mam's face.

"Pathetic," I growl.

Snatching the bottle, Mam guzzles the amber liquid. As a dribble escapes over her chin, Harriet storms into the room. Confiscating the whiskey, she addresses Mam in a careful voice, glancing at me accusingly the whole time.

"Mam, you know that's not allowed."

Mam starts wailing like a baby. Tears and snot run down her face. Harriet frowns at me and shakes her head, as if to say, *What have you done now?* Ignoring the slight, I wrap my arms tightly around myself and watch as Mam crumples into Harriet's arms.

"See how she treats me? See why I have to drink?"

"We'd better get you into bed," says Harriet, tugging Mam by the hand and steering her out of the door. "It'll be OK," she mouths back at me.

But I know better.

I jump back into bed and, tugging the covers over my head, try to zone out by thinking about nice things. Only to find there's nothing nice in my life worth thinking about. It's time to get out of here.

Chapter Thirty-Nine

Blue, Isn't It?

As I round the corner of the gym – my extended route to Maths that circumvents Mad Dog's Science class – I run straight into Maddy. She must have cut class. Luckily, my nemesis is alone.

"Just the person I wanted to see," says Mad Dog, taking a drag on a cigarette.

Her hair is in ringlets, and her feet dangle as she balances on the top rung of the fence. She looks so carefree, I almost wish we could swap lives. As I get nearer, I recognize the deceivingly gentle smile Maddy had worn on the night we shared secrets and a cigarette. It makes my toes curl.

"I've been watching your interesting diversions," says Maddy, taking another drag. "Think you're smart, hey?"

I check around me, expecting a group of girls to appear from the shadows. But this time, no one comes. We're completely alone.

"Why don't you get it over with, Maddy?" I ask. "We both know I'm no match for you."

Maddy cocks her head, throws her cigarette to the ground and jumps off the fence. Shrinking back, I prepare for the worst.

"Glad you realize it, but relax. I'm not after you this time. In fact, I've got a proposition. We have a mutual problem and I've devised a plan that'll get rid of it."

The way she talks, you'd think we were on the set of an American gangster film. It might be cheesy, but it's effective. Maddy has my full attention.

"Go on."

"You know how Jack's been suspended?"

My stomach lurches.

"Well, word has it that Mrs Snelling visited Old Mozzer and told him she doesn't think he did it. She's asked for him to be reinstated."

Feeling my palms turn sweaty, I secretly wipe them on my skirt.

"So? What's that got to do with me?"

"Patience, Comrade. I figured that when you were called to see Old Mozzer, it was to testify against Jack. But you kept quiet, didn't you? I want you to go back and tell him you're very sorry, but you were too scared to tell the truth at first. Now Jack's gone, you want to come clean. Tell Mozzer that it *was* Jack who stole the bag, and he made you look after it for him. That you were too scared to say no."

"Why should I?"

Mad Dog grins, twiddling a perfectly sculpted curl around her finger.

"Because I have information about you."

"I'm going to be late for class," I say, stepping around her. It's not brave, it's stupid – but I have nothing left to lose. "I can't help you. I'm not going to lie."

"Oh really? That's funny. I thought that seeing as you were already lying to cover your own back, another little lie guaranteed to save your skin wouldn't bother you."

I stop dead in my tracks. "I don't know what you're talking about."

"That day you pinched Jack from me, the only reason you bumped into him was because you were running away from the kitchens. That's why you were in such a hurry. I saw the bag peeping out from behind your rucksack." She reduces her voice to a threatening whisper. "Blue, isn't it?"

My cover is blown – I can't play it cool any longer.

"Can't you do your own dirty work?" The words sound much braver than I feel. My legs have turned to jelly.

"I already accused him, didn't I?"

I can't stop the look of shock from registering on my face.

"Don't tell me you didn't realize!" says Mad Dog, coming way too close for my liking. She grips my forearm. "The teachers feel sorry for you because your mam's such a loser. You back me up and Old Mozzer will be convinced. We'll look like heroes for saving the day – and we'll get the cash reward."

Burning with shame, I shake my head.

"Why do you want to stick up for Jack anyway? Don't think that because you *lurve* him..." Maddy draws out the word "love" in a mocking voice. "That he feels the same way. Forget about him. The loser ditched you as quickly as he ditched me."

Unable to speak, I stand there like a statue. I know what she's implying, but I don't want to hear it. Not if it's true.

"I take it you've heard the rumour that Jack and Sarah are dating?" she adds.

Feeling as though a cannon ball has landed in my stomach, I cough into my curled fist, trying to buy some time. Sarah doesn't even fancy Jack – she likes Chris. She wouldn't betray me like that. Feeling tears rise to my eyes, I try to push past Mad Dog. Sarah always said that the worst thing you could do was to let the bullies know you have feelings. It only encouraged them. But there's no getting past – Mad Dog blocks my way.

"Look, Liv – it's simple. Either you help me or I'll grass you up to Old Mozzer and it'll be *you* outta here. Your choice. But think how it'll affect your loser mam now she's out of the nuthouse. Think she'll cope with her daughter kicked out of school? Or will it send her straight back to the bottle?"

"Alright! Enough!"

I should be defending Mam, defending myself, but it's like something has crumpled inside me. I feel the sky bending, sagging like the centre of the chocolate cake I baked, and threatening to collapse around me.

"OK, I'll go to Mozzer. It's not like I have a choice."

Mad Dog gives me a supposedly playful shove, which is way too rough.

"I'll meet you tomorrow night, straight after school, in the smokers' corner. We'll go see him together."

"I've got to get my story straight… I need more time!"

Shaking her head, Maddy glowers.

"No point in stalling. It has to be tomorrow. We can't do tonight because it's the staff meeting so Old Mozzer won't be around. Don't worry! I have it all planned. I'll tell you exactly what to say when you return the bag, to make sure it fits with my story. I'll walk you to Maths and fill you in."

Steadying myself, I fall into stride with Mad Dog, listening intently as she dictates the course of events. Guilt eats away at my stomach every step of the way – but knowing what she's capable of, what else can I do?

* * *

During Maths, I mull the situation over. I can't believe the trouble one stupid moment of weakness has caused. I've lost my best friend, as well as a potential boyfriend, and Mad Dog is running my life. Mam and Hatty seem like they can do without me – what the hell is the point of my existence?

It's hard to concentrate on algebraic equations, and I find them even more difficult than normal. To make things worse, Mr Snipe – who usually prefers cleaning his fingernails to giving me the time of day – decides to humiliate me in front of the class.

"How did you get to this conclusion, Miss Bloom?" he asks.

"I thought—"

"A thought crossed your mind? It must have been a long and lonely journey."

The whole class falls about laughing. Even Sarah.

As soon as the lunch bell rings, I head for the library. I never skip lunch, but today I have more important matters to attend to. After booking myself in for a thirty-minute internet slot, I plonk myself at an available computer and search the National Express website. It starts off as some idle searching, but soon I'm obsessing over every possible detail.

Imagine if I could take the 23:50 direct to Victoria Station tomorrow night – it would mean arriving early on Friday morning, so I won't have to find somewhere to stay. Ideally, it would be better to wait until Friday night – I could go undetected for longer – but that would mean another day of escaping Mad Dog's clutches. Money-wise, I only have £51.80 left in Mrs Snelling's purse, so I double-check the prices. There's an adult special that's only £32 for a return – ten quid cheaper than the child's fare. I can easily pass for sixteen with a bit of makeup. So far so good – so I move onto the Tube tickets while my luck's in.

Taking out Dad's address, I check Google maps for directions from the coach station. According to a local tourism website, I'll need a £10.40 day travelcard to get me to Greenwich and back – leaving me with less than a tenner for food. But who cares? Less than thirty minutes and my life is sorted.

"Can I print three pages please?" I ask the librarian.

Mr Wagstaff is totally cool. He has blond, curly hair and a square but friendly face. He looks more like a pro-fessional gamer than a librarian, and owns the coolest T-shirt collection I've ever seen. My favourite is a blue cotton v-neck that shows a carrot attacking a rabbit. It reads: "Who's the loser now?"

"Sure," says Mr Wagstaff. "I'll set up the printer for you now."

Gathering the information, I tuck it into my bag and find a quiet corner – away from prying eyes. I rip the centre pages from one of my exercise books and make a list of everything I'll need to take with me:

Chapter Thirty-Nine

Comb, styling wax, makeup bag, Hatty's MP3
Black cords, denim skirt
Extra tees (red with blue cherries, purple rainbow, blue chequed)
Stripy tights, over-the-knee socks, underwear
Printouts, money, phone and charger

Satisfied my list is complete, I pack everything away and sling my bag over my shoulder. Now I just need to figure out how to sneak away.

The bus station is only forty minutes' walk. I have to get there early to buy my ticket, so I need to leave at 10.30 p.m. at the latest. If I get everything ready tonight and take it to school with me, I can say I'm going to Sarah's, and head straight into town. By the time they realize I'm missing, I'll be long gone.

As I'm leaving, Mr Wagstaff looks up and grins.

"I'll have some of whatever you've had," he says.

I realize how much lighter I feel now my mind is made up. Now everything is prepared. "It'll cost you a million bucks."

Checking his pockets, Mr Wagstaff pulls out a twenty-pound note.

"That's not fair – I'm just a librarian! Take this instead?"

I wish I could. That twenty quid would be more money for food.

"Sorry – not today. Maybe if the recession gets any worse?"

"Smart girl," says Mr Wagstaff, returning to his paperwork.

Smarter than you realize, I think. All I have to do now is keep out of trouble and survive another night with Mam.

Caramel Hearts

No matter how spiky people seem, they're always softer on the inside than you expect. Melt even the coldest of hearts with these golden, caramel treats and wipe your tears away.

INGREDIENTS

125 g/4½ oz golden butter
125 g/4½ oz light brown sugar
150 g/5½ oz self-raising flour
2 eggs
½ tsp baking powder
1 tsp sweet vanilla extract
70 g/2½ oz of your favourite nuts (pecans, almonds or
hazelnuts are best), finely chopped

FOR THE "SALTY TEARS" CARAMEL SAUCE

200 g/7 oz caster sugar
70 ml/2½ fl oz water
50 g/2 oz butter
150 ml/5½ fl oz double cream
tsp chunky sea salt

HOW TO MAKE THE MAGIC HAPPEN

1. Preheat the oven to 180 °C/350 °F/Gas mark 4. Place all the cake ingredients into a bowl and beat rapidly

until well combined and creamy (plenty of elbow grease required).

2. Line a baking tray with silicone heart-shaped cases and split the mixture equally between them. Bake for 20 minutes until risen and golden. Allow to cool for a few minutes, then transfer to a wire rack.

3. Now make the caramel sauce and wash those tears away. Add the sugar, salt and water to a small pan and place over a gentle heat. Stir occasionally until all of the sugar and salt has melted.

4. Turn up the heat and keep watch as the mixture boils – stir constantly to make sure it doesn't burn. After 8–10 minutes, the mixture will thicken and turn a pale almond brown.

5. Remove from the heat and carefully add the butter and cream. Return to the heat, stir, and as soon as the sauce thickens, pour lashings of it over the heart-shaped cake and serve to whichever prickly person you need to soothe.

Chapter Forty

You Gotta Do What You Gotta Do

As soon as I'm home, I sneak upstairs, remove the money from Mrs Snelling's purse and tuck it into a secret compartment inside my rucksack. Then I return the purse to the stolen bag and pack it – along with all the things on my list, except for the phone charger that I'm using – ready for the next day. I had planned to keep out of Mam's way all evening, but there's a whiff of chicken roasting and it smells good. Harriet knocks on my door as plates start clattering downstairs.

"Come on – Mam's serving up. She's making a real effort."

It does smell good, and I guess it's the last time I'll have to put up with Mam for a while, so I follow. In the kitchen, Mam looks anxious.

"I'm glad you could join us," she says, and she means it – her voice isn't fake or forced.

It's as close to "sorry" as I'm going to get.

Over dinner, I join in with Mam and Hatty's ritual of talking about their day, even though nothing particularly exciting ever happens. Recounting my own day, I carefully miss out the conversation with Mad Dog, the algebra and my library research. With a few tweaks, my life isn't that bad.

"I really am sorry, Liv," says Mam, when the meal is finished. "It honestly won't happen again."

I resist the urge to roll my eyes – how many times have I heard that? I fake a grin. Mam looks pleased with my response and gives Harriet a covert look. They think they've won me over, but they won't look so smug tomorrow when I'm gone. It'll take more than a roast dinner to put things right.

"I have a special surprise for you, Liv," says Mam, jumping up suddenly. I watch as she gathers mixing bowls, spatulas and wooden spoons. She holds up *Recipes to Make Happiness Bloom*. "Don't look so shocked – it is mine, after all."

"I-I can explain..."

"No need. Harriet's told me all about it. She was right to give it to you. Just think, if she hadn't found it like that – and had the sense to pass it on to you – it would still be gathering dust!"

I throw a quizzical glance at Harriet, but she gives nothing away.

"You don't mind?" I ask.

"Not at all. In fact, I was thinking we could bake together. Work up to tackling a Baked Alaska."

"Really?"

As Mam leans into the cupboard and starts rummaging, I nudge Harriet under the table.

"Why'd you lie?" I whisper.

"I thought it would help smooth things over."

"Wanted all the praise for yourself, more like."

We adopt innocent expressions as Mam returns to the table, laden with baking utensils.

"It's been a while, but Baked Alaska is a fabulous recipe – even if I do say so myself," she says. "Always good for impressing people – they never understand that "hot on the outside, cold on the inside" thing. But first, we'd better see how we work together in the kitchen. Here!"

Mam throws a spatula and I pluck it from the air, one-handed.

"Great catch! Now, we'll make some Caramel Hearts. Simple, delicious, and – just like the recipe says – it'll melt hearts and wipe tears away. It's my way of saying sorry for everything I've put you girls through."

"If you'll excuse me, I've got to pop out," says Harriet. She leans over the recipe book, flicks through a few pages and scribbles some notes. Tucking the paper into her pocket, she waves. "I'll be back in time for the eating bit. Have fun, you two!"

As Harriet disappears off, I find myself disarmed. Why the sudden change? It seems too good to be true. Maybe I'm being too harsh on Mam, plotting to run away.

"Are you going to stand gawping all night, or are you going to help me out?" says Mam. "Now, we need to preheat the oven, line some cases – then what?"

I snatch up the recipe book as Mam starts the preparations.

"Place all the cake ingredients into a bowl and beat rapidly."

"Can I leave that bit to you?" asks Mam, bending down and lighting the oven.

"Sure."

Why did this change of heart have to happen today, of all days – when I've made my mind up to leave?

The instant I feel the warmth from the oven, the air feels almost cleared. I fold the sponge mixture, then turn it out into the greased heart-shaped moulds that

Jack gave me. Mam lifts the sponges into the oven, and I start on the sauce as Mam stands behind me, hands on hips and a tea towel over one shoulder. Placing the sugar, salt and water into a pan, I gently stir the mixture over a low heat, but the salt grains refuse to melt. I try not to panic. Try to ignore the growing concern that I'm messing it up. Eventually, the ingredients meld together like the recipe promises.

As I turn up the heat, carefully stirring, Mam says, "Now, is there anything you'd like to ask me about your father?"

I freeze. Mam must be feeling really apologetic. My mind races. I have too many questions. They flap around in my head like restless birds, so I wait for one to tire and land.

"How did you two fall in love?" I ask.

Mam hoists herself up onto the kitchen counter. Her legs swing in time as I keep stirring. When it turns to liquid caramel, Mam tells her tale and I pause to listen.

"We met in the uni bar. Well – outside it. It was the first time I'd tried cocktails and he found me on the steps, getting some air. He helped me find my friends, and got them to take me home. He took my number from one of them, saying he'd call the next day to see if I was OK."

"That was nice."

"Yeah. Only he didn't call. Not until three weeks later, when he happened to be without a date."

"What a cheek!"

"Yeah. A real charmer."

"And you said yes? Even though it was three weeks?"

"He'd found my friends for me. And he was fine looking."

I giggle. "Fine looking". Not "fit" or "hot" – "fine".
I pull out three small plates and three spoons, and lay
them on the counter.

"I was so nervous," continues Mam. "I couldn't remember what he looked like, so I made one of my friends come
with me to identify him."

"No way!"

"Yep. But I'm glad I did. It was the best date ever. We
got on so well and hit it off right away. We liked the same
things – Johnny Cash, Russian literature, hillwalking,
cake. The conversation just flowed. You know?"

I think of Jack, and my heart threatens to crack open
like an egg.

"And you stayed together from then?"

"Not quite. We had a few dates, but Max was young.
Wanted to sow his oats."

"That's disgusting," I say, trying not to think about the
possibility of Jack and Sarah kissing.

"That's what it's like when you're that age. You'll find
out."

I look away – concentrate on the sauce. It's ready, so I
turn off the heat and let it stand in the hot pan.

"I found another boyfriend. Carl. He was lovely – but
he wasn't Max. I couldn't get your dad out of my head.
I was certain we were meant to be together."

"Fate?"

"Exactly. One day, I was in a restaurant with Carl, and
Max came in. He was on a date with a beautiful woman.
I remember her black hair trailing down her back. Her
dress was high at the front but dangerously low cut at the
back. She was a stunner. But somehow, fate intervened
and he ended up leaving the restaurant with me."

"What happened?"

"Chemistry."

I pull a face.

"You might think it's – what's that word you use?"

"Lame?"

"Yeah – lame. But chemistry is a magical recipe. Only, unlike a dessert, you can't explain the ingredients. It just – happens."

I open the oven door, checking the progress. The sponge hearts have browned nicely. Mam throws me her tea towel. Bunching it around one hand, I lift the baking tray out and set the hearts on a rack to cool. We look at the steaming desserts hungrily as the sweet, burnt-sugar scent wafts around the kitchen.

"Max was late for his reservation, so they'd given his table away. I told Carl we were old friends and he suggested they joined our table." She reaches out to prod each heart in turn. "They did – and it was like old times. Our dates melted into the background. The rest is history."

"You really loved Dad that much?"

"So much that it made me feel sad at times. I couldn't cope with all the overwhelming emotions. He was my only love. My happiness. And I was his – like this says."

She flashes me the inscription.

"Do you want him back?"

"Your dad? Sometimes I think that's the only way I'll ever be happy. Other times, I know leaving was the right thing to do. But he still tugs at me – in here."

Mam thumps her chest and jumps off the counter, changing the subject.

"These Caramel Hearts look good to go!"

I decide not to push the conversation any further. It's the most open Mam has ever been and I don't want to ruin things.

"We'll definitely try the Baked Alaska together," says Mam, as the front door slams. "How's that for impeccable timing? Hatty! Come and try some of this."

Harriet's there like a shot, a bulging carrier bag in her hand.

Grinning, I cut around the inside edges of each heart-shaped mould and tap its contents gently onto a plate. I spoon the thick caramel sauce over the top, letting it drip down the sides. The hearts are perfectly shaped and the sauce forms a creamy moat. Despite Hatty's weight fixation, I push one across the table. She tucks in and nods slowly. Mam follows suit.

"Amazing! I thought I'd never bake again but—"

"You're going to love my surprise," interrupts Harriet. "Look – I got what you needed for the Baked Alaska. It's my parting gift to you both."

A grin spreads across Mam's face but, staring at the bag of ingredients, I don't know what to think or feel. Why do they have to be so nice now I've got my heart set on London?

Maybe I should forget the whole thing? But then Mad Dog's face pops into my mind. There's no way I'm going through with her plan, so I'm dead meat. Who knows what she'll do to me next time? Anyway, I've waited a lifetime to meet Dad – and he's been in touch, so he must feel the same.

"What are you grinning at?" asks Hatty.

I shrug.

"See," she whispers. "I told you it would be OK."

* * *

I'm heading to bed when Harriet bounds out of her bed-room. Behind her, I spy piles of clothes, books, magazines and makeup. The room looks like it's been under siege and come out on the losing side.

"Packing already, I see?"

Out of respect, Harriet pulls the door shut.

"I can't believe I'm finally going back."

"Me neither."

An uncomfortable silence settles between us. There is so much to say, but neither of us can find the words. I hear Mam singing downstairs. At first I feel guilty, but then I think, *If she can be like this today, why can't she be like this every day?* Hope turns to anger. Within minutes, I'm angry at everything and everyone – especially Hatty, for leaving, and myself for nearly being fooled. Harriet obviously doesn't sense my change of mood because she nudges me gently.

"Hey, it's my last night tomorrow. Want to go watch a film as a send-off? Mam said she'll treat us to Ben & Jerry's – we could choose a flavour each and share?"

"No thanks."

"What about the bus station on Saturday – will you come and wave goodbye?"

"I can't. I'm busy."

"Suit yourself," shrugs Harriet. "But you can't keep sulking like this for ever. I've got to go back to uni – you understand that, don't you?"

"Sure," I say. "You gotta do what you gotta do. We all have."

As I close my bedroom door behind me, I put my headphones on and blast Johnny's "If You Could Read My Mind".

Staring up at the ceiling, I recount Mam's conversation. I try to stay mad, because otherwise I might lose my nerve. Maybe I'm being too harsh, but this could be my only chance to look for Dad. I can't back down now. And imagine how happy Mam would be if I brought Dad home!

I just have to face Old Mozzer and Mad Dog first.

Chapter Forty-One

Pretending Not to See or Be Seen

Mad Dog's deadline arrives too quickly and, true to her word, she's waiting for me in the smokers' corner after school.

I see Emma, Zadie and Lorna disappearing into the distance. They keep looking back and gossiping, and I take this as a bad sign.

"You've got the bag?" asks Maddy.

"In here." I tap my rucksack unenthusiastically. Knowing I'm leaving has made me brave. The purse, bills, photograph of Mrs Snelling's dead son – it's all there. Everything except the money.

"Good – you know what you've got to say, right?"

I know what to say, all right. It kept me up half the night as I tried to pre-empt every possible reaction from Mr Morrelly. And I came up with an even better version. I've decided to tell the truth. They can suspend me or do whatever they like – I'm outta here! But now, after another frustrating day of being the school leper, I'm exhausted and my brain hurts. I've given myself a worry headache and I've been jumpy all day. Every time a door slammed, I expected a teacher to haul me out of class and catch me with the bag red-handed.

"We'd better get going," says Maddy. I must look startled, because she laughs in my face. "You don't think I'm letting you go by yourself, do you?"

Maddy trots beside me, chatting away about nothing in particular, as though she's my best friend. I'm careful with what I say in return. I made the mistake of trusting her once and I'm not about to repeat it. As we cross the playground, Mad Dog suddenly goes quiet.

"What the hell is he doing here? He's got some nerve," she snarls. "And as for her – she's dead meat, I swear!"

Jack and Sarah are outside the school gates – Jack's banned from the premises – leaning in close to chat. They pause now and again to look around nervously, and seeing them together doesn't sit right with me one bit. Jack looks up and catches my eye. On cue, Sarah spins around and looks at me like she no longer recognizes me – like she can't believe what I've turned into. Unable to bear it, I pretend not to notice them, even though I know I can't pull it off. Head down, I walk in time with Maddy, pretending not to see or be seen. Maddy takes my hand and swings it as we walk, like we're complete besties. But once we're out of their line of vision, she drops my hand and stomps towards the head teacher's office with an ugly grimace on her face, cursing now and again under her breath. When we reach the office, she turns on me and flings me against the wall, holding me in place by the neck of my polo shirt. It could be worse – it could be my throat. But I daren't move an inch.

"Listen, you go in there and act as frightened as you can, cos believe me – if you mess this up, I'll make sure your life isn't worth living."

Nodding vigorously, I fight the urge to pee.

"You think things've been bad up to now, with this." Mad Dog tugs at my hair with her free hand. "Next time, you'll get more than a haircut."

"OK, I get it."

"Good. Do well and you'll never have to worry about being bullied again. And we'll get that bitch, Sarah, for interfering."

"I'd prefer not to waste my time with Sarah," I say, as calmly as I can, hoping Mad Dog will believe me. "Her and Jack deserve each other."

Mad Dog twists her mouth into a grin.

"We'll worry about that later. When we're officially friends." Pausing for a moment to give her best menacing stare, Mad Dog eventually stands aside. "I think you look scared enough now. Time to deliver the Oscar-winning performance."

I take a deep breath and smooth down my uniform.

"What are you waiting for?" asks Maddy.

"Don't you think it'll look a bit suspect if you're here too?" I say.

"I guess so," says Maddy, and saunters off, checking back on me with every few steps. "But I'll be waiting for you up there."

"Fine," I say – like I'm happy about that.

Lifting my hand to knock, I wait until Maddy has rounded the corner, give her a few seconds to make sure she's not going to check back on me, and then bottle it. I'd be mad to tell the truth and, if I follow Maddy's plan, she'll own me for the rest of my life. Racing down the corridor, I use the teachers' exit, cut through the car park and lose myself in the winding streets of the nearest estate. It's only seven hours until the bus. Only seven hours to stay hidden.

* * *

As I climb the steps of the National Express coach – changed into my skinny jeans, favourite Johnny Cash T-shirt and warm coat – I feel my heart and head calming.

This is it! I'm finally doing something brave. I'm ready to show everyone what I'm made of. There'll be no more pushing Olivia Bloom around.

Nervously, I play with my ticket – what if the driver realizes I'm underage? – but I needn't have worried. He waves me on without even looking up. I head to the back of the bus and choose a window seat in front of the toilet. I don't remember anything about living in London – I was too young –I'm looking forward to soaking up the sights along the way.

Repeatedly checking my phone for the time, I wonder how long it will take my family to realize I've gone. If they notice at all. Putting my phone on silent, I decide to ignore their calls if they do try to contact me. Finding Dad is my best hope for a happy life.

Three minutes before the bus is due to pull away, a girl in a green velvet jacket and cherry-red Doc Martens approaches, eyeing the spare seat. I adopt the best Mad Dog scowl I can and shove my rucksack so it covers the spare seat. Intimidated, the girl sits a few rows in front. As the coach pulls away, I slouch down, knees up against the chair in front, listening to "Father and Son". Things feel better already.

Chapter Forty-Two

Trapped in One Spot Isn't Fun

The National Express coach sails along the motorway. A smattering of chimney-littered industrial towns and smog-choked cities whizz by, reminding me of Egerton and the life I'm leaving behind. My favourite part of the journey is the long stretch of winding road after Nottingham. It's pitch black, but I know the darkness is filled with green fields, horses and sheep – like the countryside we travelled through on the train to Whitby.

As the coach gets further away from home, I can't stop replaying events in my head. My mind is like a film trailer, showing various scenes from my life – good and bad. After a while, it gets so muddled, I no longer know why I'm running away and whether it's the right thing to do. Then I see the stolen bag as I search for my iPod, and it all becomes clear again. I had hoped to be rid of it by now, but chickening out of coming clean to Old Mozzer means I'm stuck with it. I hunker down and try to sleep, thinking up ways I can get rid of the bag in London. Before long, my eyes start drooping, but every time the driver changes gear or brakes, I'm jolted awake.

My phone vibrates, making me jump. The screen shows "Home". I press the reject button and try to snooze again. But it vibrates a second time with a text from Harriet.

LIV, WHERE ARE YOU? H XXX

I quickly delete it. Deep down, I wonder how Mam and Harriet are feeling, but I tell myself I have to stop thinking that way, they're no longer my problem – not that it works.

To remind myself why I'm here, I reread Dad's address – even though I have it memorized. I study the Tube map, but I almost know the route off by heart too. Still, I don't want to make any mistakes.

Circle or District Line from Victoria, change at Tower Hill for the DLR to Cutty Sark, Greenwich. From there, I follow the map to the "X" I've drawn to mark Dad's house. A twinge of fear makes me shiver, and I think how different this would feel with Hatty or Sarah by my side. But the image of Sarah and Jack together pops into my head, and the thought melts away. I focus instead on the happy moment ahead – when Dad welcomes me. I wonder whether I'll hold it together or whether I'll cry. Maybe *he'll* cry? I hope not. I'm no good when people cry. That's Hatty's area of expertise.

The journey is longer and more uncomfortable than I imagined. Even though I can spread myself across two seats, my muscles ache and my neck feels snapped out of place. Six hours trapped in one spot isn't fun – it's not the adventure I expected.

When the bus pulls in at Peterborough Station, I decide to stretch my legs, but it doesn't really help. Only the excitement of London at the other end keeps me going. I'll finally meet my dad – and that is worth any amount of discomfort.

By the time the driver shouts "London, Victoria", I'm tired, hungry and agitated. But the instant the coach pulls to a stop in the huge, fluorescent-lit coach station, excitement bubbles inside me. I spot a sign for the Underground and feel a new surge of energy. Fingering the address in my pocket, I climb off the bus and head straight for the bowels of London's transport system.

Fighting my way through the turnstiles, I can't believe how many people are rushing about at such an early hour. Where could they all be going? A man with a briefcase bumps into me as I stop to figure out which direction of the District Line to take.

"Sorry!" I call after him, but he keeps walking, like I don't exist. No change there then. It seems everyone is busy and important, with places to be. Well, I have places to be, too.

"Greenwich, here I come!" I say, heading down the escalator to my first Tube.

"Get outta the way, will ya!"

It takes a moment for me to realize I'm not following etiquette – I should stand on the right. The left is for impatient people, scaling the escalator at top speed, dashing off to goodness knows where.

"Sorry!" I call, for what feels like the umpteenth time.

What's wrong with people? It's a good job the Tube is amazing – otherwise I might be put off. Wait till I tell Hatty about this, I think, then I realize – I might never see my sister again. Ignoring the lump in my throat, I concentrate on the journey.

The Tube whizzes along at top speed, sparking its way in and out of tunnels and twisting round corners like a giant, engine-powered snake. Changing lines isn't that complicated – I just keep a close eye on the stops shown above the doors. When I get off, I let myself get caught up in the crowd until a space opens. Then I stop and check my bearings. It's easier than I expected – more straightforward than the labyrinth of colours on the Tube map suggests.

But when I reach Tower Hill, it all starts to go wrong. As I exit the Tube in search of the DLR, an announcement comes over the Tannoy.

"Passengers are advised that all services to Lewisham have been terminated due to an accident at Canary Wharf. A replacement bus service is available outside the station."

Lewisham – that's the train I need! I knew it was going too well. Joining the claustrophobic throng of grumbling passengers queuing for the replacement bus, I feel like I'm swallowing dust, not air. I spot a lady in the regulation neon-orange uniform and head over to her. Waiting my turn, careful not to make eye contact or get in anyone's way, I realize my turn will never come, so eventually I jump in.

"Is this bus for Greenwich?" I ask, showing my ticket.

The attendant shakes her head.

"No, this is the 617A. You're looking for bus 617B. You just missed one, but there'll be another in the next few minutes. Are you in a hurry?"

It's bright, but still early. "Not really."

"You could always avoid rush hour by taking another route on the DLR."

As another busy person bashes into me, the idea sounds attractive.

"What route?" I ask.

"I reckon Blackheath would be your best bet. Fewer people, and you could walk through the park."

The bus is noisy and packed, and my bones ache from the long journey. I remember seeing the park on my map and a walk sounds nice. It also means I'll be calling on my dad at a more reasonable time.

"OK."

"Head to London Bridge, then get the DLR to Blackheath – you can use the same ticket. Ask someone for directions to the heath and follow the path to the big metal gates of Greenwich Park. The village is on the other side, at the bottom of the hill."

Before I can thank her, three suited workers mob her – all talking at the same time. I slip away from the crowd, heading back towards the Tube.

When the DLR pulls into Blackheath, I take a deep breath and skip out, checking the battery on my phone. There is more than half left – plenty of juice to last until I can charge it at Dad's place. I follow the exit signs and stride out of the Tube station into the cold air, map in hand. The streets are filled with people carrying newspapers, laptop cases and coffee. I stop an old man to ask for directions. He points across the main road that cuts through the shops and station, towards a side street.

I, Olivia Bloom, am getting good at life.

The heath is easy to find. It's a wide expanse of grass with a long path cutting through it – reminding me of the Rec back home. The rising sun casts long shadows on the pavement and my heart sinks as I think how much Hatty would love walking here, watching the place wake up. With every step, I think about home. What are Mam and Hatty doing? Have they called Sarah and Jack to see if I'm with them? As soon as Jack and Sarah enter my thoughts, I swallow hard and lift my chin an inch or two, shoulders pulled back.

"I don't care about any of them," I say aloud to the crisp air. "They can all go to hell."

As I repeat my mantra, the shadows seem to shrink and my heart feels free. Spotting tall, wrought-iron gates ahead, I speed towards Greenwich Park.

The park is the biggest I've ever seen. Tall trees with thick, dark trunks – big enough to hide behind – line the paths. Their leaves flutter, concealing noisy birds. One swoops from the tree – a luminous green parakeet – and I rub my eyes, thinking I'm seeing things until I spy another and another. Brightly coloured flowers bud and bloom in neatly arranged flower-beds. Red-bricked domed buildings, tiny teashops and ice-cream stands line the walkways.

Despite its size, the park feels packed. Groups of ladies in sunglasses, pushing weird-shaped pushchairs, chat loudly as they stroll. Dog walkers with multiple leads march their way across the grass, pulled by various breeds – pugs, Dalmatians, terriers and Labradors. Lines of young children holding hands jostle by, tugging at the high-visibility vests covering their jackets. They chatter and nudge each other as their mams and playgroup leaders complete headcounts or point out things of interest. It reminds me of nursery. I liked school back then. I liked lots of things.

The park opens up to an expanse of concrete littered with people taking snaps of the cityscape. I pause, taking in the view. I can't make out any of the famous landmarks I've seen online or on TV. Buildings like crooked teeth bite into every part of the jumbled landscape: gleaming high-rises and proud, red chimneys. A web of cranes lines the blue sky. It feels like every brick, block of concrete and steel rod is tumbling in on me. I turn, bumping into a Chinese lady wearing a padded jacket, a camera strung around her neck.

"Sorry! Do you know where Greenwich village is?"

The lady smiles and nods.

"Greenwich," she says, pointing down a steep, sloping path.

"Thank you!"

My heart thumps as I race towards the village. I pass people pushing prams uphill – sometimes, it takes two as the angle is so steep. I can't understand why they'd bother, just to get a view of a big, ugly city.

After a while, the long, meandering path leads to a glass building. Outside, there is a huge ship in a bottle, mounted on a concrete column, and a sign reading Maritime Museum. I wonder where I'd sail to if I could commandeer the bottled ship. Whitby, probably. The thought catches me unawares. I walk off without looking where I'm going, and bang into someone.

"Are you OK?" asks a voice in a thick, foreign accent as I stumble.

A stocky, darkly tanned man in a long coat and red scarf waits for an answer. I blush – I was so caught up in my own thoughts, I hadn't noticed him. I'll have to be more careful. Anything could happen in a city this size.

"I'm OK."

The man shrugs, then jogs towards three friends who are waiting up ahead. I sit on the concrete wall outside the museum. A water feature trickles through the centre of its blocks. Listening to the calming sound, I watch the four friends flick water from the wall at each other, then leave through the spiky black and gold gates.

I suddenly realize how close the park gates are. How small and alone I am. Feeling sick, I lean over and take deep breaths before checking my map.

Dad's house isn't far.

All I have to do is navigate the few winding roads to where "X" marks the spot.

Chapter Forty-Three

Battered Leather Suitcases
and All Sorts of Junk

As I step out of the park gates, my confidence drains away and my palms ooze with sweat. On my right, there are shops, bars and restaurants, but up ahead the street is quiet and empty. I start walking along it, heart pounding. Above me, bright red cranes loom like menacing, mechanical giants, watching my every move. I tuck in as close to the buildings as I can to escape their glare.

There's the back of a hotel to my right, flats up ahead and a road curving left – Crooms Hill. My dad's place is just off this road, meaning it's even closer than I thought. A taxicab slows and toots, looking for a fare. I wave him away and start up the hill, passing a grocery store with a big chalkboard sign outside:

PROUD TO SERVE THE PERFECT PIE, FULL OF FLAVOUR

Crooms Hill skirts the park, twisting and winding its way up so I can't see what's ahead. Every part of my brain screams at me to turn back, give up, but I know it's just fear trying to take hold, so I keep going.

Halfway up the road, I pause to look back. The grocery store is still in view but everything else – except the cranes – has disappeared. The buildings around me sink back from the road – all different heights and styles. Not like home, where each house looks the same, except for the curtains. I wonder if people can tell I don't belong here just by looking at me. A group of children tumble out of the park, almost bumping into me, and making me jump. I can't believe I'm scared of a bunch of kids.

I continue up the hill, my breath shortening with the effort. I check my map again. The turn-off is very close. I'm terrified of missing it –yet scared of finding it, too. A bright red postbox across the road catches my eye. A car obscures it from view momentarily, then turns into an alleyway between two massive houses – a cul-de-sac I hadn't spotted. High up on the side of one of the houses, I can just make out the faded street sign: Crooms Hill Close.

I've found it!

Taking a moment to gather my thoughts and my courage, I lean against the railings of the park. What do I say when Dad opens the door? I've thought about this moment for years – but now it's finally here, I'm clueless.

There's a quiet shuffling sound behind me so I turn slowly. A huge white dog stares up at me from the other side of the railings, like a lone wolf. His mouth is open and panting, but otherwise he's motionless. His nervous brown eyes connect with mine. They seem to look straight through me. Backing away slowly, I cross the road. When I look back, the dog has gone. Spooked, I hurry between the two houses into the close, shivering as the walls temporarily block the low, spring sun. I quicken my pace, desperate to return to the light and feel the sun's rays on my eyelids.

Stepping into Crooms Hill Close, relief sweeps over me. The place is gorgeous. It's a sun trap, with pretty cottages on the right and grandiose townhouses on the left. Every house has a tiny garden bordered with wild roses and neat hedges. Many have steps up to the front door, like in American movies. Hand trembling, I walk the length of the road, scouting the door numbers on both sides of the street. A small part of me doesn't want to find the place at all.

Eventually, the houses end and a row of garages begin. A shabby brick wall runs the length of the road up ahead, creating a dead end. Panic sets in. There is no number 43! I've come all this way for nothing.

Edging towards the garages, I feel as though my heart has lodged itself in my throat. This part of the road is dark, edged with tall, whistling trees and a man-sized, creaky gate. Despite my fear, I have to investigate – if I don't find Dad, I've no money for lodgings. And if I give up now, I'll have to go home and face Mad Dog and Mam – neither of which is attractive. Pushing through the gate, I heave a sigh of relief.

This is it. My dad's house.

The building is huge – four storeys high, with red-bricked walls and giant bay windows. Two white pillars flank the daffodil-yellow door. Whatever Dad does, he has a lot of money.

I follow the path and climb the steps, building up enough courage to ring the bell. I give it a good, strong poke and hold my breath. There is no reply, so I try again. After ringing the bell several times, I'm just about to give up when a window slides open. Stepping back, I look up, sheltering my eyes for a better look. A slim, olive-skinned girl with long blue-black hair peers down at me. She rubs her eyes, yawning, like she's just woken up. She's about the same age as me – but much prettier.

"Can I help you?"

"I'm looking for a Mr Max Bloom," I call.

"You'd be lucky! He hasn't been home all night."

Nausea rises in my stomach. I hadn't thought of a Plan B.

"When's a good time to call back?" I ask.

"There's never a good time. He's a workaholic."

"Can I try again this afternoon?"

The girl shrugs and starts to lower the window.

"Wait! I've come a long way."

Agitated, the girl pulls her hair back from her face, then twists it, throwing it over one shoulder. It spills down her arm like oil.

"Come back if you like, but you'd be better off waiting until tonight and trying The Bear Arms."

With that, the girl slams the window shut and lets the curtains fall back into place. I don't even get a chance to ask where The Bear Arms is, or what he'll be doing there. Mam mentioned it before – she thought he owned the place – but what if Dad's another alky? The girl said he was a workaholic, but that could be some sort of "code". Pushing the worry away, I decide to start searching Greenwich Village for the bar.

Walking slowly out of the cul-de-sac, I wait on the corner, leaning against the postbox for a time, in case someone who might be my dad suddenly appears. My rumbling stomach eventually forces me to move on, and I head back down the hill to the pie shop.

Finding my way round Greenwich is easy. It's not that big, and most of the shops and cafés are on three main streets. But there's no sign of The Bear Arms. I ask a few people, but most of them are tourists who don't speak English. The rest assume I'm begging and shoo me away. One man even shouts "Get a job!" into my face. By the time I find a busy, covered market, I'm so shaken I have to lean against the wall until my legs stop trembling.

Wandering through the tightly packed market crowd, I marvel at the latticed roof and the stalls with funny names like "Bull in a China Shop". Everything imaginable is for sale: stuffed pheasants, handmade cards, war medals and old wooden toys. There are endless rails of goth clothes I'd love – but I'd get picked on if I wore them back home. There are vinyl records (but no Johnny Cash), lamps made from coloured glass, battered leather suitcases and all sorts of junk labelled as "retro".

At one end of the market, a food area fills the air with delicious smells and I feel my shoulders relax as I watch Japanese noodles, Spanish paella, Italian sausages, Colombian coffee and Ethiopian stews sizzle and gurgle. People of all colours, shapes and sizes eat hungrily from disposable tubs, seated on concrete steps or wobbly plastic chairs. Passing below a big heart that dangles from the ceiling, I decide to ask for directions again. A seated old man looks harmless.

"Excuse me."

The old man turns, his eyes blotchy and deeply shadowed. Spit gathers in the corner of his mouth and I realize my mistake.

"Leave me alone!" he shouts, saliva dribbling down his chin. "Help! Help!"

I stand there, stunned, not knowing how to react. A friendly coffee-stall owner calls me away and hands me a cup of sugary tea. I'd prefer a milky coffee, but I'm not going to argue.

"Don't worry about 'im, love. One of the local fruitcakes. Take no notice."

"Thanks," I say, hugging the cardboard cup. After a few sips, I feel better. "I only wanted to know if he'd heard of The Bear Arms."

"A swanky joint, eh? You're in luck – I know the very place. It's not far from 'ere. Off Greenwich South Street, on Ashburnham Grove. Don't open 'til late, mind – and over twenty-ones only. Follow the blue neon lights and local glitterati after dark – you can't miss it."

Smiling, I search for the street on the map, confirm its location with the coffee seller, then head out into the sunshine. Now I know where to find The Bear Arms, I can do some exploring. What's the point of coming all the way to London if I can't enjoy myself – at least a little bit?

Chapter Forty-Four

Fake Candlelight and Long Banquet Tables

Down in the quay, the *Cutty Sark* floats above a glass building, her intricate masts dominating the skyline.

I overhear some people talking about a tunnel under the Thames, and it sounds so cool I have to follow them. We stop at a strange little circular structure – like a mini church dome – that houses a big, glass-fronted lift. It takes us down to the belly of the river.

Stepping out into the white-tiled tunnel, I gasp. It's like something out of a sci-fi film – a giant space-age cocoon. It slants upwards so you can't see what's ahead or how long it is.

My footsteps echo, no matter how quietly I creep. People's voices reach my ears long before I can see them. Now and then a muffled rumble passes overhead – probably boats, but I imagine it's the blue whale calf I saw on Sarah's TV. A cup of her Mam's hot chocolate would go down a treat right now.

The tunnel stretches out for what seems like miles. At the other end there is another lift, and within a few moments I'm standing in a small park, which looks over the Thames to the bank I just came from. The *Cutty Sark* looks much smaller from here. Too small. Just like me. My legs start trembling and I'm overcome with an inexplicable urge to get back to Greenwich Village and find my dad – and quick! I race back towards the lift and run the length of the tunnel to where I'd started.

Back in the open air, I search for somewhere snug to hang out for a while. Somewhere that doesn't need money. I see a Student's Union sign. Harriet always bangs on about hers in Edinburgh, so I decide to take a peek – hoping for a glimpse of the secret world that keeps enticing my sister away. The entrance is cool and dark, with low ceilings and sweeping staircases. Doors lead in all directions, but the doorman stops me before I can choose which one to take.

"Do you have your student card, please?"

"No, but I go to Egerton Park School. It's up North."

The doorman looks amused, then apologetic.

"Sorry, you have to be part of a University to get in here. But you can walk round some nice grounds – and the Painted Hall is free."

"The Painted Hall?"

It sounds like a consolation prize.

"Out the door, turn right – when you see the entrance to the Naval College buildings, turn right again and follow the signs. You can't miss it."

Without anywhere else to go, I decide it's definitely worth a try.

The college buildings are magnificent and I take my time wandering past, staring up at the elaborate carvings. After a while, I find the Painted Hall – a hugely ornate room filled with fake candlelight and long banquet tables. The ceilings are painted with lifelike figures, animals and angels, their expressions captured in muted pastels and rich gold.

Seated at one of the tables, I flick through the information leaflets. One claims this place was the set for *Pirates of the Caribbean.*

I wouldn't know. I couldn't afford to go to the cinema and I lost interest after that. Didn't want to look like a loser asking to borrow someone's DVD. I read about the painted figures and try to get a feel for the history of the place, but it's all so long ago, I can't relate to it. Instead, I close my eyes and imagine a banquet. I picture a huge pig roasting on a spit, baskets laden with luscious fruit and giant soup terrines with decorative silver ladles. The centrepiece is a grand layered wedding cake, with ivory icing that shines like silk. The image feels so real I can almost hear the spit crackling, taste the rich fruitcake.

Feeling a bit better, I people-watch for a while, enjoying the different languages and outfits. A long blond ponytail catches my eye and I think how much Sarah would love the detailed ceiling.

Then, my stupid brain morphs a quiet student type admiring the banquet tables into Hatty, and a nervy, quick-eyed lady into Mam. Nearby, a cross-looking man slaps a little boy's legs, his teeth bared as he mutters something under his breath. The boy looks too scared to cry and I look away in disgust. The man's just like Maddy's dad. At least Mam's never like that.

The sound of laughter makes my head swivel, and my stomach flips as I watch a mam and her two daughters pull poses for the camera before falling about in fits. I'd give anything to swap places – to have Mam and Hatty here. They could do with a break too. Instead of concentrating on starting a new life here alone, maybe I should be thinking about reuniting everyone with Dad. He certainly has enough money to look after us all and Mam wouldn't need to drink any more with Max in her life. I'd get the best of both worlds.

Without me even noticing, dusk settles over the city. The Warden waits until everyone else has gone before asking me to leave.

"See you again," he says, tipping his hat before locking the door.

I hope he will. Only next time we'll all be here – Mam, Dad, me and Hatty – thanks to my ingenious plan. The thought boosts my spirits.

But Greenwich looks different at dusk, and my momentary confidence drains away. The gates I came through are locked, so I have to find an alternative exit. My breath mists the air as the temperature drops. Huddled in my coat, I check the time on my phone – 8 p.m. Seven missed calls from Harriet and another text.

ANSWER YOUR PHONE, LIL SIS X H X

I also notice that my battery symbol has turned red. Maybe I should call back? I decide to stay strong. I'm too close to give up. I'll keep my battery power until I find Dad, then I'll charge my phone and call home. Put them out of their misery. All those missed calls tell me they've suffered enough.

As darkness falls, I keep to the main streets, pounding the same route over and over. Surrounded by people and streetlights, I feel safer.

Many shops are still open so I browse for an hour, going into anywhere that looks cosy. Hunger rumbles in my belly, but I want to make the money stretch as long as possible, just in case. Of what, I don't want to think about.

Anyway, my dad will feed me.

It's time to find him.

Even with the map, The Bear Arms is tricky enough to find. It's only a few streets away, but the streets are long and confusing and I can't tell where to turn off. The surroundings switch from loud, busy areas full of pubs to silent, residential patches filled with parked cars and inquisitive foxes nosing in rubbish bins. Both are equally spooky. Distant sirens keep setting my nerves on edge. As it turns ten o'clock, I start panicking and abandon the map, walking the streets blindly, listening out for noisy bars. After a few false leads, I spot a well-dressed crowd in high spirits. Remembering the coffee-seller's advice, I follow them.

My phone buzzes and, although I know I'm not going to answer, I check it anyway.

Home. Again.

I hit the reject button.

A third text comes through from Hatty's phone.

THIS IS MAM. WE'RE WORRIED. PLEASE LET ME KNOW YOU'RE OK XXXX

When I look up, I've lost my crowd. They've merged into the night-time city.

Spotting a flash of blue neon in the distance, I head straight for it, quickening my pace.

Two young men about Hatty's age appear out of nowhere. One is large and muscular in a white track-suit, the other is small and wiry in black jeans and hoody. They look different to the rest of the people I've seen round here. Rougher. More like people back home. They smile at me as though they've known me all their lives.

"Hey, darlin', wanna come party?" shouts the small guy in a thick, London accent.

Sweating with fear, I shake my head. If I speak, my accent will give me away.

The two guys pause, heads cocked to one side as they size me up. I don't like the way they're looking at me. News headlines flash through my mind – "Runaway Schoolgirl Found Chopped to Pieces in Bin" – so I walk on, trying to look nonchalant.

Losing interest, the tall guy grabs his mate by the arm.

"Leave her alone – she's just a kid. We've got bigger fish to catch!"

Breaking out into a cheesy R & B song, he dances away. Just like that, I'm alone again in the shadowy streets.

Holding my stomach, I blow out a big mouthful of air.

That was a close one. I try to picture what I'd be doing right now if I had stayed at home. I'd probably be sprawled on the bed reading *Cosmo*. I might even be tackling that Baked Alaska with

Chapter Forty-Four

Mam. Either way, I'd definitely be listening to Johnny.

As the memory of me, Jack and Harriet moshing rushes back, I run towards the blue neon, as though it's the only thing in the world that can save me.

Baked Alaska

Hot on the outside, cool on the inside, this is the most elegant treat you'll ever serve.

So don't get all hot under the collar when you need to impress. Stay calm and think big! There's no mountain you can't climb – it's just a case of "mind over matter".

SPONGEY DELICIOUSNESS (BASE)

55 g/2 oz self-raising flour
55 g/2 oz caster sugar
2 eggs, plus 2 extra yolks
Pinch of salt
2 tbsp warm water

SHIVERY GOODNESS (IN THE MIDDLE)

1 litre vanilla ice cream

CRUNCHY MOUNTAIN PEAKS (MERINGUE TOPPING)

6 egg-whites
300 g/11 oz caster sugar
1 tsp granulated sugar

HOW TO MAKE THE MAGIC HAPPEN

1. Pre-heat the oven to 190 °C/375 °F/Gas mark 5. Lightly grease a round 20 cm (8–9 in.) sandwich tin.
2. Make the sponge first by beating the eggs, salt, warm water and egg yolks together (hint: keep the whites for the crunchy meringue peaks), then add the sugar really slowly – a bit at a time. Bruise it all up real good until thick and dreamy.
3. Use a metal spoon to gently fold in the flour – the more love, the better the bounce.
4. Pour the mixture into the tin and bake for 12–15 minutes until swollen and golden brown. Check with a chopstick – poke it in (not all the way through – we don't want any holes) and if it comes away sticky, whack it back in for a bit longer.
5. Cool on a wire tray – but keep the oven on! When it's cold, place the sponge on an ovenproof dish.
6. Now the fun bit – make the mountain! Using a glass bowl (not plastic, otherwise it won't go fluffy) and a fine big whisk, beat the egg-whites and caster sugar together until thick and shiny. Make it gleam like snow-topped peaks.
7. Place the ice cream in the middle of the sponge (use what you need – it might not be the full litre) and swirl the meringue topping over it. Make sure it's well sealed or it'll be more "molten volcano" than "gargantuan goodness".
8. Sprinkle granulated sugar over the meringue and place it in the oven for 3 minutes, or until it is golden-brown. Serve immediately with the most tantalizing fresh fruit you can find.

Chapter Forty-Five

One of Life's Cruel Games

It's past ten o'clock, but there's no sign of any bouncers, so I slip in unnoticed. The warmth envelops me like a hug. The music is loud and the lights are even brighter than they seemed from the street. Blue neon lines the bar and beautiful, well-dressed people lean in to shout into the ears of their friends. The room smells of pineapple and spirits. Feeling safe at last, I heave a sigh of relief. It's so busy, no one will notice me.

Looking around, I realize how different these people's lives must be. No one back home could afford this much designer gear. Not even Mad Dog, with her family always on the rob. Here, people drink wine or cocktails instead of gulping pints. Behind the bar, several attractive young men and women serve an endless sea of gem-coloured drinks. I spike my fringe, smooth my eyebrows and remove my coat. Feeling very self-conscious, I suddenly realize – I don't even know what my dad looks like. He could be here, now, right in front of me.

As I scan the room, I see a girl about the same age as me tucked in a corner. She looks at home in her red satin dress and knee-length boots, her hair pulled back into a high ponytail, which makes her cheekbones stand out. She's drinking coffee while typing into a MacBook Air.

For some reason, she looks familiar. I realize it's the girl from my dad's house – so I head straight over.

"Excuse me, I don't know if you remember me – I called at your house earlier. I was wondering – is Max around?"

Raising her eyebrows, the girl peers over her MacBook.

"Not yet. He's the owner, so he should be here soon – though you never can tell with him." Realizing I'm not going away any time soon, she closes her MacBook. "I can try and call him if it's urgent. Who shall I say is asking after him?"

"His daughter, Olivia."

The words feel weird as they spill out. The girl nearly chokes on her coffee, but quickly recovers.

"Daughter? Olivia, you say?"

She makes the call.

"Dad, you'd better come over. I have a surprise for you."

My brain whirrs into overdrive. Did she call Max "Dad"? The girl hangs up and cocks her head to one side. I don't think she likes what she sees.

"So, you're one of my half-sisters. I'm Amber."

She puts out her hand – challenging rather than friendly. I accept the handshake, my thoughts tumbling. Wasn't Amber the daughter of Mam's friend Rosa? Amber's smile fades. She looks irritated by my presence, like a kid who just received last year's craze as a birthday present.

"Here – sit down. Are you hungry?"

I nod, stuck for words.

"Wait here."

Amber saunters off towards the bar. The next few minutes feel like hours. Half-sister? Harriet and I had guessed about the affair but we hadn't made *that* connection. Amber returns with lemonade and some thick,

spicy wedges with sour cream. Lemonade. A kid's drink.
I guess she's marking her territory.

"Enjoy," she says, opening her MacBook again.

I eat my food slowly, trying to look dignified and well
bred, and I sip the lemonade. She doesn't look up again
until a smooth, deep voice sounds behind me, making
the hairs on my arms stand on end.

"Amber, what is it that couldn't wait till later? You know
I hate surprises."

It's him! I spin round, eyes wide.

"Meet your daughter – Olivia," Amber says triumphantly,
like she's somehow getting one up on her dad. Our dad.

I don't care. Nothing is going to ruin this.

Max isn't as handsome as I'd hoped. He's much older and
more tired looking than I imagined. He has a really wide
jaw – like me – sleek, greying, black hair and a half smile.

His reaction isn't what I expected either.

Instead of hugging me, he shuffles awkwardly. I take a
step towards him, but he jumps back like I'm diseased
or something. Brow furrowed, he keeps his distance,
tousling his hair and looking around him, trying to find
an excuse to escape.

"Dad? Mam said you'd got in touch so—"

"I only got in contact because… I didn't expect—" he
says after a while. "Christ, you'd better come with me."

My dad leads me through a purple, floor-length curtain.
The area is VIP. Now we're getting somewhere! I wish she
wouldn't, but Amber follows. Once inside, I still don't
get the welcome I was hoping for. Dad puts all his energy
into rubbing his stubbled chin.

"It's great to meet you… but how? Why? I mean – does
your mother know you're here?"

"She only just told us where you were. Gave us your address. So I came to find you."

There's plenty of time for revealing the bad bits when we know each other better.

"Is she on about the tart you were with before Mam?" asks Amber.

The bitterness takes me by surprise. What does she have against Mam? Dad tries shooing Amber away, but she stands her ground. He smiles weakly.

"I really don't know what to say, Olivia. Where are you staying? It's late and I've got to work – maybe we could meet up tomorrow when it's had time to sink in?"

"I'm not staying anywhere. I've come to stay with you!" I say.

Dad reaches his arm around Amber and I feel like screaming, *Where's my hug, you selfish bastard? The one I've been waiting for all my life?* Amber's pretty mouth twists into a weird shape – like she's chewing on something sour. Her expression reminds me of Mad Dog.

"I can't… I mean – as you can see, I've already got my hands full with this one."

"But…"

"Olivia, I'm a busy man. You should get straight back on the bus or train and go home to your mother. Or maybe a hotel for the night. I'll get one of my staff to book you in somewhere and take you there…"

"But I've seen your place – it's huge! Just for one night? Please? I promise we'll get on."

"She's not staying with us," says Amber. Then she switches to a puppy-dog voice. "Is she?"

She's like Mad Dog all right. Got my dad twisted around her little finger.

"We just lost Rosa a few months ago – breast cancer – and we're… well, we're not ready for any big upheavals. I'm sorry – that's why I contacted your mum, to tell her – but we just… we can't."

Amber's mournful look turns icy.

"Did you think you could just turn up and play happy families?" she says.

I understand she must be upset – but it's not my fault her mam died. Me staying for a night won't make things any worse. Ignoring the comment, I turn to my dad.

"Sorry, kid," he says, glancing back towards the curtain. "Nothing personal – it's just bad timing. Maybe in a few months or something… I have to mind my own little family right now. We only have each other. One of life's cruel games."

He pulls Amber closer and she pretends to squirm away, embarrassed. But I can see it's an act. She's delighted to get one up on me. She's no half-sister of mine.

"But you're my dad. We're family too."

What was it the old letter said? "*You and the girls will always have a home with me.*" He can't turn me away, surely. Not when I've come all this way. When I'm his blood.

Breaking free from Amber, Max rubs his hands through his hair – it's starting to look a bit greasy now – and chews his lip. Just as he looks like he's about to cave in, Amber rushes to his side and starts to cry. Manipulative cow. Max strokes her hair gently.

"I'm sorry, Olivia… Look, I'll call your mother and make arrangements. I can drive you to the station or hotel myself if you like. Have you ever stayed in a five-star hotel? Here, take this for spending, you can treat yourself…"

He flicks through his wallet and holds out two £50 notes. I snatch the money, screw it up and throw it on the floor.

"I hate you!" I cry. "I should never have come."

Pushing past them, I run through to the busy bar, bumping into people along the way.

"Olivia, wait!"

But I keep running. Out in the street, I hide behind a parked car, the cold night air pinching at my face. My heart quickens as Dad races out, pulling at his face as he searches frantically in every direction. I want to go to him – maybe his reaction will be warmer this time – but something keeps me rooted to the spot.

A longing for home.

There's no chance of reconciliation with Dad, no chance of starting a new life in London – and it's time to call Mam.

When I pull out my phone, the screen is dead. I try switching it on, but the battery's gone. I scrabble around for my charger – I can swallow my pride long enough to get enough juice for a call – but it's nowhere to be found. Spilling my belongings onto the pavement, I stare into my empty rucksack. I forgot to pack it!

Now I'm completely stuck. Why didn't I take Dad's money? There's no way I'm going back just to make a show of myself in front of Amber. And I'm not giving Dad the chance to turn me away again.

Pulling up my hood, I stomp angrily into the night-time streets of London, back towards Greenwich village centre, my teeth gritted and jaw set. I glare at the first person that passes me, to make them look away. A fluttering feeling rises in my chest at the victory.

Chapter Forty-Six

Stripped Bare, Like Skeletons

The anger soon wears off and I stop in my tracks, wondering where to go next. I don't fancy going to the bus station – it's too far away and means passing through some pretty dodgy areas, even by Egerton standards. The streets are still busy and there are plenty of bars open, but the bouncers are out in force and I can't sneak in. Tiredness forces cold into my limbs and I feel like I'm freezing from the inside out. Rubbish scampers down the street, crackling off lampposts and bins, and making me jumpy. But I'm determined to keep walking until I've figured out my next move. The streets of Greenwich turn into a shadowy, unwelcoming maze. Still heaving with people, their laughter and chatter adds to my loneliness and worry.

What was I thinking? Suddenly, running away doesn't seem such a smart idea.

As 2 a.m. arrives, most places lock up for the night, and fewer people wander the streets. Straggly foxes roam free as dogs – confident, yet wary. My options dwindle and, as the misery of my situation sinks in, I plonk myself on a bench and try to look inconspicuous as homeward-bound drunks lumber down the street. They're too busy feasting on hot chips, burgers, kebabs and hotdogs to notice me anyway. I huddle in my coat, brain throbbing, as I try to figure out what to do. I never thought I'd miss anything about Egerton, but right now, I'd love nothing more than to wander up the path leading up to our front door and climb the stairs to my warm bed. Why did I put Mam through this – and so soon after returning home? Sarah's right. I'm out of control. And I've gone too far this time.

Wiggling my legs and stamping my feet to keep warm, I decide the best thing to do is to keep moving. It wouldn't be safe to sleep on the streets, and I might freeze to death. In the morning, I'll locate a mobile phone shop and get them to charge my phone. I'll call home, then catch a return coach. The thought of it makes me shudder. Harriet will be on her way to uni, so I'll have to deal with Mam alone. And there's no telling what state she'll be in, thanks to me.

As I dive into my bag looking for extra clothes, I'm confronted with the stolen bag. Angrily, I yank it out and put it on my shoulder, determined to get rid of it once and for all. If Sarah or Jack say anything, I'll just deny it – there'll be no proof.

A rowdy group of girls in short dresses and heels clatter past, squealing unintelligibly as they tuck into hot bagels. I struggle to fight back the tears, but then I cop on and realize there must be a bakery nearby, busily preparing tomorrow's bread and cakes, with hot ovens churning out heat. If I could hide out there for the night, I wouldn't have to wander the streets. It would be nice and cosy, and I could steal some breakfast too.

Jumping from the bench, I head to where the high-heeled girls just came from. Soon, I hit the market, but now the stalls are stripped bare, like skeletons. As I search the lanes leading from the square, I mull over the trail of bad decisions I've made recently. Finding my dad now feels like a totally stupid idea. It hasn't got me anywhere – except in deeper trouble. It'll tip Mam over the edge, and I'll end up in care for sure. But first, I'll have to face the bigger mess I've created.

I spy a flickering light striking the wall in the next alley-way, and peep round the corner. It's a faulty streetlight, but next to it is a sign: Stan's Bakery.

The bakery windows glow orange, like a sunrise. Inside, people scurry about unloading huge trays of golden, crusty loaves and plaited pretzels. I watch as a chubby, red-faced man with thick lips wipes at his forehead under his white hat. A short, muscular, Jamaican woman with tightly woven braids moves quickly behind him, tidying up any mess he makes. I sneak past the front door unnoticed, and search for a back entrance. There isn't one, and the shop is flanked by spiked green railings. There's no way in.

Frustrated, I remove the money from the purse and, returning the purse to the bag, fling the whole thing over the railings. It lands with a thud and I'm just about to walk away when something clatters and rolls, and something else skids across the ground. An image of Mrs Snelling's son appears in my mind. What about the photo? I imagine rain pouring down, the smiling face of Simon Snelling blistering and lifting away from the paper, his face erased for ever. I can't leave it there, so I climb the fence to retrieve the photo. Somehow, I'll get it back to Mrs Snelling – drop it in the dinner hall, maybe, so it can be found and returned.

My Converse fit perfectly between the spikes after all – making it easy for me to haul myself up and over.

Within seconds, I'm inside the bakery yard. Leaving the brightness of the shop behind, my eyes take time to adjust to the darkness. The yard is filled with delivery boxes, recycling bins and oversized trolleys for bread trays. The ventilator hums loudly as it battles to cool the oven-filled kitchen. I pick up the bag, locate the purse, but not whatever it was that rolled – despite searching round every trolley and behind every bin. Finally, I give up – I have what's important. Stuffing the wallet in my rucksack, and the bag under one of the bins, I look for somewhere suitable to rest.

Hot steam blows from vents into the night air, and I eventually settle behind a pile of delivery boxes, directly in the ventilator's path. Sitting on my bag to keep my bum off the cold floor, I let the heat warm my bones, and begin to feel safe. No one will find me here. Huddling up, trying not to think about my dad's cold reaction, my eyelids droop. I think about baking "Caramel Hearts" with Mam and wonder: *Never mind Mam's heart – what about melting my own?*

Chapter Forty-Seven

There's No Point Crying over Spilt Bagels

I open my eyes to a loud clunk. Realizing where I am, I listen carefully to the weird scraping noises from behind the stacked delivery boxes. Half expecting a scavenging fox, I kneel up as quietly as I can and peer over.

I see a squat, rotund man slotting food trays onto a trolley. As he turns back towards the kitchen door, the light highlights his features. It's the red-faced man with the white hat I saw earlier. Accidentally knocking a stack of boxes with my knee, I crouch down as he calls out.

"Hello? Anyone there?"

Hardly daring to breathe, I keep as low to the ground as I can. I hear footsteps, followed by a second male voice with a strong foreign accent.

"Talking to yourself again, Stan?"

Stan laughs. "Thought I heard something."

"Probably a fox. Bloody pests!"

"Right," says Stan, sounding convinced. "Probably just a fox. Unless my mind's playing tricks!"

Waiting until their footsteps retreat and the back door slams, I let out my breath in one big puff and sit back against the wall. I notice a patch of sky brightening and decide to leave before I'm discovered. Standing slowly, I stretch my stiff, aching limbs, and shoulder my bag.

Making sure the coast is clear, I sneak past the trolleys, snatching a couple of bagels as I pass, and climb the metal railings. As I reach the top and try to jump down, my tired foot slips from between the spikes and I topple backwards. Crying out as my jacket catches on the spikes, I tip upside down and swing like a pendulum. Stan rushes out to see what the commotion is, just as the stolen bagels spill to the ground. He helps me down, eyeing the bagels.

"You're the strangest-looking fox I've ever seen," he says.

I kick at the bagels with the toe of my shoe. "Sorry about those."

"There's no point crying over spilt bagels," says Stan. "Come inside – you've got some explaining to do."

Knowing there's no point in trying to escape – I'm too sleepy and slow – I walk towards the glowing kitchen. Stan follows close behind, whistling to let me know he's there – but at a safe distance. As we reach the door, I hesitate.

"Come on – we won't bite," says Stan, pushing his way up front and inside.

The aroma of warm bread and cake washes over me like a soothing balm. My stomach rumbles loud enough for everyone to hear, so I keep my head bent low as I follow.

"Odessa, Anatoly, we have an unexpected guest." Stan turns to me. "What's your name, pet?"

"Liv." It comes out barely audible.

"Our guest's name is Liv. Can one of you make us some tea while it's quiet out front? Bring some warm bagels and croissants too. We'll be in my office."

I sneak a daring peek as I pass. The muscular Jamaican lady I saw earlier and a tall, square-jawed man in his late fifties stare back with confused – but friendly – expressions. Then the lady jumps into action – filling up a kettle and setting it on top of a huge stove.

When we reach the office – a cupboard-sized room with a messy desk, noisy, ticking clock and three kitchen chairs – Stan perches on a chair, arms folded.

"Now, young lady, why don't you start from the beginning?"

Not knowing quite where to begin, I flop down, rub my eyes and drag my palms down my face. Then I let the words tumble out.

* * *

After two vanilla croissants, a cinnamon bagel and two cups of sugary tea, I feel much better. Until Anatoly comes in with the bag in his hand, saying "I think this is yours," and I feel like I'm going to throw up. Stan must have noticed my face drop, because as soon as Anatoly leaves, he asks me what's wrong.

"Everything," I say and start blubbering like a little kid.

He doesn't laugh, he doesn't say anything – he just listens. His silence makes my mouth spill the beans, and before I know what's happened, I've told him all about Mam, the recipe book and the blue bag, about falling out with Sarah and Jack and my disastrous meeting with Dad. When I finish, Stan rubs his chin and makes a long, low humming sound.

"You've certainly been through the wringer. What will you do now?" he asks.

I shrug.

"You know your mam'll be worried, don't you? And your dad?"

"Sure."

"It's true. You'll understand when you're older and a parent yourself. But what are we going to do with you?"

I chew my lip nervously, listening to the sound of someone punching numbers into a till in the shop.

"I was thinking I'd find a mobile-phone shop and charge my battery so I could call home. Then, I guess it's back on the coach."

"And the bag? Have you thought about that?"

"Only every day since I took it."

Stan laughs and apologizes immediately.

"I guess I'll have to take it back," I say.

"Smart girl," says Stan. "But why don't you use my office phone?" He gestures towards his desk. "Come out to the shop floor when you're finished. I'll make sure no one disturbs you."

Before I can protest – I didn't mean to call home right now – Stan strides out of the room.

I pick up the handset and hold it to my ear before slamming it down. What if Mam's wasted? I don't trust either of us to keep our temper if she is. After several attempts, I finally muster enough courage to dial home. The ringing tone seems to go on for ever. My heart thumps as someone answers.

"Hello?"

It takes a while for me to register the voice.

"Hatty?"

A huge sigh blasts down the phone, quickly followed by a muffled shout directed away from the receiver.

"Mam, it's OK! It's Liv. She's on the phone now." Then Harriet's back. "Liv, we were so worried – where are you?"

"London."

"We know that. Dad phoned. But where? Are you OK? I'm so happy to hear your voice! We were out of our minds with worry…"

A lump forms in my throat. I swallow hard to force it away.

"I'm fine. I'm in a bakery – I'm using their phone. Sorry, Hatty. I thought… I just wanted to… Dad phoned?"

"Yes, thankfully. He was worried."

"He couldn't care less!"

"He's been looking for you all night. When we couldn't get hold of you on your mobile, we thought…"

Her voice trails off. My stomach flutters. Dad was out looking for me? The journey wasn't a waste of time after all!

"My battery died. I forgot my charger. I didn't mean to worry you."

"Of course we were worried! Liv, you've got to come home. Right away. Do you have any money to get back or do I need to come and get you?"

"I've got a return ticket."

"Train or coach?"

"Coach."

A rustling sound travels down the phone, followed by a deafening bang.

"Sorry, I dropped the phone. I have the times here. Your next coach is at 11.20 a.m. Can you make it?"

I check the clock on the wall. Five hours is plenty of time to navigate the Underground.

"Yes."

"Good. I'll come meet you at the station. Hang on, Mam wants to talk to you—"

"Hatty, no – she'll kill me!"

Chapter Forty-Seven

But it's too late – Hatty's gone.

"Liv, sweetheart!"

As Mam's trembling voice rings out, I panic and slam down the phone. Leaning my head in my hands, I groan. What did I do a stupid thing like that for?

* * *

"Is everything all right, pet?" asks Stan as I join him in the shop.

"I spoke to my sister. I'm going home."

His face breaking into a big grin, Stan claps his hands together.

"Thatta girl. Not everyone sees sense like you. How are you getting back?"

"Coach."

"From Victoria? I'll drop you over there."

"It's OK, really, it's not till 11 a.m. – I can go by Tube."

"No way. I want to make sure you get there safely."

"OK, thanks," I say, eyeing some cooling shortbread Anatoly carries through on a giant tray.

"Hey, Stan, have you ever tried 'Lovers' Lemon and Choc-Chip Shortbread'?" I ask.

Stan looks up to his forehead, scanning his memory. "Nope. Can't say I have."

"Can I show you before I go? It's really nice – but the trick is to leave it in the fridge for half an hour before baking."

"Sure, why not?" says Stan, shrugging to the others. "We've got time to kill."

Chapter Forty-Eight

There's Something I Have to Do First

The journey home is painful. My stomach is in knots, and every mile closer, every time the coach lurches, I feel worse. Halfway, I open the packed lunch Stan gave me. Inside the bag there's a business card. On the back Stan has written:

> *Thanks for the recipe. If you ever want some work experience or a job, give me a shout!*
> Stan

I tuck the card into my rucksack and watch as fields of cows whizz by. I bite into one of Stan's pasties, noting the crisp crunch of the pastry, the saltiness of the corned beef. Maybe I should branch out into savouries as well? It's a bit of a leap, but if I asked nicely, when things have settled down, Mam might help. Perhaps I could create some concoctions of my own?

Then reality hits: who am I trying to kid? After this stunt, I'm screwed. Home will be worse than ever. And now I've met Dad – know for certain he's not interested – what do I have to look forward to? As I start stressing out big-time, my stomach goes all funny. An hour later, I'm retching into the coach toilet.

When the coach reaches the end of the line, I rub my eyes dry before I stand. Harriet is waiting like she promised, leaning against the wall. I wobble off the bus, a thin layer of sweat lining my top lip. As Harriet's worried face rushes towards me, it takes all my willpower not to vomit on the footpath.

"Sit down for a minute. You look a wreck!" cries Harriet, guiding me to an empty bench before tucking an arm around my shoulders. "Are you OK?"

"A bit travel sick."

I manage to avoid looking her in the eye.

"What on earth were you thinking, Liv?"

"I just wanted to meet Dad. Then I thought I might get him to come home and help Mam so you could go back to uni without worrying. Everything sucks here. You all hate me."

"I do not hate you! You're my lil sis!"

I feel her eyes on me, but keep mine focused on my knees.

"I overheard you talking to your friend on the phone about putting me in care. And you're always whinging." I affect a whiny voice and screw up my face. "*I'm fed up of you, you little cow.*"

Harriet gives a nervous chuckle.

"I might say that, but I don't mean it. We all do and say things we don't mean – especially when it comes to those we care about. You should know that…"

"See? You're having a dig already." I try to pull away, but Harriet holds on to me. "Next, you'll be cross at me cos you're not at uni yet."

"Hey! A few more days won't hurt. You're more important. OK?"

Relaxing a little, I sniff.

"You mean that?"

"Of course I do. Who else is going to make me cakes?"
I clear my throat. "I don't really think you're a fat pig."

Harriet gives me a friendly squeeze.

"Forget about it. Come on, let's go."

"I can't. I can't face Mam."

"You're going to have to at some point. She's been
worried sick."

"Sure she has!"

"Of course she has, Liv. She's not perfect, but she's
not the monster you make out either. If you dropped the
attitude a little—"

"I know. But I can't bear it. The drinking."

"Build a bridge and get over it. I know it's not easy,
but being so angry all the time doesn't help. You'll drive
yourself nuts. We can't change what's going on – only
the way we deal with it."

I contemplate Harriet's words, let them drip-feed into
my brain. My sister is right: I can't carry on like this.
Mam might not be perfect, but she's the only one we've
got.

"But what about when it kicks off when you're away?"

"The Social Services will be visiting, and I'm only on
the other end of the phone. One call, and I'll be right
there."

"Promise?"

"Promise. Sisters together, right? We'll get through this.
The truth is, Mam might never get better, but if we stick
together, we'll be OK."

"Fine," I say. "I'll try and give Mam a break. For you."

"Good – but do it for yourself. Come on, let's go."

Chapter Forty-Eight

But that's only part of the problem dealt with. Instead of getting up, I scrunch up even smaller, tucking my knees into my chin.

"What's wrong, Liv?"

"Everything! Jack, Sarah, Mad Dog, you leaving. I did something terrible and tried to put it right…"

"What could be so bad that it made you run away?"

"I can't tell you."

Harriet opens her mouth to say something, but changes her mind. After a while, she asks, "Is it something you can still sort out?"

Slowly, I nod my head.

"Then put it right. As soon as you can."

"Mad Dog will kill me," I say.

"We'll deal with her. Now you've got that off your chest, are you ready to face Mam?"

I nod my head.

"Almost. There's something I've got to do first."

*　*　*

Mr Morrelly is at his desk, browsing documents. When I enter, he looks up, raises an eyebrow and stops what he's doing.

"Olivia," he says, and a lump balls in my throat.

I hover uncomfortably. I consider turning around and leaving, abandoning my plan, but facing Old Mozzer will be easier than being under Mad Dog's thumb for the rest of my life. Plus, I owe it to Jack.

"Would you like to take a seat?" asks Mr Morrelly.

I sit, rucksack on my lap, fidgeting with my nails. The silence is like a weight suspended above our heads, threatening to crush us both, but I can't make any words come out.

"Is this about the missing bag?" prompts Mr Morrelly.

It should make things easier, but it doesn't. I want to be brave, like I felt this morning in Stan's bakery when I decided to come clean. Instead, I'm petrified and just about manage a nod.

"Do you have something to tell me?"

"Yes," I mumble.

My heart is pounding, my skin is sticky with sweat and my stomach is churning – everything is in overdrive, except for my mouth. I'm so frustrated that tears well in my eyes, and I'm mortified as one drips down my face and off my chin, onto my rucksack. Mr Morrelly stands and walks towards me, perching on the edge of his desk, right in front of me.

"It's OK, Olivia," he says. "You're doing the right thing coming to me."

I'm not so sure. I want to tell him the truth so badly, but the words still won't come. Maybe I should stick to Mad Dog's plan instead? That would be so much easier. Even as I think it, I feel my throat unblock. Quickly, I undo the rucksack, take out Mrs Snelling's bag and thrust it at Old Mozzer, brushing off a stray black mark from where I stuffed it under the bin.

"It was me," I say, and it feels like a ton of bricks have just tumbled from my shoulders.

"I'm sorry – what did you say?"

I wasn't expecting him to be taken aback. Tears threaten to fall again as I clear my throat.

"I said... I took the bag."

I expect shouting, a lecture – or a bit of a grilling, at the very least. Instead, Mr Morrelly sighs. The disappointment is visible all over the shadows and creases on his face. He takes the bag and returns to his seat. He can't stand being near me. I rub my hands together and pick at my nails.

"You know what this means?" asks Mr Morrelly.

I shake my head. But whatever it is, it can't be any worse than what Mad Dog's going to do to me.

"I have to suspend you immediately."

I nod.

"Is your mum still at home?"

"Yes," I say, and fear rises in my stomach.

What will happen when she finds out? What if she keeps drinking and it's all my fault?

"Can I go now, sir?" I ask. "Hatty's outside."

"No, Olivia – I think it's best if I call your mother and explain first. You can wait outside."

"Yes, sir," I say, trying to focus on my promise to Hatty as my heart sinks.

Whatever happens, I'll do my best to deal with it.

Mr Morrelly refuses to look at me as I leave, his gaze fixed on the bag, one hand resting on its blue leather. I pause at the door. I want to tell him that I mean it, I truly am sorry – more sorry than he'll ever know, because I've lost my best friend, ruined my chances with Jack, and now Mam's probably going to go on a bender. But I don't say any of these things. I just slip out of the door quietly and wait.

* * *

Tears stream down my cheeks in the corridor as I think about Mam's reaction to my suspension. But at least I can avoid Mad Dog and Jack for a bit longer. At least – that's what I was hoping, but I've only been outside two minutes when I hear Mad Dog call out.

"Think you're funny, do you?"

She runs at me with an angry face, Lorna keeping watch at the end of the corridor. Where the hell is Hatty? Grabbing me by the scruff of the neck, Mad Dog hauls me up the corridor, closer to Lorna, and shoves me against the wall, her bunched fist holding my top so I can't move.

"Did you do it?" she hisses.

"Yes."

She lets me go and snatches my rucksack. Opening it up, she can see that the stolen bag has gone.

"If you ever disobey me again," she says, and slaps me around the head. "I swear to God, I'll kill you."

As much as I try to fight it, more tears fall.

"Love the tears – nice touch." She glances at Lorna and I see her wink. "Let's forget all this. The deed is done. Want to hang out? We could get some cider. I won't let the girls get you."

"Why don't you just get lost!" I shout, and shove her away.

I don't know who's more surprised – me or her. At first, Maddy looks shocked, then hurt. As the realization of what I've just done dawns, she launches herself at me. But I must have shouted a bit louder than I expected, because Mr Morrelly charges out of the room.

Chapter Forty-Eight

"What's going on here?" he yells.

I stand my ground as Mad Dog releases her grip.

"Nothing, sir!" she says.

"It doesn't look like nothing to me."

"We're just playing, sir."

"Like when you cut my hair off," I say. "I'm sick of you bullying me and Sarah."

It's more effective than if I'd slapped her. Stunned, Maddy stands there, and stammers.

"W-we're just… I d-didn't…"

I glance up the corridor and see Lorna has slipped away. Instead, Hatty is standing there, watching.

"Mam's coming," she says.

Chapter Forty-Nine

Rules Are Rules

I never thought I'd see the day when Madeleine Delaney would cry. Even that time when her dad flung her against the wall for breaking her sandals, and her head bounced off the bricks with a loud crack – even then, she didn't shed a single tear. She must have been what – nine years old? Ten? And yet, here she is, in the head teacher's office, blubbering and begging Old Mozzer not to suspend her.

"You can't go around lying and bullying people and expect to get away with it," replies Old Mozzer.

"But when my dad finds out…"

Mr Morrelly pauses.

"I'm sorry, Madeleine, but rules are rules."

It's the last thing I expect, but Mam steps forward and rubs Maddy's arm.

"He can't hurt you," she says in a soothing voice. "He's still inside, isn't he?"

"Yes. But his brothers aren't."

"Like Davey? He's a nasty piece of work. Always was."

Maddy nods earnestly.

"Dad looks for any excuse to set Uncle Davey on Mam."

"You should have thought about that beforehand," cuts in Mr Morrelly.

Mam gives the head teacher a sharp look, and pulls Maddy to her. Maddy curls into Mam and her body shakes. I give Hatty a questioning look. Hatty shows me her palms and shrugs, and for a moment everyone is quiet.

Mam leans towards me and whispers, "You think I'm bad. You should see what she has to put up with."

Deep down, I already know. The way she would jump every time her parents yelled, the looks she used to give us as she walked away – me and Sarah still playing happily as though nothing had happened. You don't forget something like that.

"Is there any way you can be lenient, Mr Morrelly?" asks Mam. "There are obviously bigger issues here. Perhaps suspension isn't the answer for either of them?"

I puff up with pride as Mam sticks up for me. I ignore that she's defending Maddy too.

"They have to take responsibility for their actions," says Mr Morrelly, his fingertips pressed together like a steeple, his chin resting on top.

"But Liv's behaviour is because of me. And Maddy didn't actually steal anything. Yes, she lied—"

My jaw drops.

"But Mam, she cut off my hair!" I say.

Harriet reaches out and rubs my back. From the look on her face, she's as confused as I am. Mam considers me for a moment. Then she holds Maddy at arm's length.

"You cut off my daughter's hair?" she asks incredulously. "Why on earth would you do something like that? I thought you were friends?"

A small laugh escapes me, and I look to the floor to try and cover it up.

"Those two ditched me years ago," says Maddy, forlornly. The words curl around Mam and hook her in. "They didn't want to know."

"That's not true!" I say. "You ditched us. You started hanging round with the older kids."

"Because you kept avoiding me."

"Not you. Your dad, yes, but…"

And then I realize – she's actually right.

"You and Sarah made it clear I wasn't welcome. I had to find new friends. I couldn't go to secondary school without any. I'd get bullied."

This time I snort, and do nothing to hide it.

"You? Bullied? You've been making Sarah's life hell! Stupidly, I stuck up for you. Until this."

I point at my hair. Mam shuffles in her chair, and takes hold of my hand.

"I think there's been a big misunderstanding here, girls. Maybe you could work it out?" says Mam calmly.

Neither of us says anything. Mr Morrelly sits back in his chair and sighs.

"I guess we'd better speak to Sarah," he says.

He makes a quick call – me and Maddy stare at the floor. Moments later, there's a knock at the door. My heart pounds against my ribcage.

"Come in!" calls Mr Morrelly.

"Mrs Pearl said you wanted to see me?" says Sarah, tentatively.

Her face is flushed red. She looks from me to Maddy, then stands on the other side of Hatty, as far as from us as she can. I can't be certain, but something resembling guilt passes over Maddy's face.

Chapter Forty-Nine

"I hear that this young lady has been bullying you, is that right?"

"I d-don't know sir."

"Well, I just wanted to tell you that it ends here. Doesn't it, Madeleine?"

"Yes, sir."

"For good!"

"Yes sir."

"Madeleine and Olivia are facing two weeks' suspension, effective immediately. If and when they return to school, Sarah, I'll make sure this doesn't happen again."

Mr Morrelly glares at Maddy. "If I hear of *any* untoward behaviour from you, it'll be permanent exclusion. Do you hear me?"

"Yes, sir," says Maddy, her shoulders hunched.

"Now, you may take Olivia home, Mrs Bloom – and I expect to see her back here in exactly two weeks. I cannot condone what she has done, but owning up to the misdeed shows that there's hope for her yet. Sarah, you're free to leave too."

We all stand up to go. It's just like when we were kids – with Maddy left behind.

"Madeleine," says Mam. "You come and see me if you need to talk. OK?"

Maddy's eyes light up.

"OK. Thank you, Mrs Bloom."

"You too, Sarah."

Sarah gives me a quizzical look and I smile.

As we leave, I let Mam and Hatty go ahead. Before Sarah turns back for class, I stop her and look her straight in the eyes.

"I'm really sorry I didn't believe you about Maddy, and I'm really sorry about the bag. I'm sorry about everything. I've missed you."

She's so quiet – I realize I've damaged our friendship for ever.

I'm just about to walk away when she says, "I can't believe you owned up!"

"Neither can I," I say.

"What was London like?"

"Massive. And a bit scary. Have you seen Jack?"

Sarah nods.

"Yes. I'd give him some space, if I were you."

"Do you think he'll ever talk to me again?"

"He was worried when he heard you'd run away. But it'll take time."

"Thanks, Sarah," I say, and give her a quick hug.

As she heads off down the corridor, she gives me a wave. I catch up to Mam and Hatty.

"I know you shouldn't have taken the bag," says Mam. "But owning up and facing up to Maddy? That was brave."

I can't believe my luck, but then her mood changes. All the way home, Mam is sullen and thoughtful. I drag my feet as we walk – all three of us are in step with each other, but silent. Dreading the moment we get indoors and Mam blows, I think of the bottles under the sink – and how they won't be full for much longer.

Chapter Fifty

I Refuse to Repeat the Pattern

Reaching home, Hatty grabs my arm and says, "Mam, I need Liv to help me with something, and then we'll be right in."

"OK, darling," says Mam, her voice flat.

She disappears through the kitchen door without a backward glance. When we're alone, Hatty points her finger at me.

"Promise me: no more running away. Please? You frightened the life out of me."

"I'm sorry. I really am." I give her a guilty look. "Do you think Mam will be OK?"

"I don't know."

"Is she angry at me cos Dad phoned?"

"No. I think it actually did her some good. There's talk of him maybe visiting."

"No way! Any chance of them getting back together?"

"No chance. He has a new life now. I heard you met Amber – I had no idea she was our sister till Dad said. What's she like?"

"An awkward cow."

Harriet looks highly amused.

"Coming from you – she must be bad! But she's had her share of troubles too."

"Did Dad tell you about Rosa?" I ask.

"Yeah – Mam's gutted."

"Poor Mam. I feel bad now."

"Me too."

"Still doesn't excuse her behaviour, though," I say.

"I know. But she's trying."

Hatty pauses and we both strain our ears to see whether we can hear glasses clinking. It's all quiet, so I continue.

"I don't know how much more I can take, sis."

"Me neither," admits Harriet. "But I reckon we've got more of a chance if we stick together."

"I don't want to go into care."

"I won't let you."

"Promise?"

"Promise. Now, c'mon." Hatty nods towards the living room door. "We'd better go check on the situation."

As I follow Hatty, ready to face the music, my heart pumps furiously. Mam's cradling a cup of tea, but as soon as we enter she puts it down, stretches out her arms and hugs me. Tears stream down her face. That sets Hatty off too. Then me.

Pulling back, Mam squashes my cheeks between her cupped hands, like I'm a toddler. I don't mind one bit.

"I'm so sorry… it's all my fault – running away, getting suspended. Are you all right? Were you scared?"

So many questions, I don't know where to start.

"I'm OK, Mam. I just… I'm sorry. I won't do it again."

Mam takes me by the hand. I hope the cingi-ness wears off soon, but not too quickly. Pulling me over to the cupboard under the sink, Mam reaches inside.

"Liv, will you do something for me? If I ask really nicely?"

"Sure," I say, my heart pounding.

"Will you help me with these?"

She lifts out two bottles at a time. All six are on the counter. Only five are full. The night we argued comes flooding back, but I swallow my pride as Mam unscrews one of the bottles and starts pouring it down the sink.

"Mam, are you sure?" asks Hatty.

"It's about time I pulled myself together," says Mam. "I know what it's like to have a miserable childhood. I refuse to repeat the pattern... Here, you help too, Hatty."

Together, my sister and I step forward and unscrew a bottle each. The whiskey glugs down the sink, the sour smell rising and stinging my nostrils. We don't stop pouring until all the bottles are empty. Mam stands back and folds her arms, a satisfied grin on her face.

"OK, well that's a start. How about you go and get some rest, Liv, then we give that Baked Alaska a try?"

"Even though I got suspended?" I ask.

"Two weeks isn't such a long time," says Mam. "You can go back with a clean slate. We'll both start again with a clean slate."

"OK," I say.

By agreeing to something I know is probably impossible, at least I'm keeping my promise to Hatty.

"I bought the ingredients for you, remember?" says Harriet, winking. "I even got double of everything, just in case…"

Mam pulls the recipe book out of a kitchen drawer and hands it to me.

"Look inside."

When I open the front cover, I see the original inscription has been covered over, replaced by a new one:

To my dearest Olivia. May we have many cooking adventures together – with you leading the way. Love always, Mam (aka Happiness Bloom).

I hadn't expected this in my wildest dreams – and I know how volatile Mam is, but suddenly things seem clearer. I know what matters in my heart – my family – and as imperfect as it is, I'm going to do my best to look after it.

"Just one question," I say. "Why 'Happiness Bloom'?"

"When you were a baby, you heard your dad say my name and tried to copy. Only what you said sounded more like 'abbiness'. So it became my nickname – thanks to you."

I stare at Mam like I'm seeing her for the first time. The gentle afternoon sun softens her face and her eyes sparkle with hope. She looks tired – but beautiful.

"As for that recipe," continues Mam. "I've got a secret that makes the meringue so light, you'll think you have wings. It's all in the blending – and it's not in the book. You could add it in if you think it's worthy?"

I tuck one arm around Mam's back, the other around Hatty, and nod. I know there's always going to be temptation, and we're only a few minutes' walk from the nearest off-licence. I also know that facing up to Jack will be really difficult, and he has every right to never speak to me again. And that things with Maddy might never be fixed. But, as Mr Morrelly said – there's hope for me yet.

"Baked Alaska? That'd be really, nice, Mam."

How to Do the Right Thing - By Olivia Bloom

Forget the butterflies and blue skies, the clouds and kisses – sometimes you have to look deep inside yourself to work out the winning combination…

INGREDIENTS

Lashings of instinct
Oodles of open mind
A kind heart
Faith
A pinch of courage

HOW TO MAKE THE MAGIC HAPPEN

1. Take a big dollop of instinct and add an open mind.
2. Warm the mixture through with a kind heart, and sprinkle on some faith.
3. Add a pinch of courage and mix well.

Remember: The right thing may not always be obvious, or the easiest option – but so long as you do your best, you'll find your way.

Acknowledgements

With warm and deepest thanks to Elisabetta Minervini and the team at Alma Books for seeing the potential in this story and bringing it into the world: I appreciate all that you do.

To Jem Butcher for the beautiful cover, and William Dady for the constant support and energy – you, sir, are a gentleman.

Huge thanks to my editor, Bella Pearson, for seeing what I was trying to create and helping me to achieve it. Also my agent, Sallyanne Sweeney; a writer's journey is not always easy, and I'm glad to have you by my side.

Melvin Burgess, Malorie Blackman, and everyone on the Arvon Totleigh Barton YA writing week in 2014; your encouragement and feedback helped make this happen. Thank you, truly.

Also Tyrone Guthrie Centre, La Muse Retreat and Cill Rialaig – your wonderful spaces allowed this book to breathe.

Writing *Caramel Hearts* has meant many research trips to London, so giant hugs to my friends Angela and Abel for the spare room and great company (when I eventually ditched the notebook).

Writing this book also meant delving into to some buried feelings and memories, so the biggest thanks of all go to my sister, Tracey, who will understand parts of this book more than any other reader. You always have been, and always will be, an inspiration.

And finally, my husband Mick, without whom none of this would be possible – thank you for being you.

Elizabeth Rose Murray lives in West Cork where she writes, fishes and grows her own vegetables. *Caramel Hearts* is her first book for young adults. Her debut novel for children aged 10–12, *The Book of Learning – Nine Lives* (Mercier Press) was chosen as the 2016 Dublin UNESCO City of Literature Citywide Read for Children.

Hoping to encourage new writers, Elizabeth provides manuscript reports and online writing courses through Inkwell Writers and Big Smoke Writing Factory. She is a regular at literary festivals, and offers adult workshops on writing for children and young adults, as well as multiple events and workshops for children and teens.

Follow E.R. Murray on Twitter and Facebook at:

 @ermurray

 www.facebook.com/

ERMurray.Author

Or check out her website:
www.ermurray.com